THE
BLOSSOMING

The Third book in "The Green Man Series"

D1247245

Sharon Brubaker

ISBN: 1517255120
ISBN 13: 9781517255121

Acknowledgments: A very special thanks to Peggy, my editor, friend, and her excellent pen. To Captain Joe Musike of: www. Experiencesail.com for his gorgeous sailboat the *Voila*, charters and sailing information. Thank you to Daphne for additional sailing information. Thank you to Laura Gordon, for yet another fantastic book cover! (http://thebookcovermachine.com)Thank you to Alice and MaryBeth for their assistance with wedding 'issues.' To Susan T., my polyhedral buddy. Thank you for the catalyst of interest in platonic solids. Thank you, Alice, Barb, Bonnie, Robbie, and Sarah for beta reads and comments. Thank you to Rob, James and Robin for their love, support, and patience with 'book land.' Thank you to the 'Bayside' residents, Cheryl and Woody Jackson of Jackson Marine (http://www.jacksonmarinesales.com) and Don and Mary Green at Bay Boat Works (http://bayboatworks.com) both in North East, Maryland. Thank you to Doug and MaryBeth French for the writing retreat! And a special thanks to you, the reader.

CHAPTER ONE

Nothing will catch you.
Nothing will let you go.
We call it blossoming—
The spirit breaks from you and you remain.

— JORIE GRAHAM "TENNESSEE JUNE"

I t was early summer. The cool, early, June night gave way to a warm day as the sun rose lazily in the bright Eastern sky. A gentle breeze ruffled the crisp, white curtains so that Sylvia could see the sun glinting on the blue-gray water of the bay while the curtains billowed like sails in the early, morning breeze. The air was just on the edge of coolness. The slight breeze felt delicious to Sylvia's toes when she poked them out from under the covers on the bed. Every fiber of Sylvia's being shouted, 'Get up! Get up! It's a gorgeous day!' Every fiber of her body wanted her to get up and greet the burgeoning day, along with a large, dark-eyed poodle that sat anxiously beside the bed. Percy, a large, white, standard poodle was awake too. His large, dark, doggy eyes pleaded with her to take him outside while his cold nose nudged her hand. She was grateful he didn't whine and wake up Owen, who was snoring lightly beside her.

Sylvia stretched carefully and began to ease slowly out of bed. She was very careful not to wake Owen's sleeping form beside her. He always touched her in his sleep with a hand, a finger or the brush of a foot against her leg and she had to pull away from him slowly and gently so that she didn't wake him. She paused for a moment as her one foot touched the floor and glanced back at Owen. He was still breathing deeply and steadily. Apparently her exit from the bed did not disturb his slumber. She put her other foot on the floor and stood up, steadying herself by touching the furry head of the large, white poodle next to her.

"Okay, Percy," she whispered as she first patted and then bent to give him a kiss on his soft curly head.

Percy raced down the stairs and waited anxiously by the door until she appeared dressed and ready for his walk. As soon as he saw her he danced in excited circles, holding the leash in his mouth. He had a habit of pulling his leash from the hook by the door when he wanted to go for a walk. Sylvia laughed as quietly as she could, told Percy in a stage whisper to sit, and hooked the leash onto his collar before going outside to take a large breath of the fresh morning air. The sun glinted off the western shore of the bay, blinking brightly off the windows of homes on the far shore-line. They twinkled in the sunlight. She loved living at Bayside. She loved life on this fresh, summer morning.

As Sylvia walked Percy, she remembered for the millionth time, sweet memories of her friend Gwen's wedding. It was only a month ago and the memories were a lovely, haunting day-dream. Sylvia had been physically and emotionally spent from the kidnapping by her former neighbor, Tony, and the two men hired to hurt her. Owen, the love of her life, had seemingly disappeared and she assumed he was sulking about their off again on again relationship. Their year had been rocky, first with the murder of their colleague, Anna, and then Owen's ensuing false arrest for Anna's murder. More recently, Owen's insecurities and jealousy of Tony's interest in her had made their lives and their relationship tenuous. When he exited from their relationship a month ago, it had not been a ruse. He had to sort out what he really wanted and so had she. But, Owen realized quickly, and now told her frequently, that he could not live without her. Her friends, Gwen, Frank and their sister Claire assisted with the surprise of Sylvia's life. At the reception, Gwen made sure Claire maneuvered Sylvia to the right spot where she caught the bridal bouquet. Well into the reception, someone fixed a spotlight on the doors to the Inn. Owen emerged into the spotlight. The guests parted in a wave as Owen strode towards her looking very handsome and a rakish, sexy geek in a tuxedo, with a million dollar smile. Sylvia could only stand silently, stunned by his arrival. He took her hands, went down on one knee and asked her to marry him.

Gwen, Frank, and Claire descended upon her with laughter, tears, hugs and congratulations as soon as the word 'yes' was out of her mouth. Applause erupted from the crowd. Frank slapped Owen on the back in camaraderie. Only Audrey, Gwen's mother-in-law was disdainful. Sylvia had been puzzled but learned later that Audrey did not approve of public engagements. Audrey insisted that it was a private moment and that it should not have interrupted her son's wedding.

But, Audrey could not ruin the magic of the weekend. Owen booked a room at the Inn where the reception had taken place on the Connecticut waterfront. Sylvia could not imagine a more romantic weekend. She sighed blissfully at the memories.

Now, they were home at Bayside and 'playing house,' as her mother implied until they were married. They had not yet set a date. Yet, Sylvia began to experience what her friend Gwen had experienced, with both her mom, Mary, and Owen's mom, Anne, offering almost daily suggestions on how, when and where to plan the wedding. Gwen was having a field day with this. After many heart-wrenching conversations about Mother Audrey, Gwen's mother-in-law, overtaking the wedding plans, Gwen was in her own state of honeymoon bliss. She seemed to have amnesia about the angst she experienced while preparing her own, recent wedding. Percy tugged at the leash causing Sylvia to shake herself out of her daydream. He wanted to chase a squirrel racing through a neighbor's lawn. She scolded him gently for pulling and he immediately settled back into a walk. Percy did a high-step down the road with a jaunty bounce to his doggy trot.

Their automatic destination was one or both of the marinas at the end of her neighborhood. Owen was determined to purchase a sailboat shortly. They had been to boat shows, but even better, had the nearby marinas to aid in their search. Even with her naiveté about boats, one of her favorite things to do now was to wander among the vessels, ogling them. Owen liked to talk to the owners and get their opinions on the various vessels. He was planning to purchase a sailboat, with a comfortable cabin, so that they could sail the Chesapeake Bay for their honeymoon. Owen insisted upon a sailboat over a powerboat. He had sailed from childhood on, taking sailing lessons for many summers at the Yacht Club in North Bay. Marian and Bran had kept him busy at the camp, and were delighted when he fell in love with sailing. Sailing was something he had shared with Bran on their "Flying Scot," until Bran and Marian left for England. It was 'just right' as a starter sailboat, and day sailing was a perfect place for Owen to practice his sailing skills while Bran leaned back with his pipe and 'supervised.'

Sailboats and sailing were uncharted waters for Sylvia. She teased Owen that she was only interested in power boats because, running a power boat was infinitely easier than learning to sail — or so she thought. There was something seductive about the power boats with their sleek design and how they sped through the water. She would catch her breath when one went past the house. But, Owen was insistent on sailing and she acquiesced to his fervor about sailboats.

The peaceful morning was broken by a loud roar of a cigarette boat. Some of the cigarette boat owners had taken off their mufflers and the sound of them racing through the bay was absolutely deafening. Most were kind enough to wait until they were through the 'no wake' zone in Bayside and neighboring communities, but some were not. They sped down the bay with a fantail of water shooting from the back end and a deafening roar. The residents along the bay could not even carry on a conversation without shouting. She and Owen often wondered the percentage of hearing loss the cigarette boat owners had after spending days, weeks and years roaring up and down the bay. Some of the smaller, quiet communities like Bayside had written petitions to no avail. The county turned a blind eye, due to the millions of dollars the boaters brought into the area. Even the marina owners tried to take the cigarette boat owners in hand, but there were still enough that did not care about the noise pollution they created. Sylvia sighed. The cigarette boat would pass in a moment and the sound would subside when the boater hit the larger, more open expanse of water just south of Bayside. She held her breath, waiting for the peacefulness to return.

Cigarette boat noise aside, it was still a glorious morning. The annoying sound of the vessel was quickly a faint memory as the boat faded from sight in larger open waters. Sylvia lifted her face up to the sun that lit up the eastern sky in a bowl of peach and gold with a light, transparent cloud cover. The opposite shore of the bay was bathed in a golden light reflected from the sun in the clouds. The sun burned through the light coating of clouds leaving swathes of the brilliant blue sky reflected in the sparkling blue water.

Sylvia and Percy walked past the boat lift area and a light warm breeze blew over the point of land that jutted out into the bay. She shivered briefly just as a cloud covered the sun for a moment. Then, an unexpected cold wave of fear descended on Sylvia. The last few months Sylvia had been fighting nightmares when she had been kidnapped last spring. She had spent a horrible time locked in the little hut at the county's landfill, nearly dying of dehydration and starvation. The nightmarish memories of the kidnapping would strike her in unexpected moments. At various times during the day, Sylvia would need to stop what she was doing and breathe deeply in and out again slowly, clearing her mind from the fear and pain that descended on her. Her mantra was telling herself that she was indeed all right and that Tony and his goons were no longer around. Some nights she woke up screaming, curled up in a tight ball. Owen would soothe her and bring her back to reality. Her mother, sensing things were not all right, urged her to see a counselor or psychiatrist. Sylvia didn't feel she had the time. Also, she told herself, Owen, and her mom she was feeling better every day. They were skeptical of her bravado and, so was she, but she would not admit it to them. She stopped walking for a minute. Percy sat somewhat impatiently beside her and whined softly. His liquid brown eyes looked up at her. Sylvia took a couple of deep breaths to clear the unhappy memory that blindsided her before continuing their walk.

Traffic was already picking up as the Pennsylvania Navy poured through the neighborhood making their way to their boats. Boaters were busy working on cleaning their vessels, doing a few repairs, or preparing to motor out of the marina and get into open water. Sleepy boaters who had spent the night on their boats made their way to the bathhouses for hot showers. Others made their way to the long low building that housed the marina store and café. Owen and Sylvia had become lazy some days, paying the exorbitant price for milk or bread instead of running to a grocery store in town.

The marina store reminded Sylvia of stores at campgrounds. It held sundries as well as some basic food items. It also had generic wines and beers and an unusual collection of single malt scotch. The café, on the other hand, changed from season to season depending on who leased the restaurant. The current café staff painted it with swathes of brilliant blue with large, oval blocks of pure white. It was bright and fresh. The wall design reminded Sylvia of billowing spinnakers on sailboats and whoever had painted it, was ingenious. The new restaurant owners exchanged the heavy picnic tables that were once inside and placed them outside for guests. Now, small round café tables graced the space with the triangular flags for boats under glass tabletops. Boating flags were strung gaily across the ceiling like Buddhist prayer flags and they would flutter when someone opened the door. Sylvia and Owen found themselves walking to the marina on the weekends for brunch or lunch, or to pick up sandwiches when neither felt like cooking.

Sylvia tied up Percy outside the café and went inside for a cup of coffee. A small brass bell tinkled as she opened the door and the smell of freshly brewed coffee wafted towards her. There was something sensuous about the rich, chocolaty smell of brewing coffee that Sylvia loved. She sniffed appreciatively as the coffee perfume invaded the air just outside the door of the café. Sylvia hurried inside to purchase her first cup of the morning. Percy sat patiently while Sylvia collected her coffee and chatted with the woman at the register catching up on neighborhood gossip.

Coffee in hand, Sylvia took Percy to the huge rocks that bordered the shoreline as a breakwater. She sat on the grassy edge next to the rocks with Percy. The sunlight on the water shimmered as if hundreds of tiny shards of mirrors rode the wavelets and glinted brightly in the sun. It was so bright, it was nearly blinding. Sylvia closed her eyes. She could feel the rhythm of the earth as she sat on the sun-warmed grass. The sun reigned and showered her with droplets of warmth. Sylvia felt the sunshine light upon her like the butterfly kisses Owen had peppered her face, neck, and body with the night before. Sylvia felt centered. She seemed centered in herself and at one with all creation. It was as if an invisible net linked her with everything around her and beyond. She felt at peace. A few moments later she heard a slight rustle of leaves at her elbow. The Green Man appeared.

"Hello," she greeted him, slightly surprised.

"Good day to you, Sylvia," he said in his rich, baritone voice.

The Green Man was a great, green angel of a figure. His skin was like living wood and his body a suit of leaves that looked like brocade. There were leaves on his face and two leaves like a mustache. Sylvia felt like he was a father or grandfather figure to her. He always seemed to offer some sort of wisdom and was there when she needed him. Since his appearance last year he had helped her too, with explaining and assisting with her gifts of seeing auras and dowsing. Now, he sat with her, not speaking for a few minutes, and Sylvia closed her eyes and turned her face to the sun. She was waiting as well. She felt him watching her. His presence added to the contentment she was feeling. Inadvertently, she leaned a little closer to him.

"You are happy," he said as a statement.

She opened her eyes slowly and turned to look at him, a little surprised at this comment. "Yes," she said, "Yes, I am. I am very happy."

"That's good," he said, "you are very fortunate that you realize this."

Puzzled, she gave him a quirky look. "Of course," she said.

They sat in companionable silence. She waited patiently. Usually, the Green Man had something to tell or teach her. Sometimes his didactic comments annoyed her a little, but this time, he was silent. The silence was friendly. Sylvia decided to turn the tables and ask him a question that had bothered her for a long, long time, "Why me?"

"Pardon me?" The Green Man asked.

"Why me?" she asked again, "why did you choose to appear to me? What is my role in this subtle pattern that you have tantalized about through hints in the last year?"

"You are one of many, Sylvia," the Green Man replied gently, but seriously. "You are one of the many who are working to save this beautiful planet and universe. You are one who connects. You are a shining star in the great pattern. You feel the rhythm of this world that pulses with life and agonize over the humans that want to destroy it."

Sylvia remembered something Marian had told her the previous year about her Gran feeling the rhythm of the Earth. "Like my Gran?" she asked the Green Man.

He nodded, "Just like her," he assured Sylvia. "Think about your gifts – of seeing auras, of knowing when part of our earth is ill or in danger, of your ability to heal the Earth. Think about what you did this spring, destroying the pollution through your dowsing." He paused. "So, when you ask me that question…" He returned her look and smiled his familiar wry grin that she knew so well. "My only reply can be, why not? You *are* part of a great and beautiful pattern," he answered with enigmatic humor.

With a brief rustle of leaves, he was gone. He had a tendency to do that – just disappear into thin air.

"Aargh!" she cried in frustration. "Wait!" she cried, "I have more questions," she said to the air. Her frustrations were drowned out by the roar of another cigarette boat as it sped out of the marina and headed down the bay. She glared at it angrily and covered her ears with her hands.

When a hand touched her shoulder, she nearly jumped out of her skin. Behind her was a tall, beautiful woman with red hair and brilliant blue eyes. It was the wife of the owner of the Marina – Maureen. They had become friends in this last year.

"Maureen, you scared me!" Sylvia cried. "I couldn't hear you over that, that idiot who just roared out of here!" she sputtered before asking, "Can't Skip do something about those morons?" Sylvia asked.

Skip was Maureen's husband. They had a May - December marriage much to the consternation of some of the neighbors. Sylvia thought their marriage worked well. Skip adored Maureen. It was obvious that Maureen loved Skip. Sylvia always thought privately, that Maureen was extraordinarily beautiful. Sylvia thought she looked like a mermaid or perhaps like one of the carved figures on the bow of a ship. She wasn't at all surprised to see Maureen. Usually, she walked early in the morning when Sylvia walked Percy. It was through these early morning walks that the women had become friends.

Maureen narrowed her eyes and looked at the boat, now away from the head of the bay and into the open water due to its speed. She looked as if she was memorizing which boat was racing quickly and noisily away.

"Sorry to have scared you," Maureen answered and sat down next to Sylvia where the Green Man had just been. Percy walked over to her and put his head in her lap. She petted him.

"Oh, Percy," Maureen crooned, "I miss your pouf."

"With the heat, I had to get him clipped for the summer," Sylvia explained. "I think he looks like a lamb now."

"You're still a very handsome boy, Percy," Maureen told him, "even with your summer crew cut." She was rewarded with a lick to her hand and he gave a happy doggy moan when she rubbed his ears.

"Regarding the boat, I will speak to Skip again," Maureen told her, "We've been having some *issues* with some of the idiots," she said and she shook her head, "and I think I recognize *that* particular idiot that just roared out of here. I'll mention it to Skip."

Sylvia looked at her quizzically.

"Another time," she answered Sylvia's look. "How are you?" Maureen asked. "How are the wedding plans?"

Sylvia rolled her eyes. "Oh. My. God." Sylvia stated crisply, "Maureen, you have no idea! The moms have taken over with an overwhelming number of ideas. Personally, I want a wedding, but I don't want it to be crazy," she told Maureen. "I think I want it outside, so the question is, do we rush it for this year or wait another year? I don't think Owen and I want to hold on a year, but I don't believe that we can plan a wedding quickly. Lord, it took over every waking, breathing minute this last year for my friend Gwen who just got married."

"Why don't you have your wedding here at the marina?" Maureen suggested, "Maybe in the fall. September is always lovely and October is beautiful too."

"Hmm," Sylvia considered, "September would be nice and then we could sail in warmer weather. Do you think we could plan it in that amount of time?" she asked Maureen.

Maureen had shrugged before she answered, "What's a wedding? It's a big party. We can plan a party in a heartbeat. You didn't want a big wedding, did you?" She asked.

"No," Sylvia answered, "probably under fifty people."

"Well," Maureen replied, "Labor Day weekend would be a bit tight, but any other weekend after that would be okay. There's plenty of space here in the auxiliary parking," and she waved her hand at the small field where they were sitting, "we can set up an area so the wedding would overlook the bay. It would be lovely."

"Would that be all right with Skip?" Sylvia asked.

"I think it would be all right," Maureen told her. "I'll ask him right now." She stood up to go. "Call me later and let me know what Owen thinks of the idea. Okay?"

Sylvia felt both panic and relief. "Okay," she told her. "I'll let you know."

Sylvia led Percy home and tiptoed upstairs where Owen was still sleeping stretched across the bed, his hand resting on the warm spot where she had previously been sleeping.

"Time to get up, sleepyhead," she whispered in Owen's ear as she leaned over to kiss his cheek, "time to get our beautiful weekend started."

Owen gave a noise between a purr and a growl, "I thought we already started our weekend last night," he said huskily, pulling her down beside him and pinning her by throwing a leg over her.

Sylvia sighed happily. Bliss.

CHAPTER TWO

In summer, the song sings itself.

— WILLIAM CARLOS WILLIAMS

Their slow start to the weekend sped into a frenetic afternoon when they called their respective parents and some of their closest friends, to break the news that they wanted to wed in three months, outdoors, at the marina, instead of waiting for a year. Surprise, shock, and anxiety filled their voices. Gwen teased, Carol asked bluntly, and Sylvia's mother hinted by asking if Sylvia was pregnant, and that was the reason they were rushing the wedding. In each case, they answered "no," and continued that they did not want to wait a year. It was decided to table the discussion until they had permission from Skip to actually hold the ceremony at the marina.

Sylvia contacted Maureen, who in turn, invited them for a glass of wine in the late afternoon. So, as evening fell, Sylvia and Owen walked back to the marina with a bottle of chilled Prosecco in Owen's hand and Sylvia carrying a small tray of hummus and crudités.

Old George, the night watchman and general handyman around the marina, called out to them as they passed, "Where's the big guy?"

George adored Percy and always gave him a back rub whenever they ran into him while walking.

"At home," Owen replied, "Hopefully, he's not having a wild party while the parents are gone."

Old George chuckled in response. He reminded Sylvia of a darker elfin version of Santa Claus. His enormous belly actually jiggled when he laughed. He was a widower and gave up his house to his children when his wife died of cancer a couple of years back. He lived on his boat year round. He could always be found prowling the boatyard. If there was any nonsense, his jolly nature changed swiftly to no nonsense, drill-sergeant type of guy who barked orders. Everyone respected and listened to George. He made friends with everyone at the marina. His laughter rang out at late night card games with the fishermen and bonfires on the small beach by the marina with the regulars and the day sailors. The marina was a community unto itself and George was an important cog in the wheel. They said their goodbyes to George and walked through the boatyard to Skip and Maureen's house.

Skip and Maureen had a lovely home at the very tip of a point in the bay with the marina tucked into a cove behind their home. Light gray stone, cedar shingles, and lots of windows gave the home a New England cottage feel. Inside the home, it was sleek and modern. A local architect and builder had a sophisticated, yet distinctive style that Sylvia loved. Maureen answered the door and directed them to the patio where they had a magnificent view of the bay.

Skip stood up and gave Sylvia a kiss on the cheek and shook Owen's hand.

"Welcome," he said and gestured for Owen and Sylvia to sit down.

Maureen had disappeared into the house and quickly returned with champagne glasses and nibbles. Sylvia added her contribution to the table. The sparkling Prosecco captured the glint of the sun as Maureen raised a glass to Sylvia and Owen.

"To romance, love, weddings and years of marital bliss," she toasted.

"Here! Here!" Skip agreed. He looked adoringly at his wife.

Sylvia observed this tête-à-tête and wondered how she could ever have thought this man to be gruff and unapproachable, as she had for many years. As her friendship with Maureen grew, Sylvia realized that Skip's gruffness was a façade.

Skip turned to Sylvia and Owen. "I think it's an excellent idea that you want to wed here. In fact," he added, "we were wondering if we could use photos of your wedding to encourage others to do the same?" He looked hopefully at Sylvia and Owen.

Sylvia was flabbergasted. She shrugged helplessly at Owen, who gaped at her. He shrugged in return.

"What do you think?" he asked.

Maureen swiftly covered their confusion, "You don't need to decide this minute," she said. "Just think about it."

Both Sylvia and Owen relaxed visibly. Skip poured more wine and Maureen went to get another bottle. The Prosecco was a favorite of hers and she kept a stock chilled. A few glasses later, all had relaxed.

Maureen snuggled up to Skip. "I think this might be the chance for me to get that gazebo I've been wanting," she told her husband.

"Hmm…" Skip replied, "Maybe."

"Or a pergola," Sylvia suggested.

"Oooh," Maureen actually cooed. "That would be lovely. I can envision it draped in flowers and something white and flowing. "

Skip rolled his eyes. "Okay, okay, here we go," he said.

"Yes," Maureen stated pointedly, "here we go. And, why don't you and Owen go over to the restaurant and pick up us some sandwiches for dinner?"

"Done," Skip said. "C'mon, Owen. We're on dinner duty."

Skip and Owen's conversation on sailboats could be overheard as they stepped from the room. Maureen giggled.

"Two peas in a pod," Maureen commented.

"Owen will bend his ear about boats," Sylvia agreed.

"So, we'll get a chance to talk wedding stuff while they talk boats," Maureen said. "We have a lot to plan, Sylvia."

Sylvia sighed. "Are we crazy to do this so quickly?"

"I think it is entirely plausible and we'll make it happen," Maureen told her. "Don't worry. It will all fall into place."

"You'll need to remind me of that about a hundred times a day," Sylvia said.

Maureen poured her another glass of Prosecco. Maureen said, "Let's talk gazebos, girlfriend."

The evening continued with wine flowing freely along with good conversation, their dinner, sunset, and lots of laughs. Sylvia clung to Owen's arm as they wended their way down the quiet street heading home, to the sound of gentle waves crashing against the shoreline. She felt like a kite on the end of a string and she swayed away from Owen as they walked.

"Honey, you're like a balloon tonight. Come back here," he tugged her gently back to his side.

Sylvia giggled a silly giggle uncontrollably. Sylvia put her hand to her mouth, but the giggles still crept out.

"I'll walk Percy," Owen told her, "after I tuck you into bed."

"Thanks," she said and kissed him on the cheek. "Because, you know and I know that tomorrow's going to be a big day. The wedding circus *really* begins." Sylvia yawned. "I'm going out with Maureen and Carol to look at wedding stuff. Maybe we should elope?" she suggested, a little hopefully.

"No," Owen told her firmly. "I know we're going to get married rather quickly compared to the more traditional couples, but I do not want to elope. I want to do this right," he said.

Owen pulled her closer to him and kissed her hair above her ear.

Sylvia smiled. "Okay," she acquiesced.

The next morning, Sylvia was pacing from the kitchen to the living room, with coffee cup in hand, while Owen was stretched out on the couch, reading one of his scientific journals. Sylvia glanced at the clock and paced some more.

"I wonder where Maureen is?" she questioned quietly. "It's not like her to be late."

"Why don't you call her," Owen suggested.

"You're right," Sylvia said and went to get her phone.

But, a loud knock, knock, knock that rattled the windows in the kitchen door, startled both of them before Sylvia could reach her phone. Owen started from the couch. They saw Carol's anxious face peering in through the window of the kitchen door. When Carol saw Sylvia entering the kitchen, she pushed open the door and stepped inside.

"Syl?" Carol asked with a shrill, keen edge to her voice, "Are you all right?"

Puzzled, Sylvia answered her, "Sure, I'm okay, why? And why are you here? I thought Maureen and I were going to pick you up? "

Carol took a deep breath. "Joe dropped me off. Oh, Sylvia," she said, shaking her head, "then," Carol hesitated before stating a rhetorical question, "I guess you haven't heard?"

"Haven't heard what?" Owen asked. He had pulled himself off the couch, following Sylvia into the kitchen.

"Th-they found a body," Carol announced, "at the marina."

"What?" Sylvia and Owen gasped simultaneously.

Carol took another deep breath and said, "Joe got the call a little while ago. He dropped me off and he's meeting the other detectives to investigate. I thought," she stammered and stopped and looked uncomfortable.

"You thought Sylvia found another body," Owen finished the sentence for Carol.

Looking guiltily at Sylvia, Carol nodded her head and lowered her eyes.

"Not Maureen?" Sylvia gasped, her voice fearful.

"No," Carol answered, "I don't think so. From what I gathered from Joe's conversation, it was a man."

Sylvia took out her cell phone and punched in Maureen's cell number with shaking fingers.

Maureen answered after five rings, "Oh, Sylvia!" Her voice nearly a wail, "I'm so sorry! I...I forgot I...I...you won't believe what...what..." she stopped talking and gave a little cry.

"Maureen," Sylvia lightly scolded, "do not apologize! Carol came by and said you had a body at the marina?" she asked, her voice quavering as she asked the question.

Hiccups and the sound of tears had come through the line before Maureen said in a hoarse whisper, "George! Old George is dead."

Sylvia was speechless for a moment. She couldn't help herself. She held the phone a few inches away from her and just stared at it.

"I'll be right there," she told Maureen and hung up the phone. The color drained from her face when she turned to face Carol and Owen.

"Old George," she told them quietly.

"What?" Owen had gasped before he asked, "George? Who would want to kill him?"

"I don't know, but I told her I would come down to the marina," she said.

"Do you think you should go?" Owen asked, "It's going to be crazy with police."

"Joe's there," Carol said. "We'll be able to get to Maureen."

"Thank, God you didn't find the body, Sylvia," Owen said sharply.

Sylvia turned sharply to Owen before asking, "What did you say, Owen?"

"Thank God it wasn't you who found the body," Owen told her with a bit of an edge to his voice.

Sylvia had glared at him before she stated crisply, "You know, Owen," she told him, "I love you, but you can really be a big *jerk!*" She ended emphatically. "C'mon, Carol," Sylvia ordered before she strode out the door.

Sylvia marched down the road with Carol trotting to keep up with her.

"What an ass!" she muttered before turning to Carol. "How could he say such a thing?" she asked her.

"Sylvia," Carol admonished gently while trying to catch her breath. "He loves you! Give him a break!"

"He doesn't understand!" Sylvia cried.

"Maybe, a little," Carol said with her usual bluntness.

Sylvia glared at her only slightly mollified. They were both puffing a little as they were walking so quickly. Bayside had a small, steep rise in the middle of the road that some residents referred to it as 'Bayside's peak.' It was just steep enough for the residents to erringly call it a hill, but it also hid the myriad of emergency vehicles that were at the marina at the end of the road and neighborhood from Sylvia's house.

"Oh, no," Sylvia breathed as they crested the rise, "Look at that!"

"Joe's there," Carol told her. "He's somewhere in that mess. Come on," she urged Sylvia.

They started to slow their pace when they reached the flashing lights of emergency and police vehicles on the road that entered the marina. A crowd surrounded the macadam in front of the boat lift. A lone body was still swaying from the lift which now doubled as a gallows. George's body swung heavily from the top of the boat lift. His head lolled sideways from the knot on the rope around his neck. His swarthy face was a dark red, his eyes bulged, and his tongue lolled out of his mouth, swollen, enormous, and turning blue-black. His large body, which was usually so vibrant, swayed heavy, limply and deathly still. It was a horrible sight. Sylvia felt as though she had been kicked in the stomach. Beside her, Carol gave a gasp.

As they got closer, they saw a tall fishing boat carefully maneuvering among the boats in covered boat slips that bordered the boat lift on each side. The big fishing boat was moving through the water and myriad of boats like a car maneuvering through a crowded parking lot at the mall. Two burly policemen were standing on the fly bridge with tools that Sylvia assumed would cut down the body. Sylvia looked around for Maureen and spotted her red hair in the crowd. She was convulsing, either in tears or being sick. Sylvia rushed over to her and put her arms around her.

"Oh, Sylvia," Maureen cried jerkily as she clung to her friend. "Why? Why? Why?"

"I don't know," Sylvia said soothingly. "I don't know." She stroked Maureen's hair as if she was a small child. "Come on, Maureen. I'm going to take you home. There isn't anything you can do."

Maureen let Sylvia lead her to her house. Sylvia gently pushed Maureen to sit on the couch and went in search of a blanket. The

first thing she found was a small, lacy crocheted throw on an otto-
man and tucked it around Maureen's shoulders.

"Here, you'll need this," Sylvia told her, remembering how cold
she had felt when she had found Anna's and Joyce's bodies.

Maureen pulled the throw tightly around her shoulders and
looked up at Sylvia, her eyes large in her pale face and filled with
unshed tears. "Why?" she stated again thickly.

"I don't know," Sylvia said, "But, Joe is there and he's the best
detective," she told her stoutly. "And Carol will let us know what's
going on as soon as she can."

"Carol?" Maureen asked, not remembering at first. The realization came into her eyes. "Oh, Sylvia! Your wedding shopping!
I'm sorry!"

"Forget it," Sylvia said.

CHAPTER THREE

The day which we fear as our last is but the birthday of eternity.

— LUCIUS ANNAEUS SENECA

Despite the heat, Sylvia made Maureen a hot mug of strong tea and handed it to her. Maureen cradled it in her hands. She sipped the tea slowly and stared at nothing for several minutes. Sylvia knew exactly how Maureen felt. A light breeze blew in through the open French doors of the living room. When Sylvia saw Maureen shiver, she rushed over to close the doors. Sylvia thought Maureen looked as though she wanted to say something, but would not or could not. Sylvia waited patiently.

"I think I told you yesterday, that we were having some troubles here," Maureen said dully. "But, I never thought it might come to this," she said, shaking her head.

Sylvia had nodded before Maureen continued, "You know we have a lot of rockfish boats that use the marina, right?" she asked. "Well, it seems they have had some people extorting them for their fish and their profits."

"What?" Sylvia replied astounded. It sounded surreal – fish pirates! She almost laughed. "Fish pirates!" she returned astounded.

"Yes," Maureen agreed. "Fishing is big business here. Haven't you seen the ads for the tournaments? They're professional sportsmen. Also, the rockfish have become very popular at local restaurants. You know they advertise it everywhere. It's a steady income for many people on the bay."

"I just never thought of anything like that," Sylvia said. "But, why would George be involved. Why do you believe that these extortionists killed George?"

"George was a knight errant," Maureen said. "He was a friend to the fishermen. If he got wind of something illegal, I'm sure he tried to stop it. That has to be it!" she said. "We've had all kinds of things at the marina, boats on fire, fist fights, and even drunken boaters that fall off their boats and drown. But, we've never had a murder here!"

The whole idea of pirates of fish seemed surreal to Sylvia. Pirates on the Chesapeake didn't seem real at all –not these days. She knew there were pirates on the Delaware and Chesapeake Bays in the 17th and 18th centuries, and perhaps during the prohibition, but not now.

"Skip," Maureen stated. "Where is he?" she asked Sylvia.

"Probably answering questions," Sylvia told her. "It could be hours."

"Oh, no," Maureen said. "I should go and find him."

"Why don't you call him instead?" Sylvia suggested.

"Okay," Maureen agreed and sat back on the couch again. "Okay. That's a good idea."

Sylvia pulled out her cell phone and called Skip. He didn't answer her call and she left a message.

"Probably, he's still busy with the police," Sylvia assured Maureen.

"I don't know," Maureen sounded doubtful. "You think he's okay, don't you?" she asked with worry in her voice.

"I think Skip's fine," Sylvia told her again. "It truly could be hours of questions. On the other hand, I am just in shock about this. Who knew that a marina had a dark side?"

Maureen laughed ruefully. "Unfortunately, it's everywhere," she told Sylvia. "When I first knew Skip, we had a worker who was taking bribes for prime slips. That was an ugly mess, I can tell you," she said to Sylvia. "We almost lost the marina. In fact, that's how I met Skip. My former life was in marketing, and he was seeking an agency to bring the marina's good name back," she told Sylvia. "No one wants to believe that marinas aren't more than places of fun," she added with a slightly bitter note in her voice.

Sylvia's phone rang. The caller ID showed Skip and Sylvia handed the phone directly to Maureen.

Maureen had a brief conversation with Skip asking how he was, and asking where he was. She also told him that Sylvia was taking care of her at the house. She hung up the phone with a relieved sigh.

"He's all right," she told Sylvia with relief, "and still answering questions while they are gathering evidence," she said to Sylvia.

The doorbell rang and Sylvia went to answer it. Carol was outside and Sylvia invited her in. Her usual playful smile was gone, and Sylvia noticed that Carol had a strained look around her eyes. She came in and sat down with Maureen.

"What's the word?" Sylvia asked quietly.

"Nothing yet," Carol confirmed. "The investigation will take a while, Joe said."

"Oh," Maureen moaned. "This will be terrible for our business. I'm sure people are leaving in droves, aren't they?" she pointed her question in Carol's direction.

"Well," Carol said slowly. "They are leaving as they can. The police are asking everyone and getting contact information from everyone at the marina. Skip's trying to keep the boaters as calm as possible."

"I should be out there too," Maureen said. She turned to Sylvia, "We'll need to pick up our wedding plans later."

"We'll figure it out," Sylvia told her. "Don't worry," she assured her. There was a blip of doubt in her voice and in her heart. She hoped Maureen did not pick up on it.

Carol did, though. She gave Sylvia a quick, sharp look. She nodded briefly and then they stood simultaneously. They walked out to the chaos that still reigned at the marina. The ambulance was gone, but several police cars remained. There was a long line of cars waiting to exit the marina. The police stopped each car, interrogated the passengers before they let them go down the road.

"I need to find Skip," Maureen said, a little desperately. "Thank you, Sylvia, for coming down and helping." She reached and gave Sylvia a hug. "I'll...I'll talk to you soon."

"Thank you, Carol," she told her and put her hand on Carol's arm before she went off to find Skip.

Carol and Sylvia moseyed back to Sylvia's house. Neither spoke.

Owen rushed out of the living room after the short excited bark from Percy alerted him they were home when they opened the kitchen door. Owen immediately took Sylvia in his arms. Percy danced around them until Carol knelt down to pet him.

"I'm sorry," he whispered in her hair.

"It's okay," she said, slumping into his arms so that he had to hold her tighter. "I know you said that because you care."

"You're right," he said. "I love you."

"Love you too," she said and raised her face to him for a kiss.

He held her tightly for a few minutes before he let her go and asked, "How are things at the marina?"

"A mess," Carol answered grimly, "Everything is complete chaos."

"I thought it might be," Owen said. "I thought it best to stay out of the way. How are Maureen and Skip doing?"

"Maureen is in shock," Sylvia said, "and we didn't see Skip. Maureen went to find him when we left. She's concerned about the ramifications to their business."

"That makes sense," he said.

"Come on in here," he said and he led them to the living room. "I knew you missed your brunch, so I thought I could try to make up for it."

On the buffet was a large pitcher filled with a tomato substance and bottle of vodka and a dish of shrimp and olives next to it.

"Wow," Carol said. "This is perfect."

"And, I'll make you a superb omelet to go with it," Owen promised. He made two Bloody Marys with shrimp and olives garnishing each tall glass. "I found mushrooms, onions, green peppers and some good cheese in the refrigerator. You ladies relax a bit and I'll bring you brunch."

"I'm not arguing," Sylvia told him. "Thank you," she said to Owen as she settled onto the couch.

Owen beamed. "Marian trained me well," he commented.

"She certainly did!" Carol told him, "And Sylvia and I are glad she did!" Carol raised her glass in a salute to Owen.

He nodded with a rakish grin and exited to the kitchen with Percy on his heels.

"Well, girlfriend," Carol commented to Sylvia, "you have about eleven weeks to plan this wedding. The shenanigans today have dropped us back a few days."

"I know," Sylvia almost moaned. "I keep telling myself it will all work out, but will it?" she asked her friend.

She looked down at her engagement ring. It was platinum vines with diamond leaves that graced a central diamond. It sparkled in the sunlight that shone through the French doors. On her middle finger, next to her engagement ring, was a thick gold ring with a repeating symbol that made its way around the band. A friend had called it the 'flower of life.' It had been a final, posthumous gift from her beloved grandmother. Inadvertently, Sylvia ran her thumb against the metals on the bottom of the two rings.

"It will all work out," Carol assured her. "Immediately after brunch, we'll get online and start planning. But, first," Carol ordered reaching for Sylvia's empty glass, "another Bloody Mary is in order."

Halfway through their second Bloody Mary, Joe stopped by. He looked stressed and barely returned Carol's hug and kiss on the cheek. He sat beside her with a sigh and loosened his tie. Owen handed him a cold beer.

"Thanks," he said. He looked at their questioning faces. "I can't tell you a lot," he said. "We've started to collect evidence and have questioned numerous people. I need some time to look at the facts and mull things over. I have the feeling this investigation will take a while."

"You still have your 'cop face' on," Carol told him. "Relax now, you're among friends." She rubbed his arm steadily.

Sylvia looked at Joe. She had noticed that in the last year, sometimes his eyes had a cold, steely look. It was much different from the warm and wonderful Joe she knew. That look must be what Carol was referring too. She guessed he had to put on a tough exterior with his job as a detective. She knew he had incredible integrity and his work was impeccable. He was sipping at the cold beer and Sylvia noticed the hard look was slowly fading from his face as he began to respond to Carol's ministrations.

"Welcome back," Carol murmured.

Her comment was so soft that Sylvia only barely caught the words. Joe smiled at Carol and squeezed her hand. Sylvia had noticed in the past few months that Joe had brought a surprising change to Carol. She was still funny, blunt with her words and full of chutzpah, but Joe brought out a softer side that Sylvia had not seen before. Sylvia loved how her friend became a mellow puddle around Joe. They made an excellent pair.

"How are your wedding plans coming?" Joe asked, breaking Sylvia out of her daydream.

Sylvia grimaced as Carol answered, "They'll be getting married at the marina, but they need to find a spot for the reception," she told him. "Once that's done, they can order invitations. Things will fall into place if we stick to a strict schedule. It's a shame about the murder at the marina. Maureen, Sylvia and I were planning on quite a day."

Sylvia nodded sadly. 'This wedding stuff is overwhelming enough," she said. "But, poor Maureen and Skip," she commented, "I'm hoping they're all right."

"Give them a few hours for things to settle and then call them," Carol advised, "but, back to the wedding plans a minute," Carol ordered. "Sylvia, you'll need to find a band or a D.J. for the reception. I think I know where you could find an outstanding bluegrass ensemble that would play for you," she said looking slyly at Joe.

"Oh, Joe!" Sylvia breathed. "Would you? Could you? That would be so much fun, wouldn't it Owen?" as she turned to face him.

"It would be great!" Owen returned enthusiastically. "Can you handle being a groomsman *and* entertainer?" he asked Joe.

The light returned to Joe's eyes as he answered, "I think I can handle it," he told them. "I'll ask the boys in the band, but I think it would be just fine. Let me know the date and we'll put it on the band's calendar."

"One more problem solved and one more thing checked off the list," Carol crowed triumphantly.

After Carol and Joe had left in the late afternoon, Sylvia and Owen went for a swim in the bay. The heat of the day had built to where the water felt refreshing and cool. The bay was relatively shallow and at low tide Sylvia and Owen could walk out past their neighbor's pier and the water reached to Sylvia's breasts. As the tide came in, it would lift them off their feet. They paddled about with nylon rafts to keep them afloat. A blue heron was sitting on the pier staring intently at the water, waiting for a fish. Further down the bay, they could watch terns diving for insects in the water, and a bald eagle soared high in the sky, it's snowy, white head silhouetted against the deepening blue sky. There was a lull in the boat traffic when dusk began to fall on the bay. The light on the water changed from blue to gray to varying shades of pink and mauve as it caught the colors of the sun setting in the western sky. Boats meandered through the water heading towards their evening moorings. It was as though they were savoring the last bit of their day on the water. The lights on the boats were tiny beacons in the oncoming dusk. Sylvia and Owen walked into shore in the last dregs of evening light. They showered after their swim and went out to relax on the deck. Sylvia lit several candles and they watched the night gently turn from dusk to dark. Lights blinked lazily across the bay like a firefly's secret code.

Sylvia's phone jangled, breaking up the evening's peace. It was her mother calling about the day's progress on wedding plans.

"Oh, Mom," Sylvia said with a catch in her voice. The impact of George's death was catching up with her. "Oh, Mom," she said sadly, "It's been quite a day."

"What happened?" her mother asked concerned.

Sylvia told her mother about George's murder.

"Oh, my God!" Mary cried, "How horrible!"

She asked many questions, many of which Sylvia could not answer. Her mom expressed the same sentiment as Owen had that she was glad that Sylvia had not found the body. Sylvia repressed a small sigh. Sylvia changed the subject to the wedding after promising to let her mother know when the services would take place for George. Sylvia told her mother about Carol's thoughts to find a place for the reception as soon as possible so that they could find wedding invitations and get them so they could be expressed shipped to Sylvia. Carol warned Sylvia that the invitations should be going out in the next couple of weeks. Her mother agreed with Carol's ideas and her timeline.

"Why don't you check with the Yacht Club for the reception?" her mother suggested. "Perhaps Owen can rent a slip for the day and you can sail off into the sunset for your honeymoon?"

Sylvia had put her cell phone on speaker and Owen chimed in enthusiastically, "That would be perfect! I love that idea, Mom!"

"And I would like guests to light the wish lanterns as we leave the reception," Sylvia informed them. She told her mother to check out the wish lanterns online.

"But, Mom, we're not members of the yacht club," Sylvia reminded her, sobering a bit after her initial euphoria at the idea.

"I don't think you need to be a member to have a reception there," Mary told them. "We've attended many functions from private parties, art shows, and wedding receptions. I'll tell you what, I'll call tomorrow and find out more information and let you know what they say. Would that work?"

"That would help a lot, Mom," Sylvia told her gratefully. "And, I will call Maureen to find out more about George's services and let you know."

"So, we'll talk tomorrow," her mother confirmed.

When they ended the conversation, Owen took Sylvia's hand in his and kissed it gently. "Hmm," he murmured, "Sailing off into the sunset sounds idyllic."

He continued to hold her hand, but got up from his chair next to her and proceeded to kiss her lightly from her fingertips and up her bare arm. The light kisses tickled and Sylvia started to giggle. Owen worked his way up her arm to her neck and behind her ear where she protested with a giggling "Stop! Stop!"

He stopped momentarily to softly ask, "Why?"

She regretfully looked into his eyes before answering, "I need to call Maureen," she told him.

"Okay," he whispered, disappointment clearly in his voice, and gave her a light kiss on the lips. "I," he said emphatically, "will go online and continue boat shopping. We'll pick up this later," he told her with a promise in his eyes.

A little breathless from the kisses, Sylvia dialed Maureen's number.

CHAPTER FOUR

*Friendship is always a sweet responsibility, never
an opportunity.*

— KHALIL GIBRAN

The voice that answered the phone sounded worn and weary.
"Hello," Maureen's voice came across the phone.

"Maureen?" Sylvia asked, not quite recognizing the voice at first. "It's Sylvia, Maureen."

"Oh, Sylvia," Maureen replied. "I'm so sorry," she apologized again, "we've been caught up in funeral arrangements for," her voice caught in her throat and she sounded as if she would break apart, "for George," she finished slowly.

"Maureen!" Sylvia scolded, "Stop apologizing! What's going on with the funeral arrangements? How are you?" she asked.

"I'm actually horrible," Maureen answered honestly. "We are helping George's family and paying for his funeral," she told Sylvia. "The police want to do an autopsy before his burial," she said, "of course, so that complicates the arrangements."

"What or when are the funeral arrangements?" Sylvia asked gently.

Maureen sighed resignedly, "This coming weekend. It's sure to be crowded, so we're having a viewing Friday and Saturday with the service and burial on Saturday at eleven.

"Okay," Sylvia said before she asked, "Is there anything I can do?"

Maureen paused, "No, I don't think so," she replied slowly. "Thank you, though."

"Okay," Sylvia said, 'But, let me know if you need anything."

She filled Maureen in on checking with the yacht club for a reception, having a late afternoon wedding followed by dinner at the club. She also told Maureen about the shopping trip next weekend.

"I don't think I can go shopping," Maureen answered, "Though, something happy and fun sounds much better than dealing with death," she told Sylvia.

They finished their conversation and Sylvia thought briefly about George. She had been on his boat, a 58 foot, 1967 Chris Craft, only once. She had been impressed by the size, and how everything had been shipshape. It really was like an apartment on the water. She loved the lines of the hull and the beautiful wood. Her mom often teased, saying she had been born at the wrong time. When her mom was growing up, Chris Craft boats were 'hot' and owned by movie stars. She wondered again why anyone would want to kill George.

Before she had a moment to take another breath, the phone rang again. This time, it was Gwen.

"Hey, Syl," Gwen said, her voice light, "How did the wedding shopping go? Did you find a dress?" Gwen asked.

"Oh, Gwen," Sylvia said, her voice now weary, "It's been a day."

"What do you mean?" Gwen asked. "I thought you were going to shop until you dropped," she stated.

Sylvia filled Gwen in on George's death.

"But, you didn't find the body," Gwen asked, "right?"

"Right," Sylvia told her, again weary of the implications that she was a magnet for finding dead bodies. "Someone at the boatyard did."

"That's a relief," Gwen said. "You wouldn't want to be caught up in litigation as well as planning a wedding!"

"There is that," Sylvia replied acerbically.

Sylvia filled Gwen in on the plans to shop for gowns and reception places next weekend, after the funeral.

"I'll send you the website of the yacht club," Sylvia told her. "Is there a chance you can come next weekend?"

"I don't know," Gwen told her, "that depends on a couple of things."

"Is everything okay?" Sylvia asked her friend.

"Well, I was calling for the pictures of the dresses you and Carol emailed to me earlier. I love the meadow green dress with the empire waist the best," Gwen told Sylvia. "In fact, that's the one that would work best for me."

"I'm glad you liked it," Sylvia told her. "Carol called the bridal shop and they have samples, so we can see it 'live' next weekend."

"When I told you the empire waist dress was the best, it was for a reason," Gwen hinted.

Sylvia caught on, "No! You're pregnant?" she squealed the question excitedly. "Gwen! Can you still be in the wedding?"

"Look," Gwen said, "Frank and I are 'over the moon' about the pregnancy, but you and Frank are the only two people that know. I'm just a few weeks pregnant. The baby will be due in January.

I want to wait a bit before we tell the parents, but I needed to let you know because of the wedding. You'll probably have a chunky Matron of Honor."

"Oh, Gwen," Sylvia told her. "I'm sure you'll be glowing. You won't be very far along by the time we get married. If the empire waist dress works best for you, then that's what it will be. It's stunning online. I'll call and talk to the bridal shop this week, okay?"

"That sounds great," Gwen told her, relief flooding her voice.

"I'm so excited for you!" Sylvia went on. "Is it all right to tell Owen? How about Carol?" Sylvia asked, "They'll need to know."

Gwen laughed, "As long as they don't tell Mother Audrey!"

"I'll swear them to secrecy," Sylvia said to her friend before they hung up.

CHAPTER FIVE

"Listen to what you know, instead of what you fear."

— RICHARD BACH

At work on Monday, Sylvia broke the news of her accelerated nuptials to her boss, Mr. Carter. She laughed when he gave a furtive glance at her abdomen and quickly looked away. She assured him that she was not pregnant. When Carol came bubbling into the office bursting with ideas for the wedding, he drily asked if they would get any work completed in the next three months.

Both young women laughed and told him honestly, that the wedding would definitely be a large part of their lives and conversations. Sylvia assured him she would continue with her obligations, pull Bay Days together and her plans to distribute the letters and educational grant information just before the wedding. Carol would answer any questions while she was on her honeymoon and that they would choose the grants when she returned from the honeymoon. Mr. Carter nodded, satisfied with their responses. He nodded complacently and turned and entered his office.

It seemed to Sylvia that the week flew by and Friday evening appeared to come in the blink of an eye. They found her mother's car parked at their house and something yummy simmering on top of the stove when they walked through the kitchen door. Owen and Sylvia sniffed appreciatively. Mary was not in sight.

"Mmm," Owen murmured. "I think I could get used to this."

"Really," Mary commented as she came into the kitchen from the living room, "so, you're asking your future mother-in-law to move in with you?" she asked with a slight teasing tone to her voice.

Owen's face had momentarily frozen in shock, and a brief look of panic crossed his face before he got his emotions under control and tried to laugh at her comment. The laugh was slightly forced. Sylvia and Mary caught the look and both smiled appreciatively at his attempt to recover.

"Never fear," Mary told him as she came to give him a peck on the cheek, "I'm not planning to move in with you and Sylvia anytime soon. Even though, now that I'm retired, I could help by cooking you three square meals a day," she teased. "But, I won't move in. Not yet, at least."

His relief was palpable. Mary laughed again and Sylvia joined in.

"Go and change into something more comfortable," she told them, "and we can have drinks out on the deck before dinner."

A few minutes later they were on the porch where Mary and Sylvia chuckled again when Owen stepped onto the deck. He shook his head and his finger at them finally seeing the humor in Mary's alleged threat to move in with them. Sylvia's cell phone rang before he had a chance to say anything. Her conversation was brief.

"Gwen *is* coming," she told them, "but, she is caught in traffic. It will be somewhat late before they arrive."

"They?" Owen and Mary choroused.

"They," Sylvia confirmed. "Frank didn't want her driving this far alone."

"I can understand that," Mary said. "Well, she can sleep in tomorrow," Mary said, "while we go to the funeral. Maybe, Carol could pick her up and meet us at the yacht club for lunch?" she suggested.

"That sounds perfect, I'll text her and ask," Sylvia said and turned to Owen, "and, that will free you up to do more boat shopping. Frank can join you."

He grinned at her.

"Are you any closer to a decision on a boat?" Mary asked.

"I'm looking at a Catalina," he told her. "The thirty foot is manageable for sailing and for the cost. Of course, I love the Sabre's as well," he told her.

"What about those Nautor Swan boats you showed me?" Sylvia teased.

"Uh, yeah," he said, drily, "no problem, if I have a couple of million to spare."

"Well, it's all Greek to me," Mary said. "I wouldn't know one boat from another."

"Me too," Sylvia agreed. "But, I'm learning."

After relaxing for a few minutes, Mary got up and brought dinner to the deck. Sylvia and Owen stared at the colorful, spaghetti-like strands on the plate.

"Curry? Curried...something?" Sylvia asked looking at the brightly colored dish with lots of vegetables and small shrimp and what Sylvia thought was chicken.

"Try it," Mary said.

"Good!" Owen proclaimed as he dove into the dish.

Sylvia nodded in agreement after tentatively tasting the dish.

"Okay," she asked her mother, "what is this stuff?"

"My own heart-smart version of Singapore Mei Fun," she said proudly. "It's made from a spaghetti squash."

"Squash?" Owen questioned, wrinkling up his nose. "Squash doesn't taste this good," he told her.

"This one does," Mary told him. "Spaghetti squash is now my new 'go to' food."

They ate the meal, cleaned up and set out to wait for Gwen. Owen built a fire in the fire pit and they sat, watching a few boats and their lights meander up the bay. Mary toddled off to bed after nine and Owen banked the fire.

"Let's go inside," he told Sylvia. "Even with the fire, the mosquitoes are so hungry they're not daunted by the smoke and flame." He slapped at his arm and squashed a bug.

Sylvia didn't protest. She was tired too. They sat on the couch, and Sylvia curled up against Owen. Percy was snuggled up, dozing on Sylvia.

Gwen and Frank arrived after eleven. Gwen was clearly fatigued. Sylvia's gorgeous blond friend had black smudges of exhaustion under her eyes. She looked drawn and almost ill to Sylvia.

"Hi, Syl," she mumbled against Sylvia's shoulder as she hugged her.

Gwen slumped against her friend. "Bed," she mumbled after giving hugs.

Frank barely greeted them, but rushed their bags up to the guest room, tucked Gwen in and returned downstairs to Sylvia and Owen.

"Is Gwen all right?" Sylvia asked.

"The baby," Frank said giving them a grin. He looked almost embarrassed, but proud at the same time. His grin was rakish, and he had a Kennedy-esque aura about him. "She is ridiculously tired and emotional right now in this first trimester. She'll be okay," he assured them.

Owen gave Frank a cold beer and slapped him on the back. He sighed tiredly and sat down. They talked for a short while.

"I'm restless," Frank announced, "from the drive. Okay if I take the big guy for a walk?" he motioned to Percy.

"Of course," Owen said. "Let me get us another beer and I'll go with you."

"I think I'm going to head up to bed myself," Sylvia told the guys. She gave Frank a hug and Owen a kiss.

"See you soon," he murmured into her hair when she hugged him.

CHAPTER SIX

"To live is so startling, it leaves little time for
anything else."

— EMILY DICKINSON

P ercy whined early the next morning. It was different from his "I need to go out, *now*," whine. Sylvia woke up wondering what was happening and then heard Gwen retching in the bathroom.

She got up and tapped on the bathroom door.

"Gwen," she asked gently, "is there anything I can do to help you? I have soda, crackers and pretzels downstairs," she told her friend.

"A couple of pretzels sound great," Gwen said to Sylvia weakly. "And, I brought some ginger tea for my tummy. I'll go get it and meet you downstairs."

Sylvia went downstairs and got out the pretzels and started water to boil for coffee and Gwen's tea. Gwen came down looking pale and wan. Sylvia took the box of tea from her and made her a cup. Gwen sniffed the ginger tea gratefully when Sylvia brought it to the table. She nibbled at a pretzel very slowly.

Sylvia sat across the table from her. "Are you going to be okay?" she asked concerned.

Sylvia noticed that Gwen kept her nose away from the coffee and Sylvia subtly moved the cup out of the way.

"This will pass," Gwen said. "I'll have a pretzel, maybe two, tea and head up to bed."

"Sleep in as long as you want," Sylvia told her. "We're headed to the funeral and Carol's going to pick you up a little after 12:30 to go to the yacht club for lunch to discuss the reception."

Sylvia sat with her as Gwen nibbled and sipped. She kept the conversation light and brought Gwen up to date on the wedding plans. Gwen's pale face gradually gained a little bit of color. She still looked exhausted. Pregnancy, at least this part of it, did not look like fun to Sylvia. Gwen yawned.

"Go back to bed," Sylvia ordered her friend.

Gwen acquiesced and went back upstairs to bed. Sylvia put the water on for more coffee and took an anxious Percy, who was pacing at this point, out for his morning walk. When she returned home, Sylvia took coffee up to Owen and scooted from his searching hands, laughing as he frowned and looked petulant.

"Come on, little boy," she teased, pulling her breasts from his caressing hands, "We need to get ready for George's funeral, and the day ahead. I'm going to jump in the shower while you work on your first cup of coffee."

Mary, Owen, and Sylvia maneuvered through the early morning quietly so that Gwen and Frank could sleep. They drove to the funeral home in two cars. By the time they arrived, the line was already out the door with the number of mourners. They parked in the town's municipal lot and joined the line of mourners, now almost a block long at the funeral home. After nearly an hour, Mary, Owen and Sylvia made their way through the receiving line, giving their condolences to George's children. The line going past George's body moved painfully slow. Sylvia clutched at Owen's hand.

The mortician had done a good job. When it was their turn to view the body, George looked like he was sleeping. As sad as she was, Sylvia could not mourn "the body" of George, but thought of the laughing, kindly soul that had filled their lives. A few tears leaked from her eyes. Once again, death seemed surreal to her. Skip and Maureen were off to the side at the end of the receiving line. Skip looked grim. Maureen clung to Sylvia for a moment when she hugged her. Her eyes were red and puffy from crying.

"How are you doing?" Sylvia whispered to her in the hug.

Maureen couldn't answer. When she tried to speak, tears began to spill again. Sylvia gave her another hug, holding her own tears back, and followed her mother and Owen to find a seat. The funeral home had opened up a second room for people to sit for the service. Mary, Owen, and Sylvia found themselves packed into the back, sitting on folding chairs. It was stifling. The air seemed thick. Sylvia and her head were reeling. Death appeared to be everywhere. First Gran had died, followed by Mr. Peters down the street. Then the murders of Anna and Joyce added to the mix. Now George was dead. Was this an ordinary passage as one became older, Sylvia wondered? She could not remember a time in her life when she knew of so many people dying. Nausea washed over her and she felt a wave of heat. She had to get out of the funeral home and get some fresh air before she suffocated.

"Excuse me," she whispered to Owen. "I need some air."

"Are you all right?" he whispered the question to her.

Sylvia nodded, "I just need to get some fresh air," she said quietly and insistently, "Now!"

Owen took one look at her face, tinged with green, and shifted his legs so that she could get past him quickly. He patted her back as she went by and his eyes followed her with a worried expression.

Sylvia pushed past him and other mourners to get to the main hallway of the funeral home. She took a deep breath and headed quickly for the front door. The lovely scent of flowers that she had enjoyed when she entered the funeral home were now cloying and making her nausea greater. Sylvia hurried down the hallway towards the door, holding her breath for as long as possible. The thick, plush carpeting in the funeral home silenced her footsteps. There was still a long line of mourners, but she slipped out with a few others who were not attending the service. Once outside in the sunshine, she took deeper breaths, clearing her lungs and nostrils from the smells of the funeral home. The sun felt wonderful. She still wanted to be further away from death and the funeral home and started to walk down the street. About a block away was a small deli. Outside were picnic tables where people ate, smoked and talked. In the mornings, several of the local men sat and drank coffee and talked politics. The townspeople fondly called them 'the Senate.' Later in the day the picnic tables were filled with families including children and melting ice cream cones. As the day wore on, the groups changed to diners and local teenagers who laid claim to the two picnic tables outside the deli. Summer tourists and the boating community frequented the deli for food to take on their boats, but there were definite 'regulars' that Sylvia recognized each time she stopped by the deli. She went inside to purchase a cold drink.

She sipped at it as she continued to walk down the street. As she walked, her purse buzzed from her cell phone. It was Owen, texting her, to see if she was all right. She replied that she needed some fresh air, a bit of a walk, and would be back in a few minutes.

Just a couple of blocks away the town's community park perched at the head of the bay. It had a few pavilions, a pier for fishing, a small boat launch, a large playground and a walking path that led to the beach. Sylvia walked past a large pavilion and around a crowded playground. There, parents, babies and children created a cacophony that rivaled the small island where Great Blue herons squawked and flapped near the shore of the park. Sylvia had heard that locals suspected a rookery forming to rival that of Pea Patch Island's rookery in the Delaware River. The rusty sounding squawks of the heron blended with the joyous shouts of children playing on the playground until it created a background of white noise. Her mind still whirled and she couldn't seem to put her thoughts together with the exception that she felt that death enveloped her and her world. The world began to spin and tilt out of control. A rustle of leaves near her startled her and the Green Man took her elbow to steady her when she lost her balance.

"It will be all right, Sylvia," his baritone of a voice intoned calmly.

"How can it be good?" she cried, "I feel as though death is everywhere."

"And so it is," he replied gently, "and birth is as well. It's part of the balance of the yin/yang or black and white."

"The "Circle of Life," Sylvia murmured, thinking of the song from the 'Lion King.'

"Exactly," replied the Green Man, but not referencing the film.

"And you!" Sylvia stated, almost accusingly, "You are definitely another facet to the mix. You add the 'rebirth' part."

"Yes, I do," the Green Man agreed amiably and continued, "but, you do not know the journey you will be taking upon your 'death.'"

"Journey?" she questioned, "don't we all just 'die?' Or, is there really a heaven and hell? I know about those fascinating reports of near death experiences..." her voice broke off.

"It's a mystery I am not at liberty to reveal to you," he told her, "...yet. But, I promise you, that when your 'death' happens, your journey will be a good one."

His words comforted Sylvia. He walked back towards the funeral home with her.

"But," she argued, "death seems so senseless."

"Perhaps," he said, enigmatically, "but, it is a choice and it is very definitely a passage."

"Only to leave those behind sad, angry and frustrated," she replied.

"That's a choice," the Green Man almost snapped.

"I guess so," Sylvia said, not agreeing with him.

"Don't fear," the Green Man ordered somewhat sternly.

He had placed his arm and wrapped it around her shoulders. His touch brought waves of peace. Was that her problem? Instead of feeling the suffocation by the deaths around her, was it truly fear? Did she fear to die? That insight gave her pause, as she was not sure of her own beliefs about heaven, hell or the hereafter. The Green Man rubbed her arm and hugged her to him in a one arm hug. She relaxed.

"Birth, death, and rebirth are part of the pattern as well," he said.

For a brief instant, Sylvia had a glimpse of something that flashed through her mind. It was like the movement of the stars in the night sky, but different. It was the briefest of flashes of understanding that brought her comfort, as the comfort she felt when she first saw the tree auras dancing in the sky.

Her mother pulled up along the street and beeped at her. Sylvia jumped at the sound. The Green Man vanished instantly.

"There you are!" her mother called, as she put the window down in the car. "We were worried about you. Owen and I have been driving through the streets of North Bay looking everywhere for you."

"Sorry," Sylvia told her mother, "I had to get out of there. I had that same suffocating feeling when Gran died," she explained as she climbed into the car. "I'm doing better now."

"Good," her mother replied. "Call or text Owen and let him know you are all right and to meet us at the club."

Sylvia did as she was told and her mother drove to the yacht club. The sunshine pouring through the car window felt cleansing and Sylvia closed her eyes and thought about what the Green Man had said. She wondered again if her problem was that she feared death. But, she asked herself, how could one not fear death? She did not want to wonder what it felt like, not for many, many years to come. She had already come too close to it a few months ago.

Her mother interrupted her thoughts, "Are you sure you are all right?" she asked Sylvia as she turned into the gravel parking lot of the yacht club.

"I'll be okay," Sylvia said, opening her eyes to see the club perched at the end of a small point on the bay. Several boats were at their moorings, but then several spaces were open at the docks, and several cars were in the parking lot. People were enjoying a sail on this lovely day.

"Shall we head inside or wait for Owen, Frank, Gwen and Carol?" her mother asked.

"Why don't we go inside," Sylvia suggested.

They entered the yacht club. It was quiet. From the downstairs pub, a petite woman with dark hair and snappy, black eyes and bright smile greeted them.

"Ms. Ash? Sylvia?" she greeted them in a mature voice with a touch of a southern drawl. "I'm Beverly Maranzano, the events coordinator at the club. Welcome." She held out her hand.

"Why don't we head to the dining room for our planning," Beverly motioned for them to walk past a small seating area to a sun-drenched room filled with small tables. French doors led out to a patio area dotted with smaller tables. The patio area had awnings that shaded a large portion of the table area. Beverly led them to the only table that was covered in linen and set for six.

"The groom, my maid of honor and bridesmaid should be here any moment," Sylvia said as they sat down.

"That's fine," Beverly assured her. "Perhaps you can begin to look over the paperwork while we wait."

Beverly handed Mary and Sylvia each a folder that was filled with menus, policies, and testimonials from couples previously married at the club.

Owen, Gwen, and Carol walked into the club, laughing about something. Gwen looked much better than she had a few hours previously. Sylvia noticed Gwen had a subtle glow around her. They walked over to the table and Sylvia made introductions. Beverly shook hands with each of them.

"Where's Frank?" Sylvia asked, peering at the group.

"He's at your house," Gwen told her, "catching up on some work. A business call interrupted his weekend, so he's dealing with some work issues. He'll text Owen after this luncheon meeting so that they can go boat shopping while we head out to look at dresses."

"Oh," Sylvia replied. "Okay."

A waitress came and poured water for each of them and asked for a drink order.

When they were settled once again, Beverly asked, "Now, when I first spoke with you, you mentioned the wedding in June of next year. Do you have a date?"

"Umm," Sylvia said slowly, "We're actually moving the wedding to September of this year and we understood the weekend after Labor Day is available."

"Oh!" Beverly exclaimed softly, "I will need to double check on that." She gave a surreptitious glance to Sylvia and her abdomen.

Sylvia blushed, but Gwen was the one who spoke up, "I'm the pregnant one, not Sylvia," she stated dryly.

"Oh!" Beverly commented softly. "I see."

She stood up to get another calendar and when she left the room, Gwen and Carol dissolved in giggles.

"Her face!" Gwen stammered and lost herself to giggles again.

"Girls! Get hold of yourselves," Mary scolded in a sotto voce whisper.

Gwen and Carol tried. They took large gulps of ice water and when Beverly came back to the room, Carol pulled Gwen to her feet to look at the view over the bay.

"I'm happy to say that date is available," Beverly told them. "What is your ballpark on the number of guests for the wedding reception?"

"It's relatively small," Mary began, "only about fifty or so."

"Mom," Sylvia interjected, "Owen and I were going over the guest list and there aren't more than thirty people. Well, maybe thirty-five with the band members and the minister," she corrected, "We're keeping it simple."

Beverly nodded. "That's quite manageable. Why don't you take a look at the information while I begin to write up the contract for the event? Will you be having the ceremony here?"

They shook their heads and Sylvia explained that they were having the ceremony at the marina near their home in Bayside. Their hope was to have the reception at the club and then sail off into the sunset with wish lanterns in the early evening.

"That will be lovely!" Beverly complimented their plans.

Sylvia shared the folder with Owen and they looked at the details of décor, linens and down payment as well as the choices for the bar and the food. Gwen and Carol returned to the table much soberer than a few minutes prior. Beverly had procured another folder and the girls looked over the information as well. The waitress returned with plates of various appetizers for them to try, which they passed around.

Sylvia pushed the platter of stuffed mushrooms towards Gwen.

"Mushrooms are your favorite," Sylvia told her friend but was surprised when Gwen pushed the tray back towards Sylvia with her nose upturned and a grimace on her face.

"What?" Sylvia asked, "You love mushrooms!"

"Unfortunately, not anymore," Gwen told her sadly, "At least I'm reasonably sure the baby doesn't like them. It's very sad."

"Well, maybe it's temporary," Sylvia reassured her.

The rest of the group nodded as they sampled the tasty morsels of several appetizers. Sylvia loved the grilled fruit kabobs and Owen was adamant to have the mini crab cakes. Mary suggested a cheese tray and Carol asked for the spring rolls.

"Full bar, premium," Mary said. "You'll need to let me know if you will provide the champagne for the toast or if we need to do this. Also," she turned to Sylvia, "there is a buffet stated on the menu, but I think we would like to have a sit-down reception. Is that right?"

Sylvia and Owen nodded. Beverly agreed and they discussed food choices. Owen seemed happy, too, and was even happier when their waitress brought cups of crab bisque to serve to them.

"Delicious," he proclaimed. "We definitely want this on the menu."

"Done," said Beverly. "Choose which appetizers you would like and I'll put the crab bisque down as your soup choice. If you know of anyone with a shellfish or other food allergy, please let me know as soon as possible so that we can have an alternate available. Ahh, here are some samples of the main courses."

The waitress brought loaded platters of Snowcapped Filet Mignon, Pasta Primavera, Seafood Scampi and more. Things were portioned so that everyone could get a taste. Owen quickly chose the lump crab meat topped filet as a choice and Mary voted on the pecan crusted salmon with bourbon sauce.

"This herb chicken is delightful," Gwen commented.

"And what would the bride prefer?" Beverly asked. "You have a choice of three entrees for the reception."

Sylvia felt a little overwhelmed. "Definitely the filet," she said, "and the salmon would be two of the three," she commented. "I have no idea for the third. I need to think if we have any vegetarians in the group. If not, definitely a chicken dish."

"Well, you have the choice of Chicken Marsala, chicken saltimbocca, chicken with champagne cream sauce or the herb encrusted char grilled chicken breast," Beverly told her. "If you have a guest that needs something special, I'm sure the chef would be happy to oblige."

Sylvia looked to the group. "Well?" she asked.

They vacillated between the chicken with the champagne cream sauce and the herbed chicken, finally deciding on the herb encrusted grilled chicken breast. They went over the rest of the menu while they tried the salad and potato choices.

Beverly excused herself for a moment and Sylvia commented, "I never knew choosing a meal could be so complicated!"

"And this is just the beginning of decisions," Carol intoned, "but, we're all here to support you and to help you out."

"Do you have a florist or a baker for the cake yet?" Beverly asked her.

Sylvia shook her head.

"I have a list of several," she assured Sylvia and starred a few of her favorites on the typed sheet.

"Thank you," Sylvia said with a relieved sigh.

They discussed the band and possible dancing, and the logistics of things that sent Sylvia's head whirling. Finally, they finished their lunch and signed the papers. Beverly shook their hands.

"Please do not hesitate to call me if you have any concerns or questions," she told them. "And," she turned to Sylvia, "you should call me Bev." She gave Sylvia a warm and encouraging smile. "Don't worry," she told Sylvia. "It will all work out."

"And let me know when you find a boat!" Beverly said to Owen. "We'll check with the dockmaster on available slips so that you can dock here and sail off into the sunset for your honeymoon."

CHAPTER SEVEN

"Success is buried on the other side of frustration."

— ANTHONY ROBBINS

The girls piled into Mary's car and they were off to Wilmington, Delaware to a large bridal salon. When they arrived, the store was packed with women of all ages and a few men that looked uncomfortable. They spoke with a young woman dressed in an elegant black dress at a desk and she took down the information and assigned them dressing rooms. Sylvia asked about the bridesmaid gown. The sales associate went to pull it from the stock for Gwen and Carol to try on. While they waited, Carol and Gwen pulled several dresses off the rack commenting on some of the tackiness of the gowns. Carol pretended to vomit while Gwen teased that she didn't need to pretend, especially when they saw the netted dresses with shiny bits of mirrors sewn onto the bodice.

"If we added a bit of thread, they would be pasties to twirl!" Carol hooted.

"Carol!" Sylvia admonished, "Shh!"

Gwen doubled over in giggles once again and tried to pull herself together when the sales associate returned. They did not have the gown in the color Sylvia wanted, but Gwen and Carol tried the dress on and it was beautiful.   The dress was strapless with a wide row of beading under their breasts with embroidered vines and flowers that matched the chiffon. Godets of chiffon made the dress very feminine. Sylvia had thought about a meadow or leaf green for the bridesmaid dresses and a theme of leaves throughout the wedding.

"A perfect design to show my popping tummy," Gwen muttered acerbically.

"Stop!" Mary told her. "You girls will be beautiful in this. I love the chiffon wrap that goes with it. You'll both be floating down the aisle. Those godets will pick up and flutter if we have any breeze at all at the marina. Imagine dancing in this dress. It will be lovely."

Gwen and Carol looked at each other but agreed that they were lovely dresses.   Sylvia was insistent on green and they looked at the swatches. Finally, they decided on a dark sage green that was more autumnal than the spring greens.

Next, it was Sylvia's turn. The sales associate, Maria, asked if she had any idea of what type of dress she wanted to have for the wedding. Sylvia looked at her and shrugged. She had no idea. It was overwhelming to see the hundreds of dresses hanging on the racks in the store. The saleswoman seemed to visibly swallow her frustrations, but put Sylvia in a dressing room and told her to wait while she brought a selection.   There was a knock and Maria was armed with varieties and styles of wedding dresses. The spacious dressing room was dwarfed by the addition of satin, chiffon, lace and many furbelows. Maria helped her into the first dress that was satin and chiffon. It had a sweetheart neckline, elbow length sleeves, and a billowy skirt. She stepped out of the dressing room where her mother, Gwen, and Carol were waiting.

Catching a glimpse in the mirrors, Sylvia said, "All I need is a tiara."

Sylvia meant it as a joke. The dress looked like a Disney princess dress, but Maria took her seriously and went off to get a tiara. Sylvia rolled her eyes.

"It's a beautiful dress," her mother stated.

"If we were getting married in Disneyworld," Sylvia replied drily.

Gwen and Carol convulsed into giggles again. Maria brought back the tiara and placed it on Sylvia's head which started another round of giggles from Gwen and Carol. Maria didn't look hurt but certainly turned to look at them with a stern eye. Sylvia tried to hold back her own giggles and looked at herself critically in the mirror.

"I don't think so," she told Maria.

Maria nodded and helped her into another dress. Each dress she tried on seemed worse than the one before. Sylvia was getting a headache and also emotional. During the trying on of various dresses, Sylvia noticed the groups of females, and families and friends that gathered to 'help' other brides with their dress choices. If Sylvia thought the cacophony of the sound of the children at the park combined with the squawking of the blue heron was noisy, it was nothing to the groups shouting and adding vociferous comments about the dresses the brides tried on. Perhaps those brides were as stressed as she felt. And, she thought gratefully, her mom, Gwen, and Carol were not rude and disruptive. Carol had her own sense of chutzpah and silently made throwing up gestures at some of the dresses, but she was not loud in criticizing various real points on Sylvia nor did she make rude comments about the dresses. Gwen picked up on Carol's sense of humor and both laughed and giggled at many of the choices but did not embarrass Sylvia. Sylvia was grateful.

"I'm sorry," she apologized to Maria. "I think I need to think about what I really want in a dress. You've been a great help. Let me think about this and I can come back in the next week or so to make a firmer choice."

Maria nodded. "Your wedding is just around the corner," she warned. "You'll need to actually look for something 'off the rack' that will not require tailoring."

"I know," Sylvia said.

Sylvia's head was pounding and her emotions that had been on edge all day threatened to spill over in tears of frustration. She made her thanks again and caught up with her mom and friends on their way to the car.

When she got in the car, Sylvia nearly broke down. "That was pretty awful," she said with a hitch in her voice. "The wedding gowns, I mean," she said quickly. "I like your dresses," she told Carol and Gwen, "a lot, but the choices I tried on were definitely not what I want for a wedding gown. Lordy," Sylvia sighed loudly, "some of those were ghastly! The glitter and trim and beads seemed to weigh a hundred pounds," she complained. "And that mermaid dress!" she broke off, "I couldn't even walk in it! How do they expect someone to wear that?" she asked rhetorically. "I mean, I'm not a geisha! And...and....," Sylvia stopped and shook her head. She was babbling and very close to tears once again.

"So, I am thinking we're done with wedding dress shopping today?" Mary asked her daughter.

"I'm sorry. I know a large part of my problem is that I haven't a clue as to what style of wedding dress I want. I guess I was hoping I would try on the gowns and one would pop out at me and be 'the one.' Now, at least, I know what I'm *not* looking for in a dress," Sylvia said.

"Well, Syl, we did find the matron of honor and bridesmaid dress," Carol told her, "That's an excellent thing."

Gwen agreed, "It's HUGE," she said to her friend. "It's one big thing off that wedding list. But, you'll need to really hone in on finding a dress for yourself," she warned. "You barely have time for any alterations."

"I know, I know," Sylvia sighed again. "Maybe I can hit some of the smaller stores after work. That bridal palace was too much for me. Poor Maria!"

"She did her best, and was still kind, after you kept turning down her ideas," Carol chuckled.

"I know," Sylvia replied, "and I still feel a little guilty."

"Don't!" Gwen insisted, "It's her job."

Carol rattled off some of the other things they should really look at, like the invitations, flowers, and the cake. But, Sylvia had had enough wedding for the day. Gwen was beginning to look peaked and tired again. Mary suggested they go home. With more than one sigh of relief from the passengers, she turned the car from the Delaware traffic to the quieter roads of rural Maryland. Gwen fell asleep on the way home and Mary, Carol, and Sylvia talked quietly.

"At least you know what you don't want in a wedding dress," comforted Carol. "That's more than a lot of brides can say," she told her friend. "And, I'm speaking from experience from shopping with my cousins!" she said stoutly.

"I guess so," Sylvia said. "But, it was entirely depressing. Some of those dresses really turn a person off from even thinking about getting married."

"I will never forget your face when you tried on that heavily beaded gown!" Carol laughed.

"I know! I could barely walk and it weighed a ton," Sylvia answered her and made a face.

"I did like a couple of the more traditional gowns," her mother interjected. "I liked the one with the higher neck with – what is that fabric called – illusion over the satin of the strapless dress. It was on the lines of a halter dress. I also liked the traditional A-line dresses."

"I didn't like the halter one," Sylvia said. "The neckline was much too high and I felt like choking. I do like the dresses with a waist that flair out a little bit – not like that first Disney princess dress."

They discussed the various dresses until they pulled into the driveway. Gwen woke up and retreated upstairs to continue her nap. Mary decided to close her eyes for a few minutes as well, and Carol left to change for a Bluegrass gig Joe was playing at later that evening. She hugged Sylvia goodbye and took off in her car. Sylvia was weary too, but Percy needed to be walked. Percy and Sylvia walked down the road, up the rise and over the small hill to the marina. There was little activity at the marina. Skip and Maureen had a skeletal staff to handle those boaters who did not know old George or who did not care to attend the services and celebration of life. As Sylvia walked by the boat lift, a cold shiver of fear raced up her spine. She questioned again who might want to kill George and why? Maureen had alluded to the façade of a marina being a happy place but said there was an undercurrent that was not of the carefree boating world that Sylvia viewed. Sylvia inadvertently tugged on Percy's leash harder than usual as she turned from the boat lift. He yelped.

"Oh, sorry Percy," Sylvia told him and gave him a quick hug. "The boat lift is creeping me out today."

Sylvia and Percy headed home. Now she needed to put on a happy face. Sylvia and Owen were taking Gwen and Frank to "The Tilted Tern," a local restaurant on the water that hosted bands and dancing on the weekends.

Owen was hurrying down the road towards them. He was obviously happy and excited. Percy picked up on Owen's excitement and pulled away from Sylvia to go to him. Percy seldom pulled and she let the leash drop. Percy ran towards Owen and nosed him happily as high as he could reach without jumping on Owen. He pranced with excited, happy barks. Owen was laughing when Sylvia caught up to the two of them. He reached Sylvia, pulling her into his arms and lifting her off her feet in a happy hug. He gave her a resounding smack on the lips. His laugh partially answered the questioning look in her eyes.

"I've found a boat!" he told her excitedly.

He hugged her again and Sylvia laughed happily as well. She touched the curl that was astray on his forehead and then kissed him again, slowly, the kiss deepening until she forgot, for a moment, where they were.

Percy didn't. He barked in small yips and danced around and nuzzled both of them.

Owen gave a little groan as he pulled himself away from Sylvia.

"Stop, Percy!" he said a little sharply. "It's all right." Owen picked up Percy's leash and glanced at Sylvia. "This is what happens when you have kids, right?" he said.

"I think so," she answered, shaking her head at the dog. "You never have a moment alone."

"Promise me we will wait a little while," Owen requested, "before we have kids," He turned to grin mischievously at her, "but we can practice!"

"Oh!" Sylvia responded, blushing happily. "Now, tell me about this boat."

"It's a thirty-six-foot sailboat and it's gorgeous!" Owen said.

He continued to give her details on the remainder of their walk. Gwen was awake and yawning sleepily against Frank's arm when they came in. She gave Sylvia a sly grin after her yawn.

"Frank told me about the boat," she said to her friend. "One more thing crossed off your wedding list – the honeymoon!"

"It sounds beautiful," Sylvia agreed. "I also need to learn how to sail the thing – at least a little bit, before September."

"Well, sailboat shopping has made me ravenous for seafood," Frank complained. "Can we head to this waterfront restaurant soon?"

"As soon as I freshen up," Sylvia told him smiling. "I think you'll like the 'Tilted Tern.'"

Sylvia peeked in on her mom as she went to her room. She was still napping. She gently shook her mother awake before she went downstairs. She knew Mary would not want to be late for her dinner at Marian and Jon's. She also told her they were leaving for the Tilted Tern.

Mary, not quite awake, mumbled, "Have a good time. Be careful."

"You too," Sylvia answered her mom as she stepped through the bedroom door and went downstairs.

They drove to the restaurant in Gwen and Frank's car. Gwen commented they would be able to all party happily as she, and the baby would be designated drivers. It was relatively early in the evening and there was ample parking at the restaurant. The Tilted Tern was an old, rambling building on the waterfront in North Bay. It was flush against a storage building of one of the marinas. The other side was graced by the town's park.

Frank had insisted on a waterfront, seafood restaurant, even though Owen and Sylvia tried to convince him that the Crab Shack in town had much better food. The Tilted Tern was good but as a restaurant, not the same caliber as the Crab Shack. The Tilted Tern had become more of a drinking establishment for boaters, bikers and tourists rather than a dinner spot. It did have an excellent showcase of local bands.

The hostess led them to a table on the deck. It was a sprawling, weathered deck that was covered with a large awning and overlooked the bay and the restaurant's floating docks. The hostess seated them closer to the building in the shade and well out of the sharp, early evening sunlight. A band was beginning to set up against the backdrop of the bay and the boats. They ordered drinks and appetizers. Owen was talking excitedly about the sailboat.

Suddenly, it occurred to Sylvia, that she had not asked Owen the name of the boat. Frank started to say something, but Owen glared at him.

"It's a surprise," Owen insisted, "until I sail her home." He was unusually vehement.

"Oh?" Sylvia questioned.

"You'll love it!" Gwen baited.

"You know too?" Sylvia asked her friend. "C'mon, buddy, tell me!"

"I know and I won't tell," Gwen said to Sylvia, giving her a pretty pout.

Sylvia frowned back, "And I thought you were my friend."

"Girlfriend," Gwen insisted, "this is much too good of a surprise to spoil."

Sylvia stuck her tongue out playfully at Gwen. "Well," she admitted, "I have absolutely no idea."

"Good," the other three chorused at the same time and then laughed.

Owen asked how the dress shopping had gone. Gwen regaled him with stories of the good, the bad and the ugly side of wedding dress shopping.

"You know," Owen said, "We could have a geeky, Star Trek Next Generation wedding," he told her, "and pretend we're on Betazed."

Sylvia gave him a puzzled look. "And?" she asked him, "What would that entail?"

"Everyone at the wedding is nude," Owen told her with a sparkle in his eye, "to show that physically and spiritually people have nothing to hide, according to Peter David and a scene in his book."

"Not so good for me," Gwen scoffed good-naturedly, "with my burgeoning belly."

"Okay, okay," Sylvia told them, "I know I need to find a dress – just not at the bridezilla superstore. There has to be something better out there!"

They laughed and continued to talk. The boys ended up talking about sailboats and sailing. Gwen rolled her eyes at Sylvia and turned her attention back to the wedding.

"Syl," she advised, "you desperately need to get invitations ordered. They technically need to be sent out this week. Why, you don't even have time for a 'save the date' card. What are you going to do? Do you have any ideas on the design?" Gwen peppered her with questions.

"I was thinking of leaves or a sailing theme," Sylvia told Gwen, "But, I want to firm things up with Maureen before I order anything. I don't know what's going to happen with George's murder, the investigation and all of that. I will give her a call tomorrow."

"Good," Gwen said, "and we can look online for ideas tomorrow before we head back to Connecticut. You'll need to overnight them and work on addressing them next weekend."

The waitress reappeared to refresh their drinks and take their dinner order. The deck was getting crowded and the band started playing vintage rock and roll. For the most part, the band was excellent, but the sound level of the music was almost deafening.

"It's worse than those cigarette boats," Frank shouted across the table to Owen and Sylvia.

The band continued to play extremely loudly. They gave up on their shouting conversation and focused on eating their dinner. Sylvia looked out at the water where the setting sun was making a sparkling, golden path across the bay from the western shore to the docks. The sun was a glowing, dark, coral, red ball in the sky that was dropping in slow motion towards the horizon.

Sylvia watched as a family pulled their boat into one of the slips on the floating docks. Sylvia thought one of the children, jumping up and down in excitement, might fall overboard, but the mother saved him just in time. The Dad was busy tying up the boat and the other child was concentrating on his every move. Another ship, a cigarette boat purred to a stop at the dock. Out of the vessel climbed a blond headed woman in a bikini, who was putting on a diaphanous swim cover up. Her companion was tall, slim and had dark hair. For a moment, Sylvia thought she saw Joyce and Tony. Sylvia felt the blood drain from her face and the hairs on the back of her neck prickle. Sylvia had found Joyce's body on her beach earlier this year and Tony was in prison for killing Joyce and attempting to kill Sylvia.

Her attention shifted from the couple when the band abruptly stopped playing. The conversation drifted to silence. Everyone looked expectantly at the band leader. He approached the mic.

"Ladies and gentlemen," he said in a showman-like tone to the audience, "I would like for you to turn your attention to the sunset. We're celebrating the end of another beautiful day in the paradise of North Bay, where the sunsets are spectacular. So, raise your glasses to the setting sun," he requested.

The band leader took a beer and raised it to the audience. "It takes three minutes for the sun to set behind the horizon and leave behind a unique sky painting each evening," he told them.

Everyone watched the setting sun as it dipped down to the horizon. A cheer went up as the glowing ball dropped below the horizon line. Splashes of fuchsia, gold and mauve spread across the sky in a gorgeous painting of light. There was a gasp from some of the audience. The band leader took up his guitar and nodded to his fellow band members to start playing "There Goes the Sun," apparently an original tune mimicking the popular Beatles song "Here Comes the Sun." A few of the audience chuckled and the volume was once again turned up to the maximum level.

Owen shouted across the table, "If you are ready to go," he told Gwen and Frank, "we can probably enjoy the rest of the concert from our deck."

They paid their bill and headed back to Bayside. Indeed, settled on the deck, they could hear strains of the band wafting down the bay.

"I can't believe you can hear that band from the town, here in Bayside," Gwen marveled.

"I can," Frank said sarcastically, "at least for now. I need to go back to Connecticut and get a hearing check, to find out if I lost some of my hearing. And here I thought you lived in a quiet, peaceful, neighborhood!"

"Usually," Sylvia soothed, "it's one of the most peaceful places on earth."

"Next time," Owen said smiling, "the Crab Shack."

"Okay, okay," Frank said succumbing to the silent 'I told you so' from Owen, Sylvia, and Gwen. "Besides, you have a lovely waterfront view here."

"Indeed we do," Sylvia said, "and I'm getting better at cooking. And the entertainment is definitely 'in the air.' We won't even have the need to go out to eat on your next visit."

CHAPTER EIGHT

*"Many people spend more time in planning the wedding
than they do in planning the marriage."*

— Zig Ziglar

By noon on Sunday, Sylvia began to wonder which was more stressful – wedding dress shopping or invitation shopping. Both her mom and Gwen had firm ideas on the subject. They offered comments, sometimes simultaneously. Owen looked over her shoulder as well 'helping' with occasional pretend gagging sounds. Sylvia thought she might tear out her hair. There were just too many choices. Owen, of course, wanted a sailboat on the invitation since the ceremony and reception were taking place by the water. Sylvia found a couple of sailboat decorated, wedding invitations that were okay, in her viewpoint, but none of them clicked with her. She searched the internet for wedding invitations with leaves and found what seemed to be hundreds of fall leaf wedding invitations. The majority appeared tacky to her. Her patience was beginning to ebb when finally, after a few hours of searching what seemed to be hundreds of websites, she found a very elegant invitation. It was a washed pearly paper of embossed leaves. The inside of the invitation was a colored paper that matched the attendant dresses. An oval cutout on the front of the invitation allowed their names to show through and add a hint of color and was adorned with a small, matching ribbon. It was simple, elegant and understated. Even better, they could be printed and shipped out within twenty-four hours. Sylvia loved it.

"This is it!" she cried with relief to the group.

Her mom, Gwen, Owen, and Frank crowded around the screen. All agreed that it was lovely.

"I can fill in most of the information and double check with Maureen for final confirmation before I send off the order," Sylvia told them.

"It's a formal invitation," Gwen advised, "so you should probably be formal in your text. How about: Mrs. Mary Ash and Mr. and Mrs. Phillip Anderson request the honor of your presence at the marriage of their children – Sylvia Beithe Ash and Owen..." her voice trailed off.

"Owen," Gwen asked him, "what's your middle name?"

Owen grimaced, "Brady," he answered, "after the Civil War photographer – Owen Brady Anderson."

"Nice moniker," Frank teased. "That's just as bad as mine – Franklin Carlisle Beecher."

"Okay," Gwen said, "Enough. " She continued, "Sylvia Beithe Ash and Owen Brady Anderson on Saturday, the thirteenth of September at half-past four in the afternoon. Reception immediately following, North Bay Yacht Club."

"Perfect," Sylvia said as she typed it into the text box on the website. "Mom?" Sylvia questioned over her shoulder, "What do you think?"

"Perfect," Mary agreed.

"Your middle name is unusual," Frank mentioned, "is it a unique spelling of Beth?"

"It's my grandmother's maiden name," Sylvia explained. "It's actually an ancient Gaelic word for Birch. The language is Ogham."

Blank looks met Sylvia's eyes. She chuckled.

"Ogham is the ancient, druid language. Beith is for Birch, as in the tree," she explained.

"You might need to explain that to the invitation people," Gwen suggested. "They may think you had a typo for Beth."

"Good idea," Mary agreed with Gwen.

"Okay," Sylvia said, and she typed that into the comments section on the order form, "Let me confirm with Maureen and then I'll send for the invitations later this afternoon. Whew!"

"One more thing to check off your list," Gwen said. She looked at the time. "Oh, my God!" she exclaimed. "I didn't realize it was so late!"

"The car is packed, love," Franklin said. "We can say our goodbyes and jump in the car. If the traffic is good, we'll be in Connecticut by dinnertime."

After Gwen and Frank had left, Mary packed up to leave as well. Before she left, she told Sylvia to contact Marian. Apparently, Marian had a gift for her for the 'something old and borrowed' portion of the rhyme –something old, something new, something borrowed, something blue, for brides. Mary would not tell Sylvia what it was. Mary also mentioned that Marian had a minister to marry them. Apparently it was someone who had been at Marian's parties that Owen and Sylvia attended. Neither, Owen or Sylvia remembered such a person, but she told her mother she would give Marian a call.

Her mother leaned out the car window before she left and called to Sylvia, "Remember next weekend," she told Sylvia, "I'm headed to the beach with John and Donna. I'll see you in two weeks for the fourth of July."

A small sigh of relief escaped after her mom drove down the road. She turned to Owen and melted into a hug.

"I love you," she told him, "but, this wedding stuff might push me over the edge."

"Hey," he said, holding her at arm's length and saying with conviction, "you're doing an excellent job and it's all going to fall into place." He pulled her back into a hug. "Go inside and call Maureen. Then we can order invitations and move onto the next step."

"Okay, okay," she told him, "Pushy man," she teased.

Maureen sounded absolutely beat on the phone. Sylvia told her she would email her a copy of the invitation, but was calling to double check on the time for the ceremony and if it was still all right with Maureen and Skip to have the ceremony at the marina.

"Even though things are really, really messed up," Maureen told Sylvia, "I think it's a good idea to have the wedding here."

"Are you sure you are okay?" Sylvia asked her friend again. There was a note in Maureen's voice that Sylvia couldn't understand.

There was a catch of a sigh at the beginning of the reply. Maureen's voice was barely above a whisper, "George's murder is so scary," she admitted to Sylvia, "and, I'm not sure where this investigation is leading," she told her friend. "I—I can't talk about it right now."

Changing the subject and putting a happier note in her voice, Maureen said, "Sylvia, order those invitations. I'll check about pergolas tomorrow and email you. I said I would help you with this wedding, and I will." Maureen sounded like she was putting on a brave face.

"Okay," Sylvia said, "if you're sure. I'm sure we can switch the wedding to the Yacht Club if we need to do that."

"No!" Maureen told her adamantly, "Absolutely not! It will be lovely to have the wedding here. Order those invitations!"

"All right," Sylvia said. "Here I go, clicking the button to place the order."

They ended their phone call on a happier note. Sylvia padded out in her bare feet to Owen. He was on the deck, reading and enjoying the sunshine. The watered glittered brightly in waves of gold in the sunlight.

"Invitations ordered," she started to tell him and realized he was on the phone. "Sorry!" she stage whispered.

He looked up at her and smiled before he said to the caller, "Wait a minute, here she is." Owen handed the phone to Sylvia. "Go ahead," he told her. "It's my mom."

"Hi, Anne," Sylvia greeted. "How are you?"

"I'm thinking I am doing better than you," Anne replied. "Owen was telling me you had the bridal shopping experience from hell."

"It was something like that," Sylvia agreed. "That big bridal store just isn't my 'thing.'"

"Why don't you come up this way?" Anne asked. "There's a small bridal salon in town and we could go shopping in Lancaster too. They have some lovely boutiques in the older section of the city."

"Hmm…" Sylvia considered. "That sounds lovely. When could we do that?" she asked.

"How is next weekend?" Anne suggested, "Because, we're headed to you for the fourth of July in two weeks," she reminded Sylvia. "And," she suggested, "why don't you come solo? Owen can stay at home and do his thing with this boat he's purchasing and look after Percy too."

"That sounds like a good plan," Sylvia replied. "I take it you have already discussed this with Owen?"

Owen nodded, smiling before his mother had a chance to reply.

"I have discussed this with Owen," Anne told her, "I'll call Mary to see if she can come too and I will see you next Friday!"

They talked for a few more minutes. Sylvia told Anne that her mom was planning to go to the Jersey shore with friends next weekend. They would be on their own. Also, Sylvia told Anne that she would send the link for the invitations, and bring a sample, if they arrived in time.

After the phone call, Sylvia suggested to Owen, "Let's go for a walk. I need some fresh air," she told him.

At the word 'walk,' Percy began to prance and whine.

"Okay, boy," Owen told him, "you certainly know the 'w' word! Go and get your leash."

They automatically started walking towards the marina. Percy stopped at his favorite trees along the way to mark his spot and sniff enthusiastically where dogs had left previous marks. They topped the rise and headed down the small hill towards the marina. In the distance, they saw flashing lights.

"Oh, no!" Sylvia breathed. "Is that something at the marina again?" Her stomach clenched and she stopped, squinting to see what was happening.

Owen stopped too and looked at the flashing lights. "I don't think they're at Maureen and Skip's marina," he told Sylvia. "I think it's coming from the cove across from them. Isn't that a small yacht club?"

"I think so," Sylvia answered slowly. "I wonder what's going on."

"We'll probably find out tomorrow in the local paper," Owen said grimly, "or you can ask your source – Carol, to learn from Joe."

"Oh, yeah," Sylvia said. "Where is my brain?"

They continued to walk towards the marina. By the time they reached the marina, the police activity across the cove had dissipated. The hairs on the back of her neck prickled at the sight of the boat lift. Sylvia automatically started to give it a wide berth. Owen understood. He took her elbow and steered her away from the boat lift area and toward a grassy open space that bordered the bay. It was an alternate parking area, and it jutted up to Skip and Maureen's house, which looked dark and closed that evening. This would be the spot where the pergola would be and where they would be married. Sylvia's stomach fluttered in a good way. Owen put an arm around Sylvia and drew her tightly against him.

"Just think," he murmured into the hair by her ear, "in a few weeks, we'll be married in this very spot."

"I know," Sylvia answered huskily. "It barely seems real."

A pair of great blue heron soared and circled and landed gracefully on the small strip of beach below the breakwater rocks. They waded into the water looking for fish treats while Sylvia and Owen stood silently. Even Percy sat still. They watched the elegant birds. The twilight garnered the day turning it into night, changed the light, blue-grey birds into dusky silhouettes as night fell.

The heron squawked their rusty sounding cry good-naturedly with each other. Loud "karwack – wak – wak's" filled the air. Without warning, they lifted their great wings and flew down the bay and out of sight.

Owen turned Sylvia and pulled her toward him. He kissed her sweetly. Once again, that blissful feeling of every single thing in the universe working in synchronicity came to Sylvia. The kisses deepened and Sylvia returned them. She gave herself wholly to them until Percy whined.

"Kids," Owen said disgustedly, but with humor. His eyes darkened with desire. "Let's go home," he murmured.

And they did.

CHAPTER NINE

"The greater part of our happiness or misery depends on our dispositions and not on our circumstances."

— MARTHA WASHINGTON

During the week, Carol pushed Sylvia nearly to her breaking point. At every available free moment at work, Carol nagged at Sylvia to work on the wedding. Carol loved the invitations and said she would assist Sylvia in addressing them in the next few days. Carol also sent Sylvia an enormous number of pictures of bridal bouquets via email and text. She also set up a time for them to taste test wedding cakes at a local bakery early the next week. Sylvia threatened her good-naturedly that she was going to order business cards for Carol as a wedding planner.

Carol only grinned at the compliment and replied half-seriously and a little wistfully, "Someday…"

Maureen sent her photos of the pergola they were purchasing for the marina. It was a large, square shaped pergola with beautiful columns. Maureen also sent her pictures of breezy, sheer curtains covered in translucent leafy vines to hang from the sides of the pergola. It was lovelier than Sylvia could have imagined. She enthusiastically responded her thanks to Maureen's email and looked forward to seeing them put the pergola in place in the next few weeks. Maureen also sent her information on chair rental and covers and other details that Sylvia never would have thought of for the wedding. She forwarded the information to her mom so that she could take care of that detail.

On Friday, Sylvia skipped lunch so that she could leave a little early. She and Owen had driven separate cars to Thurmont and she was packed to travel to Phil and Anne's. It was mid-afternoon when she logged off her computer and shut her office door. Carol and Mr. Carter were discussing something at Carol's desk. They wished her luck and safe travels. Sylvia dropped by Owen's office to say goodbye. He was perched on a lab stool and busily writing notes when she stopped in.

"Hey," she murmured and rubbed a hand on his shoulder.

He jumped a little, but turned and smiled at Sylvia. "Hey, yourself. All ready to go?"

Sylvia nodded.

"Percy and I will miss you," he told her, stepping off the stool and gathering her in his arms.

"I'll miss you, boys, too," Sylvia told him.

Sylvia had hoped, by leaving an hour early, that she might miss some of the commuter traffic. She knew the roads coming south towards the bay would be crowded with boaters and had hoped that they would be clearer going north and west. The roads to Millersville were primarily two-lane roads. She forgot that commuter traffic was not the issue, but, the traffic from the Amish buggies and the farm equipment proved to slow her down more than she hoped. In many places, there were long lines of vehicles, mostly patiently waiting to pass an Amish buggy or a heavy piece of farm equipment. With the twists and turns in the road and nothing on the sides except tall, ripening corn, passing a buggy or a huge piece of farm equipment was not an option. The trip took much longer than Sylvia expected.

Finally, Sylvia turned off the main highway to a smaller road that led to Millersville. Millersville was a tiny community built around the college. Sylvia had only visited Anne and Phil a couple of times. Their house was tucked into the end of a street in the corner of the campus. It was a tall, stately, Victorian house that was tucked in behind pine trees and lower mugo pine bushes. Small pocket gardens of Echinacea and Black Eyed Susan's brightened the dark greens of the pines. Phil and Anne had restored the Victorian to its original colors of mustard yellow with red trim. It might look garish to some, but it was historically correct. It was appropriate since Phil was a history professor that specialized in the Civil War era.

Sylvia pulled into the driveway that led to the back of the house, past a small garden to a tiny parking area near a free standing garage. Sylvia got out and stretched before she pulled her overnight bag and walked to the front of the house. She raised the large, shining, brass door knocker and heard it reverberate through the door and into the house. Sylvia could hear feet rapidly coming to the door. Anne opened the door and enthusiastically pulled Sylvia into an enormous hug.

"Sylvia! Welcome!" she cried, pulling her inside.

What could have been a dark and dismal Victorian interior was bright with light paint and sparse furnishings. Sylvia remembered Phil and Anne had hired a talented art student to paint and create wainscoting for the foyer. She also remembered that Phil and Anne had not owned this property very long, perhaps for five years or less. Owen and his parents used to live across from the campus on a small suburban street of mid-size ranchers in stone and brick that was fond-ly called "Professors' Row."

Anne took Sylvia's overnight bag and set it beside the steps and led her past a formal living room calling to Phil as she did so. Phil emerged from the study. He had his usual dazed look about him and a book dangling from his hand. He gave Sylvia a hug as well.

"Come through," Anne gestured to Sylvia.

They walked down the long hallway and into the kitchen. Anne led her to a small, screened-in porch at the back of the house. Sylvia had barely noticed it when she got out of her car. It was almost hidden behind a tree and mature hosta that had a sea of light purple blooms. Anne had wine and cheese set out for them to enjoy. Sylvia brought Anne and Phil up to speed on what she knew about the sailboat and the wedding plans. Phil excused himself to make a quick phone call and returned to say dinner was on its way.

Anne added, "We're keeping it simple, if that's all right with you, Sylvia. I have a lovely salad, and the Sugar Bowl across from the campus makes the best strombolis in the world. "

"It sounds terrific," Sylvia assured her.

Anne filled her in on the thoughts for the next day, starting with the bridal shop in town and then shopping in downtown Lancaster.

"Hmm, maybe we should have saved take out for tomorrow night," she mused to Phil and Sylvia. "I'm thinking we're going to be exhausted."

They had a lovely evening on the porch, talking and laugh-ing, eating and drinking. Anne and Phil told her funny stories of Owen growing up. Some he would be terribly embarrassed for her to know, but others were quite endearing. Anne even pulled out some childhood photos to share with Sylvia. He was mortified, of course, when she called to say good night to him and teased him about one of his pictures in the bathtub.

The next morning, Anne and Sylvia left in the morning to head to the bridal salon in town. When they entered, the thick, soft, pale, plum colored carpet silenced their footsteps. Sounds were completely muffled but, a small, tinkling bell alerted the sales-woman to come from the back room.

"Good morning," she greeted Sylvia. "Welcome to 'Weddings in White.' I am Ms. Cartwright."

Sylvia introduced herself and Anne. She also told Ms. Cartwright that she needed a dress fairly quickly. Ms. Cartwright became a brisk, efficient machine and asked about her size. She pulled some things off the racks and led Sylvia to a fitting room.

"Here are some lovely gowns," Ms. Cartwright said to Sylvia. "Let me help you with these."

Sylvia tried on a lovely gown that looked like it stepped from the "Great Gatsby" era. The simple dress was of low cut silk and felt delicious on Sylvia's skin. It had a lovely fishtail train. She liked it, but it was much too low cut for her. She walked out to where Anne was waiting.

"Oooh," Anne said, "that's lovely. What do you think?"

Sylvia told Anne that it was pretty, but not exactly what she wanted. They moved onto the next gown. Miss Cartwright called it a bateau neckline, but to Sylvia it was a wide neckline of gorgeous lace that went just slightly off the shoulder. A dupioni silk bodice was covered in lace with the silk forming a long skirt and a gathered empire waist with a beautiful sash. Sylvia sucked in her breath when she looked in the mirror. This was it...but, not quite. She walked out to Anne, who breathed a happy sigh as well.

"Sylvia!" Anne cried, "You look stunning in that dress."

"I love this one," Sylvia admitted, "but, I want to keep looking."

They continued through a few more gowns. This experience of shopping for a bridal gown was far superior to the bridezilla salon. Sylvia felt elegant and beautiful in most of the gowns, and she was having fun. Anne confessed that this was something she actually craved – some girly, girl activity and she never had a daughter to experience it with. The final gown, Sylvia fell in love with. It was a creamy satin with delicate embroidered chiffon, or allusion, as Ms. Cartwright told her, overlay. The embroidery was delicate vines and a few flowers. It was just off the shoulder, had embroidered chiffon bell sleeves and was lovely. She felt like a woodland princess and she knew Anne would fall in love with this particular dress. Anne did.

"Oh, Syl!" she said, "That one is perfect. Can't you just see a wreath of flowers in your hair with that dress?"

"It's definitely on my short list," Sylvia agreed. She asked Ms. Cartwright to put it on hold and she would let her know by Monday if this was the dress she wanted.

Sylvia and Anne were practically giddy as they drove to Lancaster. Anne had snapped photos and texted them to Mary, Gwen, and Carol. Enthusiastic responses flew back and forth with the group. Downtown, there were several interesting boutiques. Sylvia felt her gaze travel from storefront to more attractive storefronts, sporting clothing, handmade soap, unusual boutiques, and antique shops.

On their trip to the city, Anne asked if Sylvia would like having high tea for lunch. Sylvia was delighted, and Anne parked nearby. They walked along looking in the brick storefronts to a small tearoom on the next block.

The tea room was decorated with floral sprigged wallpaper, antique tables, chairs, and linens. Beautiful fresh flowers graced the tables. Sylvia had never been to a high tea before. Anne made a couple of suggestions on tea varieties, and the waitress brought a steaming kettle to pour over tea leaves into two antique pots. Anne ordered a high tea for them, tea sandwiches, scones, and pastries. Soon their table was filled with the savory sandwiches of cucumber, radish, and smoked salmon. There was also a plate of delicious scones. To top it off more pastries were brought for dessert.

"We'll need to stroll the streets to walk off this lunch, and find the bridal salon I was telling you about," Anne said as she took one last bite of scone and clotted cream.

"Mmm," Sylvia agreed. "What an incredible lunch. Marian would love this. I would think it would remind her of England."

Anne agreed. "Perhaps we can have a girls' day out with your mom and Marian, and come here for shopping and tea."

"After the wedding," Sylvia intoned.

"Absolutely," Anne agreed. "After the wedding, and maybe I could talk two newlyweds into coming to our house for Thanksgiving dinner?" she hinted to Sylvia. "We could invite your mom, Marian, and Jon."

"That's a fabulous idea," Sylvia said. "And instead of the black Friday madness, we could come downtown on Saturday for shopping and tea."

"Sounds like a plan," Anne told her smiling. "I think I'm going to love having a daughter!" She grinned at Sylvia.

They paid for their lunch and poked about in several of the shops. Halfway down one block, there was a small courtyard and garden below the street level. You could stare down from the fence, and see a little garden, a fountain, and a few benches. It was quite beautiful and peaceful, but the most surprising thing of all was the giant sculpture of a Green Man on the opposite wall. Sylvia took in a breath and smiled. Would this garden Green Man bring her luck? Was it a sign? Amazingly, the courtyard was beside the store "The Mariage Jardin" or 'marriage garden.' It was the small, wedding boutique Anne had been looking for. Anne and Sylvia opened the door and an elegant woman with long gray hair greeted them. She introduced herself as Lily Dubois and asked how she could help them.

Sylvia told her how she needed a gown for her wedding in September. Ms. Dubois nodded calmly and asked if she had any particular styles in mind. Sylvia smiled at this and told her that the mermaid style and poufy gowns with tons of tulle were not her favorite. Ms. Dubois smiled in return and nodded. She asked Anne and Sylvia to sit in two, comfortable, upholstered, side chairs while she bustled towards the dresses to make some choices as she asked Sylvia her dress size.

Soon Ms. Dubois was back with a rolling cart hung heavily with several dresses. She told Sylvia and Anne that she carried a variety of vintage dresses and several of independent designers. She began to show the dresses to Sylvia and Anne. Their eyes had glowed with anticipation before she led Sylvia to a dressing room.

Sylvia fell in love with the vintage dresses. The first one she tried on was from the 1940's, made of heavy satin. It clung in all the right places, and the feel and weight of the fabric were fantastic. It had an incredibly detailed beadwork border on the neckline, and long sleeves. Sylvia had always read about ladies with their skirts rustling. This dress had a quiet 'swoosh, swoosh' as she walked.

"I absolutely love this dress," Sylvia told Anne when she walked out.

"It's stunning," Anne agreed, "but, the fabric looks heavy. Would it be too hot for early September on the Chesapeake? Usually, it's quite warm that time of year," she reminded Sylvia.

Sylvia knew Anne was right. Reluctantly she took off the dress. She tried on another that Ms. Dubois told her was a new designer who liked fashions from the 1950's. It was a sweet dress with a pleated chiffon overskirt over silk. There was simple, ribbon detail under the empire waist bodice, at the neckline and at the elbows where the chiffon blossomed into a bell sleeve. Lovely but all agreed, it was not the dress for Sylvia. They made their way through a few more dresses. Finally, Ms. Dubois handed Sylvia a lovely lace dress. She hadn't liked any of the lace dresses at the other stores, but this one was different. The lace was delicate leaves! The bodice was covered in lace and the overskirt of chiffon had leaves trailing down to lacy leaves that adorned the bottom of the dress. It was sleeveless but clever. The lace leaves climbed over the shoulder to the back of the dress.   It dipped in a lovely curvy circle low on her back with the lacy leaves cut out and stiffened a bit for detail. About thirty satin covered buttons gave access to the dress on the side. It was perfect. She knew it from the moment she saw it, and even more so when she put it on. Sylvia beamed and walked out to Anne.

Anne breathed a sigh. "Yes, absolutely, yes!" she told Sylvia. She took a variety of pictures and sent it to Mary, Gwen, and Carol.

Ms. Dubois's eyes were twinkling as well. "I can't believe it," she told Sylvia. "It's as if this dress was made for you. I don't think it needs any alteration at all! On that note," she asked earnestly, "what shoes will you be wearing?"

Sylvia had honestly not considered shoes and she admitted this to Ms. Dubois.

"It is amazing that your gown fits you so well and will not need alteration, but depending on the shoes you choose, it could be a complicated modification to lengthen or shorten the gown with the lace and illusion. This is a vintage gown and one that was created by an independent designer. My suggestion would be to purchase a shoe with a modest heel. I do have some available if you are interested in looking at them."

Sylvia looked at Anne, who nodded. Sylvia told Ms. Dubois, her size and she went in search of shoes that would fit Sylvia. She returned with four boxes. One pair was a plain, white pump that could be dyed. Another box contained an acrylic version of Cinderella's slipper. A third shoe box had a sandal and the fourth a brocade, peep toe pump. Sylvia quickly said no to the acrylic, the fake glass slipper. She tried on the conventional pump, and the sandal, but was not impressed. When she tried on the brocade, peep toe pump, both Ms. Dubois and Anne nodded and smiled. It was a white brocade of leaves and flowers with small Swarovski crystals at the centers of the flowers.

"It's not too much?" Sylvia asked the ladies, "with the crystals and all—with all of the lace?"

They both shook their heads.

"They are really comfortable," Sylvia said, surprised, as she walked around the room.

"It's that nicely rounded toe area," Ms. Dubois said. "You could dance for hours in that shoe and your toes would not be squashed. They remind me of the shoes of the 1940's," she said with a small sigh, and a smile as if she had a happy memory of that time.

"I like it," Anne said, "They look lovely with the gown. The leaves and flowers extend the design of the lace and leaves on your gown."

Sylvia lifted up the hem of the dress and smiled at the shoes. "Well, I just love them," Sold," she stated firmly.

Ms. Dubois helped her out of the gown and wrapped it up carefully giving Sylvia instructions on how to care for it. In between, Anne relayed the positive comments from Mary, Gwen, and Carol about the gown.

When they left, Sylvia made sure she looked at the Green Man sculpture on the garden wall as they walked toward the car. She quickly blew a kiss to it, as Anne turned to look at a store across the street. Now they were definitely giddy and laid the gown carefully in the back of the car, and the shoe bag on the seat, before heading back to Millersville where Phil started coals for a fabulous steak dinner.

Anne asked if Sylvia wanted to keep the gown in Millersville, but she declined. She thought aloud that Marian could keep it, until closer to the wedding. She and Jon were due back from their latest trip tomorrow, and Sylvia owed her a call.

Anne gave Sylvia an enormous hug before she left the next morning. "Oh, Sylvia," she said with emotion, "I can't tell you how much I am looking forward to having you as my daughter-in-law. Helping you choose your wedding dress meant so much to me. Thank you." Anne brushed away a small tear.

Sylvia gave her another hug, before climbing into her car. She headed back to North Bay and Bayside in an elated mood.

Owen must have been watching for her, because when she pulled into the driveway, he and Percy were at the car door almost instantly. He opened it for her and she flew into his arms. Percy whined after a minute of their hugging and kissing reunion.

"Oh, you!" she said to Percy happily giving him a hug as well. "I love you too," she assured him.

She turned back to Owen and brushed the loose curl that fell onto his forehead. "It's good to see you," she said huskily. "I missed you."

"I, no," he hesitated and gestured to Percy, "we, missed you. The house is empty without you, and I am empty as well," he admitted.

Sylvia kissed him again. Thoroughly. "Let's go inside," she suggested.

He took her overnight bag from the back seat and reached for the bag holding the wedding gown.

"Uh, uh, uh!" Sylvia teased, "No peeking!" and she waggled a finger at him.

"Okay, okay!" he said, raising both his hands, "hands off."

"Anyway," Sylvia said, "I need to ask Marian if I can keep it at her house."

"Well, that's convenient," Owen told her.

"What do you mean?" she asked, curiously.

"Marian and Jon asked us to come over for dinner tonight, that's why," Owen explained.

"Oh!" Sylvia replied, surprised, "I thought they were away until tomorrow."

"They were, but now they're back," Owen told her. "Apparently, Marian is in a fever to give you something for your bridal attire. Also, she wanted to talk to us about a minister she knows."

"I've heard bits and pieces about this from the moms," she told Owen. "I will give Marian a call to see what we can bring tonight."

CHAPTER TEN

*"Cherish your human connections - your relationships
with friends and family."*

— BARBARA BUSH

It had been a while since Marian, Jon, Owen, and Sylvia had been together due to work and travel schedules. They sat on the terrace under the large, spreading oak tree, having wine and small things to nibble on as they caught up with each other's lives. John and Marian had traveled extensively through Europe earlier in the year and now were enjoying domestic travel. Their latest trip was to New England, to the Adam's family National Historical Park. John was a descendant of John Adams, his namesake, of Revolutionary Era fame. As much as Owen was a scientist, he was raised with his father's enthusiasm for history and he asked a lot of questions. His father, Phil, was focused on the Civil War era, but Owen had many strong memories discussing the American Revolution with Marian's husband, Bran, an expert on that time period. Sylvia caught them up on wedding plans.

Sylvia turned to Marian, "Mom said you had a minister or someone who could marry us?" she asked.

Marian's eyes twinkled, "Yes!" she gushed, "you met him at one of our parties," she told them. "Dr. Luis, a very tall, dark skinned man with a mustache."

Owen and Sylvia shook their heads, not remembering anyone with that name.

"What does he do?" Sylvia asked, probing, thinking she might remember.

Marian hesitated a moment before answering, "He's a professor of sorts," she began.

"Oh, Marian!" Owen interrupted, "that's ninety plus percent of your guests. Your parties are always crawling with Ph.D.'s.!"

Marian laughed, "Yes, that's true. But, Dr. Luis travels everywhere and lectures. He's not tied to a particular institution of higher learning."

"What subject does he lecture on?" Owen asked.

"I would say its philosophy and comparative religions," Marian replied.

Sylvia wracked her brain, "I can't think of anyone like that, that I met at one of your parties."

"Maybe, it will come to you later," Marian assured her.

"But, can he marry us?" Sylvia asked.

"He has the authority," Marian told her, "I'm sorry you don't remember him. Do you want me to ask him if he would marry you two?"

"That would save us a lot of bother," Owen replied. "Anyone you know and trust, Marian, we'll trust."

"Should we call?" Sylvia asked. "I don't want to put you out."

"Mmm..." Marian murmured, "I believe he's currently out of the country. I'll contact him and let him know the particulars."

"And, let us know his fee," Owen told her.

"All right," Marian said, "But, I'm sure it will be nominal at best. He would do this as a favor."

Both Sylvia and Owen looked skeptical.

"Okay," Owen said, "if you say so."

"Carol will be delighted!" Sylvia commented, "That's one more thing to check off the wedding to-do list."

"She should be a wedding planner," Owen and Marian chorused at the same time.

"That's something I keep telling her," Sylvia agreed.

Jon went to light the coals on the grill and Owen followed him. He bent Jon's ear about information on sailboats. Sylvia and Marian took the wedding gown and shoes upstairs to 'Sylvia's room' in the house. Marian pulled a silk-wrapped package that bulged mysteriously from the top drawer of an antique bureau.

"Something old," Marian said, "that you can borrow or keep, your choice," she told Sylvia smiling.

Carefully, Sylvia unwrapped the delicate silk. The silk was a very, very old scarf that had been wrapped carefully about the object inside. Inside, Sylvia found a bronze headpiece made entirely of small, delicate leaves. She gasped in delight.

"Oh, Marian!" she cried. "It's beautiful and it is absolutely perfect!"

Marian was delighted with Sylvia's expression. "Try it on," she urged Sylvia.

Sylvia stood in front of the mirror and put on the headpiece. Marian told her it had belonged to her grandmother at the turn of the twentieth century and had been handed down through her family.

"Since you are the closest thing I have to a daughter or a granddaughter, I thought it should go to you," Marian said with some emotion.

Impulsively, Sylvia gave Marian a hug. Sylvia had looked in the mirror before she replied, "I can't even believe this," she told Marian. "First, it's gorgeous, but it is also perfect for the gown. Let me show you."

Sylvia unzipped the bag and pointed out to Marian the simple lace leaves that adorned the gown. The headpiece and the dress looked as though they had been made for one another.

"Sylvia!" Marian cried admiring the dress and headpiece, "You're right! The headpiece *is* perfect! What a gorgeous wedding dress!"

Sylvia stood in front of the mirror again, this time holding up the gown in front of her to see herself in the mirror with the dress and the headpiece. She also pulled out the brocade shoes too. Marian admired them as well, nodding with the approval of all the wedding garments.

"If you check with your mother," Marian said, "I think your grandmother had lovely pearl earrings that would look very nice with the gown."

"I will check with Mom," Sylvia promised her.

"Now, let's get both of these away safely so that I can get back to dinner," she told Sylvia.

The gown would not fit into the antique, tiger oak chifferobe that graced the room. Instead, Marian and Sylvia put the dress into a closet that was carefully built into the wall of the master bedroom before they went to join the men. They were still talking about sailing. Marian disappeared into the kitchen, and Sylvia quickly followed so that she could assist.

"We're keeping it simple tonight," Jon admitted. "You will be shocked and amazed that Marian actually picked up some pre-made items!" he informed Sylvia and Owen. "I thought the earth would come to a stop," he teased his wife.

"Oh, you!" Marian retorted, smiling as she slapped him lightly with a dish towel.

"It's all right, Marian," Owen teased, "not *everything* needs to be made from scratch or gourmet."

"You know I enjoy cooking immensely," Marian said primly, "and you reap the benefits."

"I certainly do," Jon smiled and said while patting his tummy. "I know it's the "Freshman Fifteen" for college, but I can't recall what the weight gain is for newly married couples. It's at least twice what freshman experience, I think."

Jon grilled tuna steak and fresh vegetables that were in foil packets. They continued to sit outside and ate until the twilight fell and the mosquitoes started feasting. Then, they retired to the kitchen for dessert and more conversation.

"You are coming to the Bayside Picnic next weekend, aren't you?" Sylvia asked.

"Of course," Marian said. "Anne, Phil, and Mary are coming, aren't they?" she asked.

"Yes," Sylvia said, "and our neighbors, Kim, and Craig as well as Skip and Maureen. It will be a fun group. I'm not sure if Carol and Joe are coming or not. I can find out this week."

Their evening ended on a high note, sitting comfortably in the kitchen away from the biting mosquitoes. Owen and Sylvia brought fixings for ice cream sundaes and they put together their own concoctions.

"Oh, my," Jon said, "I don't think I've had an ice cream sundae in years. That was good."

"Mmm," Sylvia agreed, "Usually, I'm a chocolate chip, cookie dough, kind of gal," she admitted, "but, that salted caramel ice cream is fantastic!" She was going to say something else but yawned instead.

"Work tomorrow," Owen reminded her, "We should head home soon."

"Work and wedding cake sampling," she told Owen.

Marian asked where they were going to sample wedding cakes. Sylvia told her that Carol had set up an appointment at a bakery in nearby, Newark, Delaware.

"There is a small bakery on the way to Havre de Grace," Marian suggested, "'Desserts by Diane,' is the name. It would give you another option."

"Thanks, Marian," Sylvia said, "I'll call them tomorrow. And, we really should be heading home."

She stood up to give Marian and Jon hugs.

"Thank you for the headpiece, Marian," Sylvia said, "It's perfect and very, very special."

Marian hugged her again, "As I said earlier," she told Sylvia, "you are the closest thing I have to a granddaughter." She turned to Owen and told him, "and you, Owen, are the closest thing I have to a grandson. How lucky am I that you are together!" She bathed them both with a radiant smile.

CHAPTER ELEVEN

"I don't think it's possible to have a wedding without it being stressful!"

— DEBRA MESSING

As Sylvia suspected, Carol wanted to pepper her with wedding questions the next day. They were swamped with work for the upcoming 'Bay Days' and some other projects, and the wedding conversation had to wait until lunch. On the way to the cafeteria, Sylvia filled Carol in on details of the gown, headpiece and shoes being stored at Marian's. She also told Carol that Marian had found them a minister.

"Wow!" Carol replied, "You're checking things off this list pretty quickly. I can't wait to see your gown!"

"Are you coming over for the Fourth of July picnic at Bayside?" Sylvia asked, "If so, maybe we can scoot over to Marian's to take a look."

Carol sighed, "I'm learning what's it's like to be in a relationship with a cop," she told her friend, "I'm still not sure of Joe's schedule for the weekend."

"Just come yourself, if he can't make it," Sylvia told Carol. "It's casual and fun. It's potluck."

"Okay, okay," Carol said, "Mom's going to the beach, but I guess I can hang here with Joe or without."

They entered the cafeteria that was getting crowded with the lunch hour. Fortunately, Owen had arrived before them and had saved them a table. Both women stopped talking about the wedding dress. Owen stood up, gave Sylvia a quick kiss, and waited until they sat.

"How are your plans coming?" Carol asked Owen.

"Plans?" he asked, looking puzzled.

"For your part of the wedding planning," Carol asked, "Best man, tuxedos, rehearsal dinner, you know…that stuff for wedding planning."

Owen laughed. "Carol," he said, "you actually lost your calling. You definitely should be a wedding planner," he chuckled. "My best man is my friend from college, Scott. We spent many years together as roommates. We don't get together too often because he's all over the country for his job. He'll be here for the wedding. Sylvia hasn't had a chance to meet him yet, either."

"Good," Carol said, "and…"

Owen sighed, "Marian is insisting on the rehearsal dinner. Mom and Dad and I are arguing with her that we'll only agree if she has it catered." He looked at Sylvia and said with a sardonic tone, "you can imagine how well that's going, but Jon agrees, and I think he'll talk her into it. Mom's been looking up caterers by the dozens. Regarding the tuxedoes, what do you want me to wear?"

Sylvia looked at him and smiled, "Well, I loved you wearing the tux with the tails when you proposed, but I think it will be much too hot for that at the wedding. Since it's a waterfront and sort of a beach wedding, do you just want to wear a suit or just a dress shirt and pants?" she asked.

He pondered this for a minute, before he answered, "I think I would like to wear a tux," Owen said and smiled at her before he continued. "How would a light gray tuxedo be with a tie or cummerbund to match Carol and Gwen's dresses?" he asked.

"Ooh!," Carol agreed, "the light gray would look fabulous with the sage green dresses."

"And if you want to keep it more casual," Sylvia suggested, "you, Scotty and Joe could get light gray suits. I'm sure you could find a sage green tie. Maybe you could purchase it as their groomsman's gift?" Sylvia suggested.

Owen nodded, thinking about it. "Okay, I get it. No tuxedo is your wish. Keep it a little casual. I guess we'll have to have a 'boys' shopping date soon. I'll get in touch with both of them."

"Where's Scotty now?" Sylvia asked.

"I think he's in Canada this week," Owen said, "he's taken his geeky self and created an empire with his Geeky Conventions. Being a geek has made him a lot of money and he's guest geek at the Star Trek museum in Vulcan, Canada."

"Lucky him," Carol said, "The suit idea is great. Cake decisions this week and flowers next week."

"Yes, Commandant," Owen saluted Carol.

She laughed, "Back to the grindstone," she reminded Sylvia before she said to Owen, "See you this afternoon for cakes."

Sylvia and Owen followed Carol to the bakery in Newark, Delaware. It was an old building and Sylvia suspected it dated to the nineteen fifties or early nineteen sixties. When they walked into the bakery, the aroma of sweet baked goods wafted out to them in a wave. They all sniffed appreciatively. They introduced themselves at the counter and were asked to sit at the decorative white iron table and chairs at the front of the bakery. In a moment, two young women arrived, one with binders and a clipboard and the other one with a tray. The young lady with the binders and clipboard put them down on the table and held out her hand.

"Hello, I'm Lauren Hirsch," she introduced herself, "and I'm the bridal coordinator at the bakery."

The other young woman put the tray down on an adjacent white, wrought iron table and went back to the kitchen. She returned a moment later with plates, forks, and napkins. Lauren had them fill out an informational sheet with their personal information, wedding date, and the number of guests. Sylvia did this while Carol and Owen browsed through the books with photographs of beautiful cakes. After Sylvia had finished the paperwork, Lauren discussed the various cakes and fillings.

They tried eight different kinds of cake and ten different fillings. Lauren looked hopefully at Owen and Sylvia after they tried the various combinations. Carol voted for chocolate cake with a pineapple filling. This was no surprise to Sylvia, as she knew Carol had a penchant for tropical drinks. Carol and her mother, Amber, visited the islands nearly each year. Carol loves Pina Coladas and other fruity, tropical drinks. It was a surprise to Sylvia that Owen liked the red velvet. Sylvia couldn't decide on her favorite.

"I think we need to think about this before we make a decision," Sylvia said. She turned to Owen, "I think a smaller cake would be sufficient, don't you?"

He nodded and answered, "The cakes are stunning," he said as he gestured to the book of photographs of cakes baked and decorated by the bakery, "we'll need to talk about what type of designs we like as well."

"Thank you so much," Sylvia said to Lauren, "you have given us a lot to think about and decisions to make."

They left the bakery and walked to their cars. Sylvia looked wistfully at one of her favorite restaurants across the street. It was a Thai restaurant that catered to the University in town. It would be nice to be able to go to dinner, but they needed to get home to Percy.

Owen caught her wistful glance and suggested take out. She agreed by nodding enthusiastically and asked Carol if she wanted to join them.

"Thanks, but no," Carol said. "I need to get home too. Do you want to go to Costco tomorrow to check on cakes?"

"Honestly, Carol," Sylvia told her, "I'm not sure I can do cake tastings each night. I know it's a holiday, but maybe we could go somewhere on Sunday?"

"Sure," Carol agreed, "but, you really need to make a decision very soon," she pushed.

"I know, I know, I know," Sylvia said slightly petulantly, "Next week cake *and* flowers. Mom and Anne will be here over the weekend, so I'm sure they'll have a lot of suggestions as well."

"You're right there," Carol agreed. She yawned her response, "Time to go home. Here comes Owen with your food." Carol nodded in the direction of the restaurant across the street where Owen emerged with a small box and a bag.

Owen and Sylvia were quiet on their ride home. Just on the outskirts of North Bay, they both started a conversation simultaneously and then laughed.

"You first," Sylvia told Owen.

"No, you go ahead," he replied.

Sylvia was going to argue and decided against it, "I wasn't impressed at the bakery," she told Owen. "It just didn't feel right," she said with a shrug.

"I was going to tell you the same thing," he admitted. "Although, I'm really not sure what we're looking for. Those cakes were too ostentatious."

"That's it, exactly," Sylvia said. "I don't know what we want either, so, I think I'll take Marian's suggestion and contact that bakery near Havre de Grace and look at the list from Beverly - next week."

They arrived home and a grateful Percy ran outside to the yard. Sylvia set their dinner out on the deck and lit some candles to keep the insects away. She watched Percy gambol like a lamb in their front yard. He went down to the beach to lap at the water and yap at a wave that came in and surprised him. Owen laughed a deep laugh at this and Sylvia couldn't help but laugh as well. She went inside to prepare Percy's dinner and brought it to the deck as well.

Once again, the feeling of connectedness filled Sylvia. She could almost envision the invisible cords that connected her to Owen, to Percy and all that was around her. In her mind's eye, they seemed to glimmer until the connections had so many ties that the world appeared to be brighter. It was a golden light in her mind. Deeply, Sylvia knew Bayside always had that effect on her. The place was in her blood, her bones, and her soul. Perhaps it was that siren song that called to her when she saw the edge where the water met the sky. Perhaps it was the peacefulness of the community itself. She didn't know. She also knew she was deeply connected to Owen. She loved him, but it was deeper. It was a much deeper connection that she couldn't put a name to it. She stared dreamily beyond where Percy and Owen were playing, imagining once again, and the brilliant, golden ties that bound them to her. She did not realize they had come up from the beach until Percy's wet nose bumped her hand and Owen's footstep on the stairs to the deck broke her out of her daydream.

Owen laughed, "Syl, where were you?" he queried, joining her at the deck railing.

She nodded at the glorious vista before them as she snuggled into his shoulder. His arm tightened around her.

"Aren't we lucky?" he murmured into her hair.

"Oh, yes!" Sylvia whispered back softly and huskily with an almost imperceptible nod.

They stood mesmerized as they watched the sunset paint the sky.

CHAPTER TWELVE

'A good neighbor increases the value of your property.''

— AN OLD CZECH PROVERB.

H er mother returned to their house on July third for the an-
nual Bayside Fourth of July picnic. Each year the community had a Fourth of July picnic where friends and family of community members gathered for a potluck smorgasbord of dishes,
grilled burgers, and hot dogs. There were games for the children
and fireworks afterward.

Sylvia had often participated in the festivities when her
grandmother was alive. She had fond memories of the children's games, and probably still had one of the coveted prizes
from the three-legged race or "egg on a spoon" relay stashed
somewhere. Her Gran had vehemently vetoed her participat-
ing in the turtle races, and so each year she wistfully watched

as people cheered on box turtles they had found in the woods. Gran staged a protest when members hot glued tchotchke baubles, silk flowers or painted on the turtle shells. Sylvia understood, but part of her still wanted to participate in the race. She had always likened the Fourth of July picnic at Bayside to a Norman Rockwell painting. It was a slice of Americana that didn't exist in many places today.

Last year, they had declined to participate since they were in the throes of Owen's indictment for Anna's murder. He had been released on bail, but their stress level had hit a pinnacle and community events were not a priority.

Though preparations had been in the works for weeks, the morning of the Fourth was the culmination of the community's efforts. Owen joined the men of the community and assisted in hauling and setting up long tables created from sawhorses and plywood that had been stored for the last year. Other crews gathered grills, encircled like a wagon train from the old west, with the gas and charcoal grills in the middle and the serving tables all around. An area for the children's games was cordoned off, and community members staked out favorite spots in the open space for their group. Mary had given Owen strict instructions where to set their folding chairs, and a small card table for their relatively large circle of friends to gather.

Mary and Sylvia helped cover the food tables and decorate with bright bunting in red, white and blue. Sylvia rolled a few hundred bundles of plastic silverware while her mother tied gay, patriotic ribbons around the bundles. When Sylvia finished with her bundles of plastic silverware, she left her mother to chat and catch up with the neighbors.

Sylvia had dithered on what potluck dish to take. The request and unspoken rule was to bring a quantity of food that would feed those you invited and more. In the end, Owen had decided on the dish, requesting an herbal vinaigrette potato salad. She would need to prepare it this morning so that the flavors had a chance to meld before the picnic at five o'clock.

The day was hot, but not overly oppressive. Sylvia pulled out the largest pot in her cache and washed off ten pounds of red, white and blue tiny potatoes. She then set them to boil with a good amount of kosher salt. She went out to her flower pots on the deck where she snipped a handful of herbs and went inside to create vinaigrette from fresh lemon juice, mustard, olive oil, herbs, and spices. Once the potatoes were done, she drained them in a whoosh of steam and put them back in the warm pot and stirred in the vinaigrette. It would need to cool a little before she placed it in the refrigerator. Sylvia poked at a piece of potato with a fork and taste tested the salad. It was delicious. She went into the living room to wait for her mom and Owen to return. She settled with a book to wait until she heard a sound in the kitchen and went to investigate. Percy had been a little too quiet for her comfort. Usually, he didn't surf the counter, but she didn't want to take the chance with food for the picnic. She stood up and went stealthily to the kitchen only to see Owen poking a finger into the potato salad and filching a couple of potatoes.

"You!" she said accusingly, surprising him enough to have Owen jump a little. "That's for tonight," she scolded him.

"But, it's so good," he pleaded. "Maybe, I can have just a little?"

"No, no and no," she scolded lightly.

"Okay," he said slyly, "so, you'll need to distract me from the food," he said as he pushed her up against the refrigerator and started nibbling at her throat. His hands roamed her pleasurably.

Sylvia closed her eyes, she thought she moaned out loud, but their reverie was broken by a loud knock on the kitchen door.

"Oh, my," she breathed, straightening her blouse. "Look at the time." Sylvia flashed Owen a grin.

He groaned this time. He pulled away from her as his parents came through the door along with Jon and Marian. Phil and Jon carried a large bag and box. Anne and Marian followed, chatting amiably, and carrying bottles of wine. Hugs and kisses went around, and Sylvia stowed the food and drink, as Owen led everyone to the deck. Sylvia pulled glasses and pitchers of iced tea, and lemonade from the refrigerator. The afternoon passed by languidly. Percy was in his element, trotting to all of his favorite people for treats and pets. He finally settled down at Sylvia's feet. Carol had texted her earlier, and when she arrived with Joe, their jovial group loaded the garden wagon with their potluck dishes. They carried the bottles of wine. Percy whined at the door when they all exited. Sylvia gave him a last pat on the head and told him to guard the house. His huge, brown eyes followed her every movement, and he put his paws up on the door so that he could watch them walk down the road. Their next door neighbors, Kim, and Craig, as well as Maureen and Skip, had beaten them to their picnic site. Almost immediately, the men of the group, along with Carol, went to fill plastic cups from the chilled kegs of beer temporarily housed in a canoe that had been filled with ice, soda, and kegs. Mary passed around the wine to the remaining group. They sat together and talked for a short time until Mary noticed the lines to the myriad of dishes getting longer and longer. They went to join the picnic attendees and fill their plates as well.

Part of the community of the picnic was the catching up and co-mingling of everyone's lives, as well as the intermingling of the summer and year round folks. Sylvia greeted people that she knew, and nodded and smiled, but was surprised when the efforts were not easily returned.

As they took their filled plates back to their circle of chairs, Carol asked acerbically, "I thought this was a *friendly* community."

"Oh, Carol!" Sylvia said, giggling. "What are you thinking?"

Carol shrugged nonchalantly, and sat beside Joe and dug into her food. But, Sylvia ate slowly and watched the people at the picnic. It was common for people to mingle, and go from circle to circle, with their drinks and to share appetizers. Their circle stood as an island, and people did not approach them. Sylvia had never experienced this before. She remembered the previous years when there was a steady stream of people visiting their circle when Gran was alive. Today it was very evident, that people averted their eyes as they walked past, or rushed by their circle without greeting.

Sylvia turned to Carol saying, "Carol," and she paused, "as usual, your instincts seem to be correct."

"What are you talking about?" Owen asked her.

"Carol was noticing that people were not overly friendly to us this year," Sylvia explained to him, and to the group at large.

Puzzled looks met her eyes. Carol raised her eyebrows to Sylvia and nodded in agreement. Everyone stopped eating for a moment.

Craig, Kim's husband, broke the silence, "It's because you are sort of a black widow to the community," he said.

"Craig!" Kim expostulated.

"Well, it's true...sort of," Craig said, looking sheepish. "Sylvia and Owen brought murder and mayhem last year, and this year," he nodded to Maureen and Skip, "Maureen and Skip brought the murder and mayhem. You are the flies in the ointment, so to speak, or possibly jinxes to this private, quiet, little haven along the bay."

"That's a little harsh," Kim admonished her husband.

"True," Craig returned, looking a little sheepish. He raked his hand through his hair, as a guilty look settled on his face.

"But, you are likely correct," Jon added in his lawyerly tone.

Suddenly, the food in Sylvia's stomach turned into one giant boulder. Craig's comments had struck a chord, and she silently agreed with Jon that the murders were why they were being shunned. Their neighborhood was usually peaceful and almost seemed to exist outside of the anarchy of the rest of the world. That was one of the reasons why she loved it so much. But, what could she do about it? The encroaching violence sickened her as well. Other than minor burglary, that happened on rare occasion, particularly to the seasonal homeowners, crime was non-existent in their community. Was she a jinx? That thought was uncomfortable. She would need to ask the Green Man.

Sylvia jumped when the loudspeaker came on, and the treasurer of their community association called for everyone's attention. The laughter and chatter came to a quiet hush. The Treasurer thanked everyone for coming to the picnic and for the fabulous dishes. He asked for applause for the volunteers and for those cooking the hamburgers and hot dogs. After the applause had died down, he asked people to pull out their raffle tickets. With great flourish, with the community association's president, he pulled out ticket by ticket for the raffle prizes and for the 50/50 raffle. Cries of surprise by happy people ran up to claim their prizes. When the prize giving was completed, the treasurer reminded everyone that the children's games would begin in fifteen minutes, to stop by the fabulous dessert table, and not to forget their leftovers and chairs. He wished them a happy Fourth of July. Polite applause thanked the Treasurer, and people returned to their conversations.

Craig turned to Joe, "Since I'm the one who keeps putting their foot in his mouth, I'll bring up another uncomfortable question. Is there any news on old George's murderer?"

"Not anything I can talk about," Joe answered him.

"Possible fish poachers," Maureen added, her eyes downcast.

"What?" Marian and Kim cried simultaneously.

"It's a possibility," Joe commented. "Poaching fish and oysters in the bay are big business. Those investigations are with the Coast Guard, and not our offices. But, we hear stories..." his voice trailed off.

Jon raised a quizzical eyebrow at Joe. "There were rockfish poachers that were recently prosecuted in Baltimore. To my knowledge, the fish poachers are not usually prone to violence. But, there's always a first time," he added enigmatically.

"People have killed for less," Carol added, "We are all too familiar with that scenario."

The group became quiet again.

"I forgot to ask you, Joe," Sylvia said a couple of minutes later, "there were a bunch of police cars at the marina across the cove a few days ago. Are they related?"

"Not that I know of," Joe said, "That was a prescription drug sting. People are going to Florida's pain clinics for painkillers, and bringing them north, and later selling them on the street. Oxycontin and Oxycodone are two of the favorites to bring up. The boats seem to be a popular way to sell the drugs."

"There's been a lot of chatter about an increase in drug traffic in the county," Jon commented.

Joe had on his cop face.

"We are on the I-95 corridor. Everyone knows we're in the pipeline. Why, I've been told one of the high schools near I-95 has high heroin usage." Jon mentioned.

"Heroin?" Sylvia queried, wrinkling her nose. "I couldn't do that. Ugh. Needles." She shrugged her shoulders.

"Be that as it may," Jon told her, "Heroin has become a cheap high."

"And Deerton, has the highest illegal drug usage in the state," Carol comment.

"Really?" Mary asked. "I had no idea."

Carol and Joe nodded their heads simultaneously, and grimly. Joe still had his 'cop face' on.

Sylvia wanted to change the subject to a more positive one. She turned to Skip and commented that she really liked some of the new boats he was selling at the marina.

He nodded. "They are beauties," he agreed, "and with the fuel prices coming down again, we are selling more."

Sylvia sighed dreamily, "I love the design of those Buick power boats."

Skip looked blankly at her. Puzzled, he asked, "Buick power boats? We don't have anything by Buick. That's a car. What boats are you talking about?"

Owen chuckled and ruffled Sylvia's hair. She lightly slapped his hand away. "Sylvia is referring to the Regal power boats," Owen explained.

Skip realized Sylvia's error, and started to chuckle, then guffaw and he laughed loud and long until tears streamed from his eyes. "Oh, Sylvia," he told her when he had recovered himself. "I will have to remember your comment. That was good." He slapped his knee and went off into another gale of laughter.

His laughter was contagious and soon everyone was laughing, except for Sylvia.

"An honest mistake," she started to say, trying to recover from her embarrassment. But, Skip's laughter was contagious and soon she became caught up in the genial mood as well.

Jon whistled, "You have excellent taste in boats, Sylvia," he told her. "Regal yachts, those are definitely dreamboats."

Sylvia had wanted to lighten the mood. She had inadvertently done so with her blunder. For the remainder of the picnic, they laughed and talked with pleasant conversational topics. Every time Skip glanced her way, he would smile. As evening began to fall, the picnic began to break up. Skip and Maureen hurried home to help with the boats heading out to the boat parade. Many of the other community members disbanded to get to their own boats or beaches. Sylvia's guests retired to her deck to wait for the fireworks.

Sylvia could hardly believe a year ago they were somber from Owen's possible erroneous charge for Anna's murder. A year ago he had been out on bail. Their Fourth of July celebration was quelled by the stress of the reality of the situation. She looked around the group, relieved to know that everyone was happy and well. Jon's hand was resting on Percy's head. Percy looked up at him adoringly, before he settled at Jon's feet.

Percy. A year ago she could not have imagined having a dog in her life. All that had happened with Joyce's murder and Tony's crazed obsession flashed before her eyes. She gave an involuntary shiver.

Owen, whose arm had been lightly resting on Sylvia's shoulder, felt the shiver. "Are you all right?" he asked.

Sylvia nodded.

"Penny," he whispered to her.

"Just remembering," she whispered back. "And, I'm very happy how things have turned out in this last year."

Sylvia nestled closer to Owen. Beatific glances from Jon, Marian, and their parents were sent their way. They watched the parade of boats gather in a group at the head of the bay near the border of the town park, but a safe distance away from the barge that held the county's fireworks. A loud crackle and boom exploded in the air as the fireworks show started from the town park. The sky was alight with colorful, blossoms of light and shooting rockets brilliant against the dark, blue-black sky. Boat horns squealed with delight and excitement but were soon drowned by the thunderous booms from the fireworks show.

"We'll need to make our own fireworks in a bit," Owen whispered in her ear.

She shivered, this time, in pleasure, as her insides melted at his suggestion and he trailed a finger over her ear and down her neck. Now the evening began to feel interminable as she looked forward to Owen's promise.

When Jon, Marian, Phil, Anne, Joe and Carol had left, Mary yawned loudly.

"Whew! What a day!" she said as she yawned and stretched again. "I'm exhausted."

"Mom, why don't you head up to bed," Sylvia directed her mother. "Owen and I will be happy to clean up."

"All right, if you insist," Mary replied, not really protesting, and starting to head out of the room to go up the stairs.

"We insist," Owen told her. Behind her back he raised up his eyebrows with intent at Sylvia.

Another shiver of pleasure went through her. Mary went up the stairs, calling out 'good night' as she went. Owen commanded Percy to go up to bed, assuring him they would be up soon. He went up and they could hear him do the magic turn, turn, turn as he settled into a circle to sleep.

"Alone at last," Owen told her quietly. He came up behind Sylvia, who was putting plastic wrap on the food and putting it in the refrigerator.

"Shh," she warned him.

"The whole house fan is on," he reminded her. "Your mom can't hear us." He let his hands roam over her and nibbled at her neck again.

Sylvia laughed lightly. "Let me get this cleaned up first," she said, "and then you can have your way with me." Her voice trailed off huskily.

"Promise?" he asked, hesitant to take his hands from her.

"It will just be another couple of minutes if you help out," she suggested.

They cleaned up the kitchen in no time. Owen took another chilled beer from the refrigerator and poured another glass of wine for Sylvia in one of their heavy acrylic wine glasses. She held up a hand in caution and stood silently, listening.

"I think everyone is asleep," she whispered.

Owen nodded in response and they tiptoed out the French doors, down the steps of the deck to a Mayan hammock that was strung between the trees at the edge of the property near the little grove where Sylvia had found the Green Man's mask. They settled into the hammock and balanced their drinks. Owen had his arm around Sylvia's back and she leaned against him looking up at the dark shapes of leaves silhouetted against the starry night sky. All was quiet and peaceful. The bevy of boats that had paraded up the bay to see the fireworks had moved back to their moorings. Lights and low fireworks flashed off and on, like colorful fireflies, across the bay. Sylvia became lost in the starry sky and the breathing patterns of the tree auras above them. She could just faintly make out the tree auras, as they reached higher into the sky. It was a slow and sensual dance. Owen began his slow and sensual assault on her, running his other hand under her blouse and teasing her nipples. She groaned softly and he stopped the cries of pleasure with his mouth nibbling on her lips at first and then deepening the kiss. Sylvia's hand lost its hold on the stem of the wine glass and it fell to the ground with a soft plunk. She didn't care. She returned Owen's sensuous assault with one of her own towards him.

CHAPTER THIRTEEN

"Contentment is the only real wealth."

— ALFRED NOBEL

It was nearing dawn when they returned to the house and into their own bed. Owen fell into a deep sleep, but Sylvia was restless. She had slept a few hours in the hammock, cuddled into Owen, their circadian rhythms, syncing them to a deep, restful sleep. Even though she had slept only a few hours after their lovemaking, Sylvia felt refreshed. Percy was alert, so she motioned for him to follow her down the stairs. She made a cup of coffee and let him run in the yard while she returned to the hammock with a steaming cup. Eventually he settled just underneath her, keeping silent and watching the bird activity on the bay with interest. Sylvia mused contentedly while sipping her coffee when she heard a rustle of leaves and a leafy face tickled her. Sylvia smiled and turned her face to the Green Man.

"You always know when I'm thinking of you, don't you?" she asked him.

His chuckle was deep, and he pulled her more tightly into a hug. "Something like that," he assured her.

Sylvia told him about Craig's comment from the previous day that she was some sort of a jinx. It still niggled at her, unhappily. The Green Man listened to her worries.

"There always needs to be a balance," he told her. "There will always be good to match the wrong in life. You can't stop the balancing act."

"Okay," Sylvia said slowly. "But, I thought you were here to overcome the evil."

"I am," he replied. "I strive to create more good in the world. But, there still needs to be a balance."

"So there will always be bad things that can happen?" Sylvia asked.

She could feel his sadness before he answered, "Unfortunately, yes," he told her. "You see, every little thing you do, no matter how minute, whether it is a thought or an action, affects the balance. And, it's not just you," he explained, "It's *everything* -- even the smallest thing in this universe. The balance is constantly shifting ."

"A shifting sea of sand," Sylvia quoted softly, not remembering where she had heard it.

"Exactly," the Green Man said before he added with a little exasperation in his voice, "and you humans, who have the brain power that you are dearth to use, consistently make choices that affect the balance in a negative way."

Sylvia ruminated on this for a few minutes. She and the Green Man swayed in a gentle rhythm in the hammock.

"And me?" she asked quietly. "Why me?" she asked him again.

The Green Man's sigh tinged with frustration at her lack of understanding and said, "You are one of many beings that help the balance. You are a blessing," the Green Man assured her.

They continued to sway slightly, neither talking, just having the pleasure of the closeness of friends. Sylvia was absorbed in his compliment and kept trying to form questions or ideas of how she could help. But, the words were muddled and did not develop clear thought. She sank into a happy, dreamlike state with the Green Man next to her, enjoying his presence.

Mary's voice broke the stillness, "Syl?" she called out to the yard, "Sylvia? Where are you?"

The Green Man's leaves rustled, and he disappeared in an instant. Sylvia sighed. She was just starting to get a few answers to the myriad of questions she had for the Green Man. She sighed again.

"I'm here, Mom," she answered, "In the hammock."

Percy ran over to Mary as she stepped from the deck into the yard. "Oh! I was wondering where you were. Did Owen's snoring chase you from bed?"

"Sort of," Sylvia said. "but, I also just love coming out to enjoy the morning. It makes me happy."

Sylvia sat up and her mother joined her on the hammock, sitting next to her.

"You are *so* much like your grandmother," Mary told Sylvia. "When I was growing up, she was always the first one up. Sometimes it was like a game to find her in the morning," her mother reminisced. "Usually, she was outside, fiddling with the plants."

Her mother didn't often reminisce and Sylvia listened with interest.

Her mother continued, "Sometimes, I remember, I thought she was talking with someone, but no one was ever around. When I was little, I would run to find the person she was talking to and no one was ever there. She would laugh and remind me she would talk to her plants to make them grow better. Sometimes, I even imagined there was a voice that answered her. It was a man's voice. But, it was my imagination," her mother mused, shaking her head.

It *must* have been the Green Man, Sylvia thought to herself. It had to have been him. She would need to remember to add that question to her long list of queries for him. They continued to sit quietly for a few minutes watching the sun and the water and the sky. The dappled sunlight from the trees above made patterns on them.

Sylvia finished her coffee and stared into her empty cup before she said, "I really miss Gran," she told her mother.

"Me too," her Mom returned quietly. "She would certainly have loved helping to plan this wedding. We should go in and get some breakfast before we head out. Aren't Carol, Marian, and Anne joining us? "

"Yes," Sylvia said perfunctorily, "back to wedding plans."

She put a hand under her mother's elbow and helped her get out of the hammock.

"Come on, Percy," she told her dog, "time to go inside."

Percy heard her but raced around the yard and down to the water in a wild streak. Sylvia and Mary laughed.

"Come *on*, Percy," Sylvia ordered.

He looked up at her when she called his name. Sylvia patted her hand on her leg and he raced around the yard in one last circle before he trotted up to her and into the house obediently. She shook her head at him.

Awhile later, Sylvia and Mary picked up Anne and Marian. They were to meet Carol at the bakery in Havre de Grace. The owner, Diane de Franco, had asked them to come after nine and before noon. They had settled on 10:30 to meet to discuss cakes. Diane seemed surprised, but not upset when the entire group descended upon the tiny bakery that was a restored, vintage gas station. The inside of the old gas station had been gutted. Diane led them through the door from the sales area into the old garage bay that now held ovens, sinks, storage and long counters of work space. What had been the small retail store of the gas station was transformed into a quaint bakeshop. It had buttery yellow walls and bright recessed lighting. Lighted cases held pastries, cookies and cupcakes and a small rack held baskets of fresh bread and rolls. There was a small table that held a Keurig coffee machine with racks of choices. It smelled divine.

They crowded into the small conference room. One of the bakery assistants told them to help themselves to coffee or tea and went to get additional chairs. Photos of brides, grooms, and their wedding cakes were on the walls and a thick scrapbook of photographs of Diane's cakes lay on the table along with a legal pad and pen. There were a few issues of a magazine called, "Cake Craft" devoted to wedding cakes. They settled in. After introductions, Diane picked up her pad of paper and pen.

"So, Sylvia," Diane began, "tell me about your wedding. Tell me when, where, colors, your dress, and your ideas about the cake."

So Sylvia told her. She told Diane about the pergola and the curtains, the marina, the yacht club and her dress. Carol pulled out her phone and shared photos of Sylvia's dress, shoes, and the attendant dresses. Diane asked her about numbers of guests and thoughts on cakes. Sylvia paused at this. She admitted to Diane that she did not have many ideas about cakes with the exception that she wanted to keep it fairly simple.

"Well," Diane replied, "first question -- round or square?"

Sylvia looked at everyone. Anne, who had been looking at the cake scrapbook with Marian, pointed out an elegant square cake to Sylvia. Everyone oohed and ahhed.

"All of these cakes are lovely," Anne commented.

"But, I do like the square ones," Sylvia said.

"You mentioned leaves as a sort of theme," Diane commented and asked, "in the curtains on the pergola and in the lace of your dress. Do you want leaves on your cake?"

"Well..." Sylvia said slowly, "I don't want the autumn leaves theme. I didn't like any of the cakes with fondant leaves that I looked at on the internet."

"Show Diane your wedding invitation," her Mom suggested. "It almost looks like the lace on your dress."

Sylvia pulled the invitation from her purse and handed it to Diane. Diane studied it for a minute and then began to sketch quickly on her notepad. She turned it so that everyone could see.

"How's this?" she asked. "You could have a square cake of two or three tiers. I can tint the icing to a pale sage green, like your attendants' dresses. I can create a lacy effect from icing with the leaf design that's on this invitation."

"Oh!" Sylvia exclaimed, "That sounds perfect!"

"Do you have a topper?" Diane asked.

Sylvia wrinkled her nose. "No. I don't like a lot of the bride and groom ones," she admitted.

"You can put on anything you want," Diane assured her. "Also, I can do a lovely fondant bow." She borrowed the scrapbook to show Sylvia an example.

"Why don't you think on it," Diane suggested and let me know. "You have plenty of time."

"You are the only person that thinks that!" Sylvia told Diane and glanced at the women at the table before she laughed a little ruefully.

Diane smiled at her, "No worries! Now the fun begins," Diane said. "Excuse me a minute."

Diane stood up and left the room.

"She's AWESOME," Carol stage whispered.

"I love her design idea," Marian said. "I think your cake will be just lovely."

Sylvia agreed. Diane was back in a moment with small white china plates, forks, and some samples. They all tasted the various cakes--chocolate, white, carrot and red velvet. Sylvia was particularly fond of a pound cake with mini chocolate chips inside.

"I think this is my favorite," she told Diane. "Owen would love this."

"And I can make up an icing between the layers that is like cookie dough. I add lots of brown sugar to the icing and more mini chocolate chips," she told Sylvia.

"Sounds divine," Sylvia said.

Everyone nodded in agreement. Diane went to get a contract. With paperwork settled, they left the bakery and Sylvia felt a weight off her shoulders.

"Way to go, girlfriend," Carol told her. "One more thing completed. Now, we need to address those invitations. Can we all go back to your place and have an assembly line to get them ready to go out in tomorrow's mail?"

Sylvia laughed. "Is that okay with everyone?" she asked, knowing her mom, Anne and Marian would be more than happy to help.

They spent the afternoon putting together the invitations that had arrived on Friday. Their assembly line worked and it only took a couple of hours to complete the task.

Owen called her on her cell phone. She knew he had been working things out with the purchase of the new boat.

"Hi!" she answered the phone. "How are you? Where are you?"

"You sound happy," He said, "You must have had a successful morning."

"We did! We did!" Sylvia exclaimed. "Wait till I tell you about the cake. And," she added, burbling on, "the invitations are all addressed and ready to go."

"Great!" Owen agreed. "But, I need you to do me a favor."

"Anything," Sylvia answered. "What do you need?"

Owen's reply was teasing and his voice dropped to a husky drawl, "You're dangerous, do you know that? I can think of a myriad of things that I need..." his voice trailed off.

He paused a moment while Sylvia's heart flip-flopped.

"I need you to get into your bathing suit," he told her, "and meet me out front in about fifteen minutes."

"Okay," she sounded puzzled. "I'll see you soon."

CHAPTER FIFTEEN

"My she was yar,"

— Tracy Lord (from The Philadelphia Story)

She hung up the phone and turned to the group and told them what Owen had asked. Marian and Anne knew something. Both had a twinkle in their eyes. Mary came with another pitcher of iced tea and asked if they wanted to sit on the deck. Sylvia scooted upstairs to change. She joined the ladies in more casual clothes and accepted a glass of iced tea from her mother. She sat on the deck where she could look into the driveway for Owen, but he did not come. She tapped her foot a little impatiently. Finally, a car pulled into the driveway. Phil emerged, but no Owen. Where was he? She was about to call out her question when Phil pointed to the bay. Motoring as close to the shoreline as possible was a sailboat. It had a gorgeous dark hull and the sails were down, but it was still lovely moving slowly through the water. At the helm was a man who was waving at her. It was Owen! It must be his new boat. She grinned and waved back. His happiness was evident all the way to the shoreline.

He maneuvered the boat as closely as he could to the mooring he had placed in the water a couple of weeks ago in preparation for the vessel's arrival. Jon's head popped up and he went up to the bow of the boat. He had a long tool in his hand and he somehow finagled the device and the mooring and the boat was secured. Owen dropped a ladder. He and Jon climbed down and waded to shore. Mary had thoughtfully rushed in to get towels as Sylvia still stood, a bit stunned at what was happening. Marian rushed down to the shoreline to meet Jon and Sylvia, waking from the surprise, ran down as well and threw herself into Owen's arms.

"She's beautiful!" she told him.

His grin was from ear to ear and he beamed down at her. "Yes, she is and so are you," he told Sylvia before giving her a kiss.

"I can't wait to see her," Sylvia told him anxiously. "Can we go? Now?"

Owen laughed, "Yes," he told her. "We'll go out for a quick tour. And then we can get the dinghy and take everyone else who wants a tour. I think Phil stopped by the liquor store for some champagne. Maybe the moms can rustle up some snacks and plastic cups?"

Mary and Anne went inside.

Carol prodded Sylvia. "What are you waiting for, girl? Get on your boat!"

Owen and Sylvia waded into the water. As she got closer to the boat, Sylvia felt a small shiver of apprehension. It was so big!

"Before we go on board, I want to show you something," he told her.

Owen pulled her through the water to the stern. They were treading water now. Sylvia looked up to see fancy scrollwork spell out "True Love." Her mouth dropped open and tears came to her eyes.

"Now you know why I had to get this boat," Owen told her, "One, because you are my true love and two, because of your infatuation with "The Philadelphia Story.""

"Oh!" Sylvia breathed. She couldn't throw her arms around him in the water - not easily. She would need to wait until they got aboard. "Oh, Owen!" was all Sylvia could say.

"Come on," he said, "let's get aboard."

He helped her over to the ladder and she climbed up the ladder and went, not so gracefully, over the side of the boat. When Owen had his feet on the deck, she threw herself into his arms.

"It's beautiful," she said before correcting the statement, "no, it's yar," Sylvia said using the term from "The Philadelphia Story."

"*She's* beautiful," Owen corrected her. "But, you have to see the rest of her. He led her below down a small set of stairs. Below he pointed out the equipment, the galley, the bathroom or 'head' Owen corrected himself. He also showed her their berth where they would be sleeping.

"You know that sailors are a superstitious lot, don't you?" he asked as they were checking out all the nooks and crannies.

"What are you talking about?" Sylvia said distractedly. "And, you are the least superstitious person I know," she commented.

"Well," Owen told her with a grin, "I like this particular superstition. You know it's bad luck to have a woman on board."

"What?" Sylvia asked. "Are you kidding?"

"Bad luck," he paused, "unless they're naked," he told her with a grin. "So, guess what," He suggested, "you'll have to be naked, a lot when we're sailing."

"I suppose it means I'll be spending a lot of time in the berth with you?" she said coyly. "Wanna' give it a try, sailor?" she teased.

"If only," Owen groaned. "I know the rest of the pack will be coming on board in a couple of minutes. Later," he told her, "we'll have plenty of opportunities to check out the good luck you can bring to the vessel."

Owen began to reach for her when a voice floated down to them, "Ahoy!" It was Phil. He had rowed half of the group over to the boat and was headed back for the rest. Owen rushed up to give a hand to Mary, Anne and Carol to get aboard.

Mary, Anne, and Carol crawled all over the boat and asked Owen a million questions while they waited for the others to arrive. Phil and Jon held the dinghy steady for Marian to nimbly come up the ladder, followed by Jon and later Phil, who tethered the dinghy to the boat for their return trip.

Sylvia stayed on deck with Jon while Owen gave the rest of the group a tour of the stateroom and cabin. Sylvia could hear their praises through the hatch as they poked around. Jon busied himself with getting champagne and nibbles from a tote bag they had brought along.

"So what do you think of your surprise?" he asked with a twinkle in his eye.

Sylvia looked at the boat from bow to stern and at the sparkling water in front of her before she answered, "It's totally amazing!" she told him with a touch of awe in her voice. "It's -she's beautiful," she told Jon.

"Just wait until your first sail," Jon told her. "She's a dream of a boat. You and Owen will have many happy years sailing this vessel."

"I think so," she agreed and before she could say anything else, Marian's head popped up out of the hatch.

Jon rushed over to give his wife a hand. Everyone gathered on deck. Owen was at the helm, beaming with pride and happiness.

"It's time to christen this vessel," Jon announced. He turned to Owen, "I assure you, Owen, I will not harm this beautiful boat by breaking a bottle of champagne against the side, but I will pour champagne on it to assure you safe passages."

Jon proceeded to hand plastic cups filled with champagne to everyone before he opened another bottle.

He raised his cup and toasted, "To the 'True Love,'" he said, acknowledging the boat, "and to true love," he raised his glass to Sylvia and Owen, but looked so deeply at Marian that she blushed.

"Here! Here!" Mary raised her glass.

Everyone toasted. Jon poured the champagne on the edge of the boat. Everyone cheered when the last drop of champagne left the bottle and splashed onto the gunnel.

Anne and Marian passed around platters of cucumber sandwiches and cheese and crackers. Phil and Jon refreshed everyone's plastic cup with more champagne. The afternoon ebbed towards evening with suggestions of sailing destinations, as well as catching up the men on the latest wedding information. A plaintive bark came from the shoreline.

"I think we need to head home and let Percy out," Sylvia told Owen.

"And I need to get home as well," Carol answered, smiling, "and make dinner for my man."

Carol gave Sylvia a huge hug. "I'm taking off as soon as I get to shore. I'm so glad you were surprised," she told her friend. "I'll see you in the morning."

Sylvia hugged her friend back. "I know, I know, flowers this week."

Carol gave her a thumb's up as she went down the ladder to join Phil, Mary, and Anne in the dinghy. In a short while, Phil had returned and gave over rowing to Jon as he and Marian got into the dinghy.

"We'll be right in," Owen told his Dad. "We're going to swim to shore."

Phil nodded to his son and they cast off. Sylvia and Owen watched Jon row to shore. He and Phil pulled the dinghy out of the water, put the oars inside securely and pulled it away from the high tide mark and turned it upside down. Owen went to double check the boat one more time to make sure everything was secure before he and Sylvia jumped into the water. The tide was high and the water a good bit deeper now. They didn't struggle, but swam and rode some of the wavelets to shore from a passing cigarette boat. They pulled themselves out of the water and as they stood, they could still feel the pull of the tide. Between the pull of the tide and the champagne, Sylvia was a little unsteady on her feet. Owen took her by her elbow and steadied her. They took large steps through the shallow water to reach the shoreline where Percy waited anxiously. He pranced and yipped at them until Sylvia put a calming hand on his head. Mary was heading towards them with a couple of beach towels.

"I have an idea," she called when she knew they could hear her, "what if I drive to the ice cream stand up the road while you two clean-up. I can pick up some takeout. They say their pulled pork is amazing, but they have all kinds of sandwiches to choose from in addition to the ice cream," Mary told them.

Sylvia looked at Owen and shrugged. "Okay with you for dinner?" she asked.

"Fine with me," Owen answered. "Sounds great."

"Okay!" Mary said, "Decision made. I'll get my keys and see you in about twenty minutes."

She hurried to walk to the house for her keys and purse. Owen's eyebrows lifted when he looked at Sylvia.

"Twenty minutes," he said hopefully to Sylvia.

"Oh! You!" she returned with a swat of her towel to his bottom playfully. "Race you to the shower," she challenged.

About twenty-five minutes later, Owen was putting the wet swimsuits and towels into the washing machine, when Mary returned laden with plastic bags filled with their food. A smile played at his lips and his curly hair was still damp from the shower and the July humidity.

"You're having quite the day," Mary remarked to him.

"I am indeed," he returned.

"I'm so glad the boat worked out so well," she told him kindly.

Sylvia stepped into the room, her hair damp as well. She had left it loose to dry in the summer air.

"Deck for dinner?" Mary asked.

Sylvia and Owen nodded. Owen took the bags from Mary while Sylvia got drinks and Mary took out silverware and napkins. They were just settling into their food when Owen's cell phone rang.

"It's Scotty!" he cried. "Excuse me," he told the women. Owen took himself to the Adirondack chair in the yard, where he could talk and watch the sunset provide a dramatic backdrop to the 'True Love.' He returned a few minutes later with a broad grin on his face.

"Good news!" He announced. "Scotty will be in the area next weekend!"

"Terrific!" Sylvia replied, "I can't wait to meet him! Is he going to stay here?" she asked.

Owen was finally getting a chance to eat. His mouth was full of pulled pork and he had some lukewarm beach fries in his hand. He swallowed and answered, "No, he's going to be in the Inner Harbor in Baltimore. He'll be at a Sci-Fi convention and he wanted to know if we could go down and meet him to have dinner and a night out on the town."

Owen had snagged a few more beach fries before he continued, "I thought that we might want to sail to Baltimore to meet him there. It would be a great test for the 'True Love.' We could dock at either the Inner Harbor or Fells Point."

Owen looked at Sylvia hopefully. She replied with a nod, but then glanced at Percy.

"Oh," Owen murmured understanding, but he turned to Mary with pleading eyes and said, "Mary, would you mind grand-dog sitting?"

Mary laughed and said, "Of course not!"

"When would we leave?" Sylvia asked Owen.

"Well," he said thoughtfully and chewed another beach fry before answering, "we could sail off into the sunset on Friday evening. I'm hoping we could get one-third to one-half of the way on Friday night, find an anchorage and then sail into the harbor on Saturday. Or, we could leave at dawn on Saturday morning," he offered.

Sylvia turned to her mother, "Why don't you just spend the week here, Mom? You wanted to be here to check out flowers for the wedding, right?"

Mary thought it over. "I could have John and Donna pick up my mail and newspaper. They would keep an eye on the house too," Mary answered. "If I need to, I can head up on Thursday and be back on Friday before you leave."

Both Owen and Sylvia nodded happily.

"While you ladies are flower shopping tomorrow evening," Owen said, "I'm going to pick up a few things for our trip this weekend. We need to start stocking the larder on the boat."

They spent the evening talking about the boat and their first sail. Owen pulled out a chart book and showed Sylvia and Mary their route to Baltimore. Owen called Scotty to let him know of their plans. He was staying in a hotel adjacent to the convention center at the Inner Harbor and said he could meet them anywhere in the area.

As they lay in bed that night, Owen pulled Sylvia tightly to him. "Like the boat?" he asked her.

"She's perfect," she told Owen. "I can't wait to go on my first sail."

He chuckled softly, "You know, this is a Buick boat too," he teased.

"What?" she exclaimed, "I didn't know Regal made sailboats!"

"They don't, as far as i am aware," Owen informed her, "but, this is a Sabre."

Sylvia looked confused.

"Buick La Sabre?" Owen teased.

"Oh, you! You and Skip will never let me live that down," she complained.

"Probably not," Owen agreed, "but, you keep us smiling."

Sylvia was about to say something, but Owen covered her mouth with an insistent kiss. "You keep me smiling," he said huskily.

And she gave into his kisses with pleasure.

CHAPTER SIXTEEN

"A well-spent day brings happy sleep."

— Leonardo da Vinci

W ho knew that flowers could give you a headache, Sylvia thought. She rubbed her temples and listened to the chatter between the florist the yacht club recommended, her mom, Anne, Marian, Maureen, and Carol. It was the cake crowd, now working on the floral arrangements for the wedding. Sylvia had not had a clue as to the sheer number of flowers needed at a wedding, nor the outrageous expense. Her mother, thank God, just waved a hand at the cost, but Sylvia blanched when she looked at the prices. Her bridal bouquet was fairly simple and consisted of white roses, ranunculus, stephanotis, Queen Anne's lace, rosemary, and holly. It was a full bouquet, hand tied with ribbon and lace that would match the gown. The holly was to honor her grandmother and the florist had suggested Queen Anne's lace to add an airy feel to the bouquet instead of baby's breath. For Gwen and Carol, the florist suggested green hydrangea, sage green spider mums, rosemary and Queen Anne's lace. Sylvia was pleased with her designs even though the florist blanched visibly when she brought photos she had printed from Pinterest. She recovered and told the group that Pinterest was a nightmare for florists. People had no idea what flowers were available during a season and the incredible expense of many of the exotic bouquets.

What Sylvia hadn't thought of, were the flowers for the ceremony itself and for the mothers, groomsmen, etc. Ideas flowed around the table. Every single woman had a different opinion.

Marian, who had been relatively quiet during the conversations, finally spoke up, "Sylvia, you love the urns of herbs at your house, why don't you have urns with varying green herbs - like variegated sage, rosemary, and trailing thyme. You could use those small garden flag holders and put small hanging baskets of herbs and flowers at the end of the aisles."

The florist nodded enthusiastically at this. "I also have green, Spanish glass vases that sit on a wrought iron base you can put in the ground. We could fill the vases with white and green hydrangea, spider mums and some trailing greenery. The vases could be tied with sage green bows to match the attendant dresses," she suggested.

They all took a moment to think while the florist went to a storage room to bring out an example of the vase. On seeing the vase, all agreed it would be lovely. The florist asked if there would be an altar for the wedding. She made several suggestions for the pergola of several, opulent designs. Another round robin of discussion with all the ladies ensued. Sylvia wanted to keep it simple. She liked the urns of herbs that Marian suggested. Sylvia also agreed that she didn't want the curtains to blow wildly during the wedding. She decided upon a simple floral arrangement to tie back the curtains. Maureen suggested hanging Japanese lanterns in sage green and white as a backdrop to the bay.

Regarding the yacht club, the florist had had much experience with floral arrangements for various events at the club. She suggested a small, oval dish planted with dark blue and purple pansies on each table and crystal sailboats riding the wave of flowers. She also suggested flowers or ribbons for their walk from the club to their waiting sailboat for the honeymoon. She brought out dark, sapphire blue and navy and cream ribbons to show the colors.

The flowers were coming together and Sylvia's relief was palpable. The florist caught her eye and smiled at Sylvia.

"A little too much wedding?" she asked Sylvia softly when she handed the floral contract to her to sign.

Sylvia gave a nod in acknowledgment. The florist chuckled.

"It will all work out," the florist told her. "Your choices are lovely."

Sylvia straightened her shoulders and looked back at the florist. "I think you're right," she said thinking a moment, "We are actually pulling it together."

The evening ended with excited chatter at the Crab Shack in town. Carol was talking about a shower and a bachelorette party. She texted Gwen frequently and hooted with laughter at some of the responses. Sylvia was glad her friends got on so well together.

But, Sylvia noticed, that Maureen was unusually quiet that evening. She had approved of the flowers at the marina with a nod and a faint smile but added little to the conversation.

Sylvia gave Maureen a quizzical look and asked her, sotto voce, "Are you all right?"

Maureen shrugged. She actually shrugged. Shrugging was not a gesture Sylvia had *ever* seen from her friend.

"Later," whispered Maureen.

Leaving the florist, Sylvia suggested that Maureen ride back to Bayside with her. Mary had carpooled with Maureen to the florist.

Hugs, kisses, and good wishes went round the table as the merry party broke up. Sylvia led Maureen to where her car was parked. Once inside, she turned to her friend.

"Okay," Sylvia told Maureen, "confess. What's going on?"

Maureen visibly swallowed. "Remember we thought fish poachers may have turned violent on George?"

Sylvia nodded and Maureen continued, "Please keep this confidential. It may have been oyster poachers that George stumbled upon. There are some arrest warrants out for the fisherman who have overfished the oyster beds south of here. They apparently covered up their damage and filed false health reports about oysters! I heard that their actions were felonies. They *have* to be the murderers! It makes perfect sense!" Maureen cried.

"So, you think George discovered they were overfishing the beds?" Sylvia asked Maureen.

"Yes!" Maureen cried.

"And, they killed George because he found out?" Sylvia continued questioning.

"Yes!" Maureen confirmed with conviction.

They were heading into Bayside. The summer brought long days and they drove towards the sunset that was painting the sky ahead of them. The high clouds were lit from behind and color washed the sky in deep mauve. They were both quiet for a couple of minutes as they drove to the marina.

"Have you voiced your ideas to Joe?" Sylvia asked.

"Oh, you know him," Maureen began, "he's a pretty sharp guy. I know he's checked with the Coast Guard. I think he was looking at the environmental health agencies for the bay too. I can't remember the name of the office, right now."

Sylvia nodded but needed to concentrate on the road as a large SUV with a boat trailer speeded past them and the trailer swung into their lane.

"Damn, tourists!" she muttered.

"Hey, hey," Maureen scolded lightly, "Those are our people. They keep the marina alive and well."

"I know, I know," Sylvia grumbled, "but, I wish they would learn to drive their huge cars and trailers on this narrow road. You never know who is going to be walking or biking here. It's amazing no one has been killed!"

"I agree with you," Maureen acquiesced. "Sylvia," she continued, her voice riddled with concern, "I can't help wonder how this could affect our business."

"Is Skip worried?" Sylvia asked her.

"We're both worried, but I think in different ways," Maureen said. "It's definitely not been a good couple of weeks for us. I feel brittle and Skip is testy. He won't really talk about his fears with this. He wants to keep the information from me to 'protect me,'" she added with a bit of sarcasm. "It's one of the few downsides to marrying an older man who has actually forgotten that women can walk and talk and think."

"That doesn't sound like Skip," Sylvia said. "I'm really surprised."

"He's very conservative," Maureen confided. "His Dad was a martinet that kept his sons in the military mode most of the time. His mom was a domestic queen and his Dad worshiped and protected her from everything."

"So, the apple doesn't fall far from the tree," Sylvia murmured.

"Exactly," Maureen finished as they pulled into the driveway. "On a happier note, your wedding details are all coming together. That's so exciting! Skip and I cannot thank you and Owen enough for having the wedding here, especially after George's murder. It will brighten the mood. I just wish it was sooner than later."

"Huh!" Sylvia said, "It's coming soon enough!"

"I know," Maureen said, "but, it's at the end of our summer season. I would love to capture some good things during the throes of summer boating. Business has been a little thin."

"Give people some time," Sylvia said reminding Maureen, "We all loved Old George."

Maureen nodded, emotion getting the best of her. She exited the car and headed into the house with a wave.

Sylvia drove home, thinking about all Maureen had said. When she pulled into the driveway, Percy barked excitedly. Owen wasn't in the house and Sylvia let Percy out into the yard and stood at the deck railing looking out at the "True Love." The dinghy was tethered to the sailboat. She thought briefly of swimming out but decided to sit on the deck and watch for Owen. When he emerged from the hatch, Percy barked and danced excitedly on the shore. He glanced towards the shore, smiling at Percy and spotting Sylvia, and waved. It was only moments before he descended to the dinghy and rowed back ashore.

"How are you?" he asked her, enveloping her in a hug.

"Good," she told him. "The flowers are done and it's going to be gorgeous."

"Good," he replied, "and I've started getting things ready for our first sail. The chart books, propane, cleaning supplies, towels, bedding, dishes, and silverware and...," he smiled at Sylvia, "the most important thing -- champagne."

"Wow," Sylvia told him, "you've been busy."

"Yup," Owen said happily, putting an arm around her and turning so they could look at the boat, "and more tomorrow."

Sylvia smiled at Owen's pure joy of owning the sailboat. He was like a little boy with a brand new toy. The old rhyme of "the bigger the boy, the bigger the toy," rang inside her head. She held back a giggle and kissed him on the cheek instead.

"I'm glad you're happy," she said.

"I am," he replied, and pulled her tightly to him.

CHAPTER SEVENTEEN

*"Life is like sailing. You can use any wind to go
in any direction."*

— ROBERT BRAULT

The week flew by as Sylvia organized and completed final details for Bay Days the next weekend. Every evening was filled with cleaning and stocking the boat. Her mom went home overnight to check on her house and run some errands but returned Friday morning. Owen and Sylvia skipped lunch so they could get home an hour early. Mary had ordered a pizza and salad for a quick dinner before they packed up the last few personal items. Sylvia gave Percy a hug and a kiss on his pouf, telling him to be good for his grandmother. Mary gave them both hugs and told them to be careful and to have fun.

When they were on the boat, Sylvia waved gaily to her mother and Percy, standing on the shore. Percy gave a mournful howl as they motored off. Sylvia watched and waved to her mother and Percy were small sticks on the shoreline and then looked out to the bay. Owen was at the helm and the evening sun was warm and bright. Sylvia had never sailed but found this first foray of moving through the water, enjoyable. Owen wasn't sure if they would catch a good wind for this leg of the trip. They passed the camp and convention center south of Bayside where people were swimming and paddle boating. Personal watercraft zipped everywhere. A few came fairly close to the boat. This frustrated Owen as he headed to the larger expanse of open water of the bay. The majority of personal watercraft stayed closer to the shoreline with a few braver souls that rode through the channel. Many boaters were heading towards North Bay to the marinas and Sylvia thought of the interstate, except this was on the water.

She watched, open-mouthed, as Owen unfurled one sail that he called the mainsail and then a smaller sail at the front of the boat that he called the 'Genoa.' Their sails were crisp and white with a border of navy that matched the hull. The wind picked up in the sail and began to pull them along. Sylvia gasped in delight. She knew, at once, why Owen loved sailing. There was absolutely nothing like this feeling. It was a feeling of freedom, of flying and of joy.

"Can you go below and grab me a beer?" Owen asked Sylvia.

"Sure," she said, breaking out of the reverie.

Sylvia hesitated at using her sea legs. She found it wasn't too bad to climb through the hatchway and pull a cold beer from their small refrigerator. She took the time to pour herself a glass of wine in a plastic cup. It was an odd feeling, to feel the boat moving through the water beneath her. She didn't have anything to compare the feeling to. The only comparison was the moving sidewalk at the Philadelphia airport, but that was definitely a poor comparison. This was more like flying while standing. She liked it - a lot. Smiling, Sylvia ascended the stairs and handed the cold beer in a cozy to Owen, who was standing proudly at the helm. She sat on the bench near him. He took a swig from the bottle and placed the beer in a holder near the wheel. Sylvia sipped and looked at the vista before her. On her left were tall cliffs in varying oranges, terra cotta and buff shades. It looked as though someone had taken a wet brush and ran through parts of the cliff like a watercolor.

"Those are the clay cliffs near Turkey Point," Owen informed Sylvia.

"They're beautiful. They look like primitive art of some kind," Sylvia said.

There were a few people on the beach and a couple of small sailboats anchored from the cliffs.

"It's a favorite spot," he told her, "but, the hike from Route 272 is very, very steep. We can hike down sometime. It's near the lighthouse."

"Okay," she agreed, intrigued by the cliffs.

The wind pulled them along and Sylvia asked Owen how fast they were going, not really knowing how it would translate into miles per hour.

"We're sailing between five and six knots," he told her. "That's about five miles per hour. It's a beautiful, leisurely sail."

Sylvia thought they were going quite fast. She never dreamed that this feeling would only be five miles per hour. But the world continued to go past her. Owen pointed out the cliff and the light-house. She felt the boat shift just after that. Owen told her it was because of the Elk and the North East Rivers meeting, therefore causing the currents to merge. He bit his lip and concentrated on maneuvering the boat. He was busy at the helm adjusting for the changing current. Sylvia was quiet and a little tense until they were smooth sailing again. It took a few hours and Owen pointed out various sites from his charts, but they reached the anchorage Owen had planned as the sun was beginning to set.

Owen told Sylvia he wanted to steer clear of the shallow inlet at Churn Creek. He told her the tide turned somewhat dramatically and he tried not to run aground. He seemed tense as he maneuvered the boat between what he called 'day markers' and crab pots. Sylvia saw them but really didn't understand the challenges. Sailing was going to be an education for her.

There were six other boats at the anchorage. They waved to the other cruisers when they were settled. Owen dropped anchor and took down the sails, explaining to Sylvia what needed to be done and how.

"Is there going to be a test?" she teased him.

"Absolutely," he told her raising his eyebrows and he gave a seductively, low laugh, "and totally 'hands on.'"

"I'm not sure if that's good or bad," she continued to tease him. "This sailing stuff is daunting."

"Don't worry," he said, "You're in good hands."

He went below to refresh their drinks and he brought up some crackers and cheese that he had in the refrigerator.

"Ahh," he said, relaxing on the seat cushions. "Now, I can relax."

Sylvia went over to him to rub his shoulders. She was surprised at how tense his muscles were.

She looked at him, "Are you okay?"

"Absolutely," he told her, "but, I haven't done this in a long time. I love every millisecond, but I have to get used to sailing again."

"Okay," she said, "just wondering. It was a fabulous, first sail for me. It's gorgeous here." She looked at the sandy beaches and the wooded shoreline in the protected cove. Sylvia could see where it got its name of Still Pond.

There was an occasional rocking of the boat from the traffic on the bay outside of this protected cover, but other than that, it was quiet and still. As the sun set, Owen pointed out some bald eagles, roosting in the trees, near the edge of the water. Civilization seemed far away. They had pulled into the southern portion of the cove. Sylvia could see some high bluffs on the western part of the cove that was a natural protection for all of the boats.

"On another sail," Owen told Sylvia, "we can sail here, anchor, and then take the dinghy to shore to swim and explore."

"That sounds like fun," Sylvia said.

"No time for it on this trip," he said, "We'll need to get up early to get started on our journey to Baltimore."

"Have you talked with Scotty this week?" she asked.

"No, just emails. He's been on the road again," Owen told her. "We'll give him a call as we approach Baltimore and give him an estimated time we'll be arriving."

Owen stood up and stretched and gave an enormous yawn. "Lord, Sylvia, I'm tired!" he told her. "I'm headed below."

Sylvia followed him through the hatch and down the stairs. Owen had warned her about limited water resources, so their ablutions were brief. Owen headed to the bunk, stripping off clothes as he went. Sylvia went to one of the cupboards in the salon and pulled out an adorable, yet, sexy, lacy baby doll nightie. She had wanted to surprise Owen on their first-night sailing. She put on the nightie and brushed out her hair. When she went to their berth, Owen was sound asleep and snoring like a freight train. Smiling, she sighed and shook her head.

With another sigh, Sylvia went to where she stowed her clothes and pulled out a very, light robe. She filled up her wine glass and came out onto the deck. When they had first pulled into Still Pond, they could still hear many boats zipping up and down the C&D Canal. Owen had commented that it was just like home. As the light faded in the western sky, the boating traffic became lighter and lighter. All was quiet and peaceful. Occasionally, she heard a muffled sound from one of the other boaters, but she couldn't hear the conversation. Insect song overtook the boating sounds. Everyone seemed to be enjoying the quietude. Stars that had just been popping out earlier, one by one, had filled the sky with a sparkling brilliance. The water reflected the starlight in a dark, dazzling beauty. Sylvia sipped at her wine until she was tired and slipped below. She crawled into bed next to Owen and snuggled against him, despite the warm weather. The boat rocked gently and Owen's arm automatically reached out to touch her as well as a toe on his foot. Sylvia smiled in the dark and went to sleep.

CHAPTER EIGHTEEN

*"The voyage of discovery is not in seeking new landscapes
but in having new eyes."*

— MARCEL PROUST

S ylvia wasn't used to waking up slowly, without the cold nose of
a dog on her hand. The boat had rocked them gently and she
had slept deeply. She thought she smelled the coffee and when
she opened her eyes, she was disoriented. After a moment, she
realized she was on the "True Love." She *did* smell the coffee and
heard a quiet whistling. Owen. Sylvia smiled. She pulled herself
from the berth and pulled on her robe and peeked out of the
hatch. He was nowhere to be seen in the cockpit. She climbed
out and stood and searched for Owen. There he was, at the bow of
the boat, whistling away, cleaning the 'bright work' as he called it.
    "Good morning!" she greeted.

"Morning!" he replied, smiling from ear to ear. "Did you sleep well?" he asked.

"Mm-hmm, like a baby," Sylvia nodded.

Owen grinned in reply. Sylvia didn't see anyone up and about, so she let the robe she was wearing slip open, revealing the sheer, baby doll, nightie beneath. Owen's eyes widened. His mouth dropped open and the sponge in his hand dropped to the deck. He stepped over some ropes and the cleats at the bow of the boat and came toward her.

"Wow," he murmured as she leaned back on the cushions of the cockpit.

Sylvia just smiled. She got up and went down the hatch to their berth. Owen followed.

Somewhat delayed, their trip to Baltimore was uneventful. Sylvia was amazed at the amount of boat traffic on the bay. She thought the tankers were enormous and scary. Owen kept well away from them, explaining to Sylvia that the tanker captain would be hard pressed to see their small boat, except at a distance. Owen successfully tacked across the bay towards Baltimore. Once across the bay, Sylvia saw floating, yellow barrels in the water.

"What are those?" she asked Owen.

"A warning," he said grimly. "They tell sailors to keep away from the army post, Aberdeen Proving Ground. We're lucky they're not shooting any ordinance today. There are several pages of 'do's and don'ts' for being near this place."

All Sylvia could respond with was an "Oh!"

Owen pointed out Poole's Island and the lighthouse that stood starkly against the extensive wooded shoreline. Sylvia wondered about what parts of American history were buried because of unexploded ordinance and God knows what, at the edges of the Army post. They sailed around Hart-Miller Island and then started up the Patapsco River. Owen referred to his sailing charts frequently and his happy whistling turned to an almost grim countenance.

The boat traffic increased, and the expanse of water narrowed. Sylvia wished she could help. Warehouses and buildings and expensive houses dotted the shoreline. As they sailed closer to Baltimore, Sylvia could see huge container ships in port as they approached. Her eyes grew big when she saw the enormous crane used to unload the ships. The area was littered with grain elevators and piles of rock, sand and gravel. She could see trucks moving along the shoreline and the smell of diesel fuel wafted from the shore. After the industrial area, they sailed past Fort McHenry. Owen told her he had sailed with Bran there as a child. They had anchored and had a picnic and were able to tour the fort. It was quite different from the open expanses of the Eastern Shore. There had been houses, of course. Lovely houses, on the Eastern shore, but as with any cityscape, it became more crowded as they approached the city.

Owen dropped the sails and motored through the boat traffic. Sylvia's thought that it was like a crowded interstate rose up again in her mind as they traveled with power boats, cruisers, water taxis and other sailboats to reach the inner harbor. Sylvia had held her breath as Owen maneuvered their boat through luxury yachts, safely tucked into their boat slips. What Sylvia would call a watery roadway, Owen called a fairway. She wished she knew more about sailing to help him, but she was clueless. She sat back and was quiet as he maneuvered the boat and radioed the marina for instructions. A dock hand came out to assist because Owen had radioed ahead that they were arriving. He had made reservations earlier that week. Owen gave him a generous tip before he went ashore to the office to register. Docked successfully, they both felt relieved, at Henderson's Marina in Fells Point. They were moored at one of the floating docks. Sylvia looked at the large brick building ahead of them on shore. Owen told her it was an Inn and part of Henderson's.

Owen was anxious to meet Scotty. He urged Sylvia to get ready quickly. She took a brief, 'sea' shower and changed out of her shorts and t-shirt into her linen sundress that she had bought a year ago. She still loved it with its bright irises decorating the cloth. The dress made her feel pretty.

"C'mon, beautiful lady," Owen told her as he reached for her hand. "Let's go ashore."

She smiled at his comment. He had secured the boat and they stepped onto the wharf. Sylvia's legs felt funny and she wobbled. The floating dock seemed to shift under her feet and she was afraid she might fall into the harbor.

"Whoa," Owen said, steadying her and taking her arm. "You don't have your land legs yet," he warned.

Sylvia took a steadying breath. Owen helped her walk up the floating dock to real land. Sylvia had never felt so glad for her feet to walk onto the solid, wooden wharf that bordered the inn at the water's edge. Owen had taken a moment on the boat to text Scotty. Scotty was at the Convention Center that was nearby in the Inner Harbor. Owen wasn't sure if he was taking a water taxi or if he was walking to Fells Point. They began to walk up Thames Street, one of the oldest streets in Baltimore and Fells Point. Owen hurried by many of the shops that beckoned Sylvia's eye. There were many pubs and restaurants, but Sylvia admired the beauty of the historic buildings of this restored portion of Baltimore.

Sylvia was enjoying the walk. She loved the boat but was beginning to feel a little confined. Walking felt good, even at the pace that Owen created.

"Slow down, a little," she complained lightly to Owen.

Owen slowed his pace only slightly, "Sorry," he told her. "I'm looking for the pub Scotty asked us to meet him at."

"Which one?" Sylvia questioned, "I think there are a hundred here."

"Probably," Owen agreed, "It's an Irish pub called Slainte."

All of a sudden Sylvia spotted it and pointed it out to Owen. There were small tables with white umbrellas and flags flying just below the red sign with its name. They crossed the cobblestone street. The tables outside were filled. Celtic music wafted out from the doorway. Inside was cool and dark, and they were temporarily blinded from coming in from the bright sunshine. Seemingly from nowhere, a hand clapped Owen on the back. He turned in surprise and broke into a huge smile.

"Scotty!" Owen cried, slapping his friend on the back as well.

Scotty was not quite as tall as Owen, but had long, brilliantly, red hair that was tied in a queue. He wore a black tee-shirt emblazoned with "You are what you Geek" and his company's website underneath and black jeans. Sylvia wondered if he was broiling in his dark clothes on this humid, summer's day. Owen introduced Sylvia. Suddenly, she felt a little shy. This guy had a lot more history with Owen than she had. This guy was pretty famous for his successful Geek conventions. She wondered what she would talk to him about. The hostess sat them in a comfortable booth. Owen ordered a Black and Tan and Scotty ordered a Scottish Ale that had a raspberry finish. Sylvia was unsure of what to order. She vacillated about ordering her favorite - a Blood Mary, a glass of wine or to branch out and to try something new. She asked for water and patience while she decided. When the waitress brought the drinks, Scotty urged her to try his ale. She took a sip and was very surprised that she liked it. She liked it very much and ordered one for herself.

As they sipped their drinks, Owen asked Scotty about his latest convention. He regaled them with stories of the sights and events at the Baltimore Convention Center.

"You'll have to come back with me after lunch," he urged.

Owen looked at Sylvia and she nodded replying, "Sure."

Scotty sat back for a minute and cocked his head, "Listen," he told Sylvia and Owen, "it's the High Kings they're playing."

"You like Celtic music?" Sylvia asked him.

"I love it," Scotty told her. He rattled off some of the names of his favorite bands.

Sylvia in turn shared some of her favorites and Owen sat smiling at their enthusiasm. They ordered their lunch. Scotty ordered Shepherd's Pie. Despite the Irish specialties, Owen ordered a specialty burger, and Sylvia a Salmon burger. Owen pointed out to Sylvia that the restaurant was open for breakfast, lunch and dinner. He suggested they could skip their paltry fare on the boat and eat at Slainte for breakfast or brunch accompanied by a Bloody Mary.

Talk turned to the wedding and Owen asked Scotty for his thoughts regarding a suit or a tuxedo. Scotty preferred a suit, and Owen told him that it was the choice of the other Groomsmen as well. Owen said he would move forward on finding a gray suit, light gray shirt and sage green tie to match the attendant dresses.

Scotty asked about places to stay in North Bay. Sylvia asked if he wanted to stay in a hotel or bed and breakfast.

"I'm not overly picky," Scotty told her. "I'm used to hotel rooms. But, a bed and breakfast might be nice for a change. That is if it's not too frou-frou," he added.

"There's one in the neighborhood," Sylvia told him, "just at the marinas. They have a dog and a couple cats if you're not allergic. You could walk over to our house," she suggested.

"That sounds great!" Scotty told Sylvia and Owen. "I'll probably fly into Philadelphia or BWI and rent a car to drive to your place."

They finished their lunches and began their walk to the Baltimore Convention Center. A breeze from the water kept some of the humidity from cooking them. Even with the breeze, Sylvia felt the back of her neck grow damp with perspiration. The streets were crowded with tourists. They walked to the Inner Harbor and then turned towards the baseball stadium. A couple of blocks from the waterfront, a huge building, filling a city block, rose in front of them. Scotty led them in, flashed a badge and led them towards the section where his convention was going on.

It wasn't easy to miss. Even in the summer heat, people were in full Sci-Fi costume regalia, Anime costume, and costumes from various video games. They were funneling in, as best they could, through turnstiles. Others were dressed in street clothes and many were gawking and asking for pictures with those in costume.

"This is amazing!" Sylvia told Scotty.

Scotty beamed. They spent the afternoon wandering through the vendors. Scotty and Owen seemed to be catching up on everything that had happened since they left the university. Sylvia interjected an occasional comment, but mostly looked and listened. They left the convention and wandered the streets to Little Italy and found a restaurant that Scotty had researched on his phone as they walked.

"It's supposed to be one of the best restaurants in the country," he informed Owen and Sylvia.

Sylvia, feeling a little road weary and sweaty, worried she wasn't dressed appropriately for the restaurant. But, she needn't have worried. It wasn't a stuffy restaurant, just a good one. They had an outstanding dinner, sipping on fantastic wine as they sampled delicious pasta dishes.

With no room for dessert, they wandered back out onto the Baltimore streets. Scotty gave them both huge hugs before turning towards his hotel. Owen and Sylvia made their way back to the bustling streets of Fells Point. The pubs in the area were going full blast with Saturday night revelers. They made their way back to their boat.

"Home, sweet, home," Owen said as they stepped into the boat and into the cockpit.

It was Sylvia's night to yawn and stretch. "I think I've eaten enough food for a week," she complained to Owen, "but, what a beautiful day. I can see why you and Scotty are such good friends."

"He's a really, good guy," Owen told her. "I didn't realize how much I missed being around him. But, it seemed like no time had passed since we were last together."

"That's the sign of a really, good friend," she said. "Excuse me, while I go and pass out."

"I'll tuck you in," Owen said, "but, I'm still restless."

"Are you going on a pub crawl?" she asked teasing him.

"Not without you," he promised. "I'm just going to sit on the deck and enjoy the evening."

"Okay," she said, "but, don't be too long."

He tucked her in and kissed her slowly. Sylvia yawned again and fell asleep almost instantaneously.

She woke up first on Sunday. She was beginning to feel more comfortable on the boat. She dressed and fiddled with the propane stove, praising herself when it was lit. She boiled water and used their small Melitta pour-over coffee filter to make herself a large mug of coffee. She took it out on deck and smelled the morning air.

City air was definitely not like the fresh air they experienced at Bayside. She smelled the water, but there was an undercurrent of city scents. Sylvia wrinkled her nose. It was a beautiful morning, but it was already warm with a promise of a scorching and humid day. The air seemed unusually heavy.

Sylvia let Owen sleep while she pulled together a ditty bag and went in search of showers. She used the code he had given her to get into the woman's shower room. She spent a long time under the hot water, enjoying every moment. She dressed in light capris and a t-shirt and combed her hair. She was going to let her hair dry naturally in the sun.

Returning to the boat, Sylvia found that Owen was up. He gave her a kiss good morning before he left to get his own shower. Owen asked if she wanted to head to Slainte for brunch before they headed for Bayside. They walked through the now quiet streets of Fells Point to the pub.

Owen loaded up on coffee while Sylvia enjoyed a Bloody Mary. Owen pointed out that they have bottomless Bloody Mary's from Monday to Friday. Sylvia laughed and asked how soon could they return during the week?

"Honeymoon?" Owen suggested. "Honeymoon with a night at the inn here at the marina?" They had looked at the inn's brochure, and both had zoned in on the Romantic Getaway package.

"It's a deal!" Sylvia told him, eyes sparkling. "I can hardly wait." She had fallen in love with the pictures of the high poster beds and the amenities the Inn offered. The rooms reminded her of Marian's house. She was sure these were pseudo antiques and Marian's were the real thing, but the pictures of the rooms were still lovely. Each one had a vista of the marina, the bay or the small garden the inn created in a courtyard.

Relaxed and happy, they motored out of the Harbor and made their way down the Patapsco River towards the bay. The boating traffic was relatively heavy with tankers, pleasure boats, and personal watercraft. As they made their way down the river, the air became denser and denser.

Sylvia became nervous. She could see darkening clouds gathering in front of them. The bevy of boats that were zooming back and forth now seemed to be heading up the Patapsco River towards marinas while they were headed for the open bay. The power boats sped past them on a regular basis creating choppiness to the water. Sylvia was regretting her second Bloody Mary, and her huge breakfast. She prayed she wouldn't get sick. Owen was looking stressed. She wished for the hundredth time that she had boating experience and could help Owen out in some way. She remembered that the yacht club had sailing lessons for kids and adults. She put them on a short mental list of things 'to do.'

"Owen?" Sylvia asked him tentatively, "Do you think we should go back to Baltimore?"

Owen wore a determined look. "No," he answered. "I think we'll be all right."

Suddenly, the wind seemed to change. The smell of a storm was in the air, as the scent of ozone enveloped them. Sylvia's nervousness grew as the shoreline in every direction became indistinct. Black clouds rolled in and Sylvia's stomach clenched.

"Owen?" she asked tentatively, but he couldn't hear her above the wind that had begun to blow. "Owen?" she shouted, an unspoken question in her voice.

"Come here! Quickly!" he shouted to her. His stubborn look had taken on a look of determination.

He gave her directions to secure the main sail. She was to put a rope around the boom and secure it with square knots. The wind was blowing fiercely. The sail was flapping madly. She crawled across the roof of the cabin to get to the sail. Rain began to pelt them in hard, heavy drops. It felt good at first, cooling her from the heat and humidity of the day, but the raindrops became harder and they hurt. The boat was rocking wildly in the wind. Owen was doing all he could to steer the boat and keep it on course. Sylvia now dragged the wet, heavy rope and secured the sail as best she could. She could barely see in the driving rain and held on for dear life as she crawled carefully back to the cockpit. Owen still held the helm tightly, his knuckles white against the helm. Sylvia was scared out of her wits.

"I have to get out of the shipping lane!" Owen shouted. "Get below and look at the charts."

Sylvia's stomach plummeted. Look at the charts? She *really* didn't know what she was doing. She pulled out the chart book, remembering they were near the mouth of the Patapsco River. She frantically looked at the chart and saw a cove called Old Road Bay. It looked like it would be a good place to get out of the storm. She yelled over the wind to tell Owen to head North towards Old Road Bay.

Owen put in the coordinates and began to follow the GPS directions to take them to the cover. Out of the shipping channel and in the cove, Owen dropped the anchor to ride out the storm.

Now shivering, he went to Sylvia sitting with her arms around her knees on the couch in the cabin. He held her tightly telling her it was going to be all right. The boat still rocked wildly. Sylvia hid her head in Owen's chest.

"I don't like this! I don't like this!" she cried as she clung to him.

He chuckled. "It's just a little storm," he told her, holding her more tightly.

"But, you were scared too, weren't you?" she asked.

"Some. I haven't done this in a long time," he reminded her again.

"I know," she said, "but, I think you are doing a damn, good job, keeping us safe in this storm!"

"Thank you," he said, kissing her on the top of her head. "Now, I just need to get us home safely. I think the storm is letting up."

He had changed into dry clothes and it was just spitting a little bit of rain.

"I'm going to try this again," he called to Sylvia. "It's clearing!"

She went above and indeed the clouds were rolling away almost as quickly as they had come. Behind the gray, rolling clouds, clear blue sky and puffy clouds adorned the sky. It was as if the storm had not existed over that part of the bay.

"You'd better start the phone calls and texts," he said. "We're not going to make it home tonight. I'd like to head to Still Pond again if we can get there by dark."

"Okay," Sylvia agreed. She called her mom and explained what had happened, assuring her they were safe and that no other storms seemed to be in the area.

"It was an anomaly," she assured her mother. "We've had a great weekend. We just need to extend it by a day. We're hoping to anchor at Still Pond again, and head home in the morning."

After hanging up with her mother, she texted Carol, letting her know she wouldn't be into work in the morning. She texted Mr. Carter what had happened as well.

There were fewer power boats on the water since the passing storm. The day wended its way towards evening. The water was still choppy for a while, due to the change in the storm front. But, the wind had dropped. It was very, very slow going using the motor, against the tide and the choppiness left by the storm. They bounced along instead of gliding, slamming the waves instead of riding with them. The sun was going down behind them quickly. Sylvia had made them sandwiches and brought them up to Owen as twilight began to fall.

CHAPTER TWENTY

Dum spiro spero. (While I breathe I hope.)

— LINDSAY CLAN FAMILY MOTTO (SCOTLAND)

"I don't think we're going to make Still Pond this evening," he told her. "We're close, but I don't want to travel in complete darkness. I'm not familiar with the bay anymore and have a lot of relearning to do."

As twilight descended, he scoured the charts. They had just passed Fairlee Creek and darkness was falling fast. Clouds began to gather in the West, blotting out their usual treat of an incredible sunset. Sylvia just hoped that the storm would not return. She voiced her fears to Owen and he told her they would find another protected cove.

"There are a couple of places we can anchor at Worton Creek," he told her. I don't think anyone would care."

"Fine with me," Sylvia said. "I'm looking forward to a quiet night."

They motored into Worton Creek. Owen had talked about making it to Tim's Creek as there was a marina they might be able to slip into for the night. But, when they looked up the information, a website was no longer available, nor did the cell number listed work.

"Well, that tells me its likely empty," Owen told her. "Let's still try to make it there."

It was getting quite dark and boats don't have headlights like on a car. Owen had her walk to the bow of the boat with a large, search light. She heard him swear softly.

"What's wrong?" she asked.

"The damn masthead light is out," Owen grumbled. "Once we're below, no one can see that we're here," he told her.

"Do you think anyone will be motoring about in the middle of the night?" Sylvia asked incredulously.

"No," Owen replied, "but, it's something we need to get repaired as soon as possible."

"I think that's the marina ahead," Sylvia told him.

The shoreline was completely dark and they could just make out pilings and older docks.

"I don't want to go much closer," Owen told her. "I don't know how long this marina has been abandoned. I know there are a couple of other marinas up the creek, but I don't want to take a chance motoring completely in the dark. We're tired and I don't want to do anything stupid."

"Sounds good," she said.

Owen dropped the anchor. They went below. Owen poured drinks for each of them, and the settled on the couch.

"What a day! You know, you didn't have to give me all of these crazy sailing scenarios in one weekend," she told Owen accusingly.

"Honey, this was nothing. But, we're out of the woods. I'm pretty sure that storm is not coming our way. We can relax, sleep and head home in the morning," Owen assured her.

"I've really enjoyed this weekend, but I'm going to be really happy to see our house," she told Owen. "Percy, our bed and our deck seem like a cozy dream right now."

"Well, scoot into the berth and you can dream about it tonight and see it tomorrow," Owen told her.

They settled in for the night, holding each other. They both slept dreamlessly and deeply until an odd sound woke them both, startling them from sleep.

"What the hell?" Owen said, propping himself up on one elbow.

"Sounds like a car or a boat," Sylvia said sleepily. "What time is it?" she asked Owen.

Owen looked at his watch before answering, "Just after four thirty," he told her.

"Maybe it's fisherman heading out to check their crab pots," Sylvia said dreamily. "Didn't we pass some of those?"

"Yes," Owen agreed, "but, with the masthead light out, they won't be able to see us," he said worriedly. "You stay below and I'll go up and take a look around."

Sylvia drifted into a half-sleep state as she heard Owen's steps head up to the cockpit. Then she heard his voice question, "What the hell?" again with an odd note in his voice.

"What's wrong?" she called up to him.

There was no answer. She thought she heard him pulling on something. It was as if something was rubbing on the outside of the boat opposite from their berth. Was it the anchor? What was he doing? Thinking he likely did not hear her, she grabbed her robe and went through the hatch.

"Owen!" she started to call, "What are you..."

He interrupted her with a stage whisper of panic, "Get below! Now, Sylvia!"

"What?" she said more to herself than to Owen.

It was then that she noticed activity at the old marina. Red flashlights were bouncing in the darkness. There was a boat pulled up to the pier. It was a large power boat that looked like it could go fast. In the weak light that was the beginning of dawn, things seemed hazy. Sylvia had a difficult time seeing anything clearly. She squinted in the almost darkness. The red lights bounced from the boat and up the pier as if people were carrying something. In the dim light, it looked like boxes. She could hear the men on the shore grunting, so she thought they must be relatively substantial. Sylvia could hear the boat's motor going and saw the lights going back and forth, and back and forth. They seemed to be going to a building that was up a small hill. She thought she could see a long, low roof. She could smell something odd. What was going on?

Dawn was beginning. The sky was starting to lighten behind the trees on the shoreline. Owen had pulled up the anchor and was now crawling as best as he could on his belly, back to the cockpit.

"Sylvia!" Owen cried again, not so quiet this time, but ordering her, "get below!"

That was when all hell broke loose. She heard the sound of a loud 'crack' in the air. She jumped at the noise. There was a second crack and something hit the side of the boat, just below the gunwale. She could hear the splintering of fiberglass. Another crack and Owen made a loud, indescribable sound, something like a moan and a cry of pain all rolled into one. She saw red spreading at his left shoulder. It suddenly dawned on her that Owen had just been shot! The boat had been hit too.

"Start the boat!" Owen yelled. "Quick, Sylvia!"

He groaned in pain, as he made his way to the cockpit. He sort of fell into the cockpit and slumped down in a heap near the helm.

"Stay down and get us out of here!" he told her.

Sylvia didn't really know what to do. She turned on the boat and took the helm to steer the boat up the creek. Was this a good idea? From the charts she knew there were marinas ahead. Maybe she could get help there. Her cell phone and Owen's cell phone were below. She couldn't take the time to go below to get them. Owen was holding his shoulder, trying to staunch the blood. He looked very pale and woozy from the pain. Sylvia knew she couldn't scream aloud, only inside her head. A couple of more shots rang out, and thankfully, the powerboat sped away, out to the bay and to open water. She tried to focus on the water ahead. Fear of running aground loomed in her mind.

Sylvia thought of the Green Man and wondered why he wasn't there to rescue them. She panicked, but in the back of her mind, she remembered him saying a few weeks ago, that he couldn't come to her if she needed him on the water. Had that been a premonition or a warning? She didn't know.

Inside her head, she could hear him say to her, "Steady on. It will be all right." She heard his voice! She glanced at the shoreline. In the light beyond the leaves of the trees, it looked like a face. A green, leafy face created by branches, trees and the light of the burgeoning dawn. She kept on, confident that it would be all right.

The early morning light helped Sylvia see more clearly. She could see boats up ahead and floating docks. She headed that way. She could see someone standing on the bow of their boat, with a foot propped up on what looked like a railing, a cup of something steaming in his hand. Owen had called it something, something that had to do with a church. It was the bow pulpit, she remembered. This fact astonished her as she couldn't even begin to think at the moment.

She headed for the man with the coffee cup yelling "help!" as loudly as she could. She must have shouted it two or three times. He finally heard her.

Startled, the man looked up. Sylvia relayed to Owen what she was seeing. He gave her instructions for slowing down the boat.

"Try not to hit another vessel," Owen groaned. He coughed and more blood seeped from the wound. He was breathing oddly as if he could not get enough air. He told her gasping, "Go into neutral. Let me know when the RPMs go down to zero."

His voice was weaker, and Sylvia did as she was told. Owen's voice was barely a whisper when he told her to go in reverse. The 'True Love' groaned and bounced on the water. It frightened her.

"It's okay that it's bouncing," he told her weakly, glancing up at her face.

They floated near the other sailboat. Very near. Now, Sylvia was close enough to the man to see him.

"My fiancé has been shot!" she yelled at the man, "Please, please help me! Call 911!"

The man pulled out his cell phone and dialed something, and talked to someone. Owen was slumped over. There was more blood on his back. His breathing was becoming more labored. She didn't know what to do. Tears were streaming down her face. She knew she couldn't leave the helm until the boat was secure. The man somehow had pulled their boat over to his and secured it to his before he came on board. He was tan, tall, and bearded. Sylvia guessed him to be in his late thirties or early forties.

"I called 911," he told Sylvia. "What happened?"

In a shaky voice, she explained the sequence of events a short time ago.

"I'm Mike, by the way. I heard the shots," he told her. "I thought there were some kids or someone hunting out of season. Let me help him. It looks like he has a collapsed lung. I need to move him so he doesn't drown in his own blood."

Sylvia looked at the man in horror. By this time, Sylvia was on her knees checking out Owen. She tore at the thin cotton of her robe and balled it up and pressed it to the wound that was weeping blood. She tore off more of her robe and put it on his back. Owen was groaning in pain by this time. The man moved him, and another horrible sound came from Owen's lips.

The man was calm. He told Owen he would be all right and to hang on.

Flashing red and blue lights were coming down the road towards the marina. The man quickly navigated hopping between the boats, went down the pier to greet the emergency personnel and the police. Owen was barely conscious. He was very, very pale when they put him on the stretcher, and carefully took him from boat to boat, and to the pier. Moans of pain escaped his lips with each bump and jostle. Sylvia felt she couldn't move. This was a nightmare and she was hoping she would wake up any second and find herself nestled in Owen's arms. Mike had put out some sort of bumper between the boats and tied their boats together. Mike's deep voice broke her trance. He suggested she might want to change before they went to the hospital. She looked at herself in her skimpy night-gown and torn robe. Horrified, she hurriedly threw on the first clothes she could grab from the cupboard. She pulled on shorts and a t-shirt quickly, grabbed her purse, cell phone and thrust her feet into flip-flops. Mike was going to stay with the boat, but the police told him he needed to come along until all the statements could be given. He went reluctantly. The police guided them to the back of one of the squad cars and they followed the ambulance.

"Where are we going?" Sylvia asked faintly.

"The hospital in Chestertown," the cop told her.

They hurtled down the road, following the ambulance, swiftly and silently, with lights blazing. The back of the squad car was creepy to her. There were no door handles. It smelled funny. She had ridden in the front of a police car with Joe, but she had never been in the back. Even with air conditioning, the vinyl seats were sticky. She introduced herself to their rescuer and thanked him for coming to her aid.

Mike told her he was a family man who chartered boats for a living. His first aid experience, he told her, came from teaching boy scouts. Sylvia told him this was her first sail. This had been their maiden voyage on their new boat. Her voice cracked when she said this.

The ambulance and police car continued to drive swiftly through the low, flat country of Maryland's Eastern Shore. Farm fields full of corn and sunflowers grew almost up to the road. The sky was brightening with the dawn and the sun shone. To Sylvia, it was a dark sun. Sylvia and Mike were silent for the rest of the ride to the hospital. Sylvia looked out anxiously as they left the farm fields and civilization encroached upon the flatness.

Sylvia had gone to college in Chestertown. She vaguely knew where the hospital was situated in reference to the campus. It was only a stone's throw from the main campus. Fortunately, she had never had reason to find the hospital during her four years at Washington College. Occasionally, she had seen an ambulance or two turn down the road towards the hospital. Otherwise, she would not have known of its existence or the close proximity to the college.

When they arrived at the hospital, another flurry of activity enveloped them. The police officer escorted her into the Emergency Room's waiting room. It was relatively small with under two dozen chairs. Bright summer sunlight did its best to brighten the sterile waiting room of tile and plastic chairs. Sylvia filled out mountains of paperwork. The police asked her to accompany them to a small room adjacent to the waiting room, just past a couple of vending machines. She talked, and talked and talked to the police. When the police interviews were completed, she went back out to the waiting room, where Mike was sitting, looking rather anxious. He had a charter that evening - a sunset sail. Somehow, he needed to get back to his boat. Somehow, Sylvia realized, she needed to get their boat home. Mike asked if she could call someone. He also asked if one of the cops could take him back to his boat.

"Of course," she answered him, shocked when she looked at the actual time. "Oh, my! They're expecting us home any minute."

She pulled out her phone to call her mother. Mary answered on the second ring.

"Hi, Syl!" she greeted. "Are you pulling up to the house soon?" she asked. "Percy and I have been out on the deck, keeping an eye out for you."

"Not exactly," Sylvia said. The shock was beginning to wear off and emotions were threatening to come to the surface.

"Where are you?" her mother asked.

"Chestertown," Sylvia answered.

"You went up the Chester River? What, are you visiting your alma mater?" her mother semi-joked. "When are you planning to come home?"

"Well, that's the thing," Sylvia told her mother. "I have a little story to share with you."

"That doesn't sound good," her mother replied.

"Well...not all of it," Sylvia agreed.

Sylvia told her exactly what had happened that morning. Other than a shocked gasp, when Sylvia told her of the gunshots, her mother was silent until Sylvia finished her story.

"What do you need me to do?" Mary asked.

"Please call Phil and Anne and let them know what happened. Also, can you call Jon and Marian, and have them go to the Worton Point Marina. Please ask Jon if he would sail the boat home. If you could come to Chestertown to the hospital, we would really appreciate a ride home," she told her mother.

A nurse came out and motioned for Sylvia to follow her.

"I've got to run, Mom. See you soon," she said.

She motioned for Mike to follow her back. Owen was sitting up in the hospital bed. He seemed slightly groggy. There was a tube coming out of his chest and it was attached to a machine. He seemed to be covered in tubes and wires.

"Owen!" Sylvia cried, rushing up to his bedside.

She grabbed his hand and clutched it to her, trying to avoid bumping any tubes. She gave him a kiss.

"Hi, Syl," he said weakly.

Sylvia introduced Mike as the man that saved them. Owen looked abashed but grateful.

Sylvia filled Owen in on how the boat would be sailed home by Jon, and how Mom would be picking them up.

"Can you go home?" she asked.

"I don't think so," he told her weakly. "I don't know."

The nurse came in to take his vital signs. "Don't wear him out," she told Sylvia, "the police have already been here to ask him questions. We'll let you know when he's headed up to a floor. A gunshot and a collapsed lung..." she paused and shook her head, "Let him rest," she nodded at Owen, whose eyes had closed.

Sylvia and Mike exited the emergency room and went back to the waiting room. Mike had given his statement, and now one of the cops offered to give him a ride back to the marina.

"Will you be all right?" he asked Sylvia, concern in his eyes.

"I'll be fine," Sylvia said, more bravado, than truth in her voice. "My Mom will be here soon." She paused, took his hand and looked into his eyes, "I don't know how or where to begin to thank you."

Mike told her, "No problem. You have my contact information. Let me know how Owen is doing."

The policeman was obviously impatient. He looked away but was tapping his foot. Sylvia noticed.

"I will," she told him, "and thank you, from the bottom of my heart." She leaned over, and gave him a kiss on the cheek, her emotions threatening to spill over. She turned, blinking, to the policeman, and thanked him as well. Mike and the police left the emergency room.

Sylvia sat down in one of the hard, plastic chairs again. She didn't know if she had ever felt so alone in her life. A television babbled world news. She dully watched as people with various illnesses and injuries came into the Emergency Room. The background noise became white noise with the occasional faint sirens growing louder and louder as they approached the Emergency Room. The crackling voice over the intercom paging doctors jolted her awake every few minutes. Sylvia sat, not really staring at anything in a trance like a state. She leafed languidly through old, tattered magazines, but did not actually read. Finally, after what seemed like hours, one of the nurses called to her. Owen had been moved to a medical, surgical floor of the hospital. Sylvia hurried up to see him, but the nurses were setting him up with the monitors and machine. She stood outside the door, making sure she didn't get in the way. Owen was still asleep, and he moaned deeply when they moved him around.

Tears threatened to spill from her eyes again. The stress of the day was catching up with her. When the nurses were done, they asked her if she needed anything, and she asked, quietly, if she could have a blanket. She was so cold, her teeth were nearly chattering. In a few moments, one of the nurses brought her a blanket that was warm.

"This is wonderful!" she told the nurse. "Thank you so much."

"Let us know if you need anything," the nurse told her. She offered her a sandwich, coffee, and cold drinks.

Sylvia declined the offer of food and beverages. She was not very hungry. The nurse's name was Barbara, Sylvia was grateful for her kindness. Barbara left the room and Sylvia pulled the warm blanket more tightly around herself. The stress of the day seemingly caught up with her all at once. She was asleep within seconds. It only seemed a moment later that her mom was shaking her gently.

"Sylvia? Syl? Are you all right?" Mary asked her daughter.

Sylvia felt like she was swimming through thick water. She pulled herself out of the dream she was having, and back to reality.

"Mom?" she asked, faintly.

"Oh, Sylvia!" she said, bending down to give her daughter a half hug.

Tears did spill out this time, just pouring down her cheeks without a sound. Her mom held her. Sylvia couldn't speak. She looked over at Owen. He was still asleep from the pain medications they had given him. His breathing sounded ragged and odd with the tube sticking out of his chest. There was a suction thing attached to the tube that gave a steady, but strange, whooshing sound as he breathed. It was a little frightening to see and hear.

"Oh, Mom!" Sylvia cried, "I'm so glad you came!" She started crying all over again.

Mary waited until Sylvia calmed down. She handed her the thin tissues, from the box by Owen's bed, one by one until the tears stopped. Sylvia excused herself to the bathroom where she splashed water on her face. While she was in the bathroom, her mother had pulled up another chair. Sylvia sat back down with a sigh. She pulled the blanket around her again.

"Tell me everything, from the beginning," her mother told her.

So, Sylvia told her. She told her about the weekend's highs and lows. The docking at Still Pond, how much she loved sailing, the meeting with Scotty, the marina, the inn and the horrific sail home. She rambled. She babbled. Sylvia didn't think she made any sense, but she kept on talking. Her mother kept quiet, listening to her, and holding onto her hand. Sylvia finally stopped. She was exhausted from her story and from crying. Mary continued to hold her hand. Sylvia slumped in the chair.

"Sylvia?" a weak-voiced Owen called to her.

Sylvia sprang up from her chair and ran to the side of the bed.

"Owen?" she asked him, her voice ragged with emotion and exhaustion. "Owen?" she asked again, "how are you feeling?"

He looked up at her, eyes still heavy with the pain medications they had given him, "With my hands, I think," he croaked, trying to make a joke.

"Oh, you!" she cried in exasperation, but she peppered his face with butterfly kisses. She moved and accidentally bumped the tube that came from his chest. He groaned.

"Oh! Owen!" she cried, "I'm sorry!"

"It's okay," he gasped. "It's all right."

"Do you remember what happened?" Sylvia asked him.

"I think I remember," Owen started and took a breath before completing the sentence, "getting shot by someone."

Sylvia nodded, but could not speak. The few tears she had left streamed down her face. Owen tried to raise a hand to touch her face, but could not. He let his hand sink back to the bed.

"Oh, Sylvia," he whispered weakly, "don't cry."

"I know, I know!" she sobbed, just on the edge of hysteria, "but, I thought I lost you! I don't know how, or why this ever happened."

Owen patted her hand.

Sylvia took some deep breaths before telling him, "They said the gunshot went through your shoulder area but punctured your lung. That's why you have a tube in your chest. You will be all right. The machines are helping you to breathe, right now. But, you will be fine," she assured him, trying to convince Owen as much as herself.

Owen tried to smile at this, but the pain medications were pulling him back into a sleep state. Another nurse came in to check on Owen. He woke up briefly, barely acknowledging her presence, and went back to sleep almost immediately.

The nurse, Barbara, turned to Sylvia, "Why don't you get some food and some rest," she advised.

"I don't know what to do or where to go," Sylvia said faintly. "I don't want to go to North Bay tonight. I don't want to leave Owen."

Barbara looked at Mary. "There are some lovely restaurants in Chestertown, why don't you leave for a little bit. There's a bed and breakfast, just down the road."

"But, what about Percy?" Sylvia asked Mary and then turned to Barbara to explain, "Our dog, Percy, is home alone."

Mary turned to her daughter, "I can call Marian and Jon to take care of Percy, or maybe you can call Carol. We have lots of support. We'll figure it out."

Mary turned to Barbara, "Can you recommend anywhere we can stay?"

Barbara grimaced, "Most of the motels have only a few stars on their reviews. As I said, there's a bed and breakfast within walking distance."

Mary put her arm around Sylvia before she said, "I think we need someplace nice. This girl has been through a lot in the last twenty-four hours."

"Walk out to the desk with me," Barbara told Mary and Sylvia, "I'll get the number for you and you can make a reservation before you go. It shouldn't be booked during the summer and at the beginning of the week."

They made a reservation, with Sylvia still protesting.

"Sylvia, I am your mother, and *I* am telling you that you need some food and some rest," Mary said to Sylvia in a firm voice.

Barbara nodded. "Don't worry, Sylvia. We'll take good care of Owen."

Sylvia nodded a little shakily with tears threatening to spill over again.

Mary led Sylvia to the car. She drove to a nearby discount store and pulled Sylvia inside to get some toiletries, nightgowns for each of them, an outfit for the next day and a small bag to carry it all in. Once they were checked in, her mother took her to a restaurant in town. Sylvia wasn't hungry at all, but her mother ordered a bottle of wine and some appetizers. Sylvia nibbled disconsolately.

"Why don't we have this packed up and we can take it up to the bed and breakfast?" her mother suggested. "You are exhausted and we have some additional calls to make."

Sylvia didn't protest. It was only a few minutes to the bed and breakfast. Fortunately, her mother talked with the innkeeper, while Sylva hung back. She was overtired. She didn't want to speak to any more people.

As tired as Sylvia was, she didn't feel like she could sleep. Fragments of thoughts of the day's events buzzed continually in her brain. Her mother insisted she lay on the bed and she did. She felt too tired to think. She felt too tired to move. In a haze she listened, while her mother called and let Jon, Marian, Carol and Mr. Carter know what had happened. She heard her mother's voice talking in soothing tones to Phil and Anne. The cadence and tone of her mother's voice was like a lullaby. It eventually lulled her to sleep.

Sylvia slept dreamlessly for a few hours. But, the peacefulness of dreams left Sylvia, and the nightmares began. Over and over, in her dream, she replayed the scene of Owen getting shot and the blood spilling everywhere. Red lights flashed off and on and on and off. Lights, blood, gunshots replayed over and over in an unending nightmare.

Mary woke up when her daughter began moaning in her sleep. Tears sprang to her eyes as Sylvia mumbled words of angst. Mary could only guess at what Sylvia was dreaming about. It was when she cried out in anger and pain in her sleep, that Mary put her arm around her daughter and whispered, "It's all right. You're safe. Owen's safe," over and over again until Sylvia settled down again.

It was mid-morning when Sylvia woke up. Sunlight streamed through the sheer curtains at the window. She squinted. Sylvia was confused, not remembering where she was, at first. When the realization hit her, her eyes widened.

"Syl, it's all right," Mary told her daughter when she was awake, "I called the hospital and Owen had a peaceful night. When you get dressed, and have breakfast, we can head back to the hospital to see him."

Her mother had been sitting in a lounge chair next to the window in the room. She got up and sat on the edge of the bed and put her hand on Sylvia's arm as she spoke.

"What time is it?" Sylvia asked.

"Just after nine-thirty," her mother told her, "Since its mid-week and they have no other guests, the innkeeper was waiting until you woke up to start breakfast. I'll just slip downstairs and let her know you're awake while you get dressed."

Sylvia lay back a moment to look around the room. She barely remembered crawling into bed last night. It was a lovely place, feminine, but not 'frou-frou' as Scotty said over the weekend. She smiled, remembering his face about the 'frou-frou' comment. There were lace curtains at the window and lots of pillows, but it was clean, light and airy. She smelled coffee brewing and something baking reminded Sylvia she needed to get up and get ready for the day.

The innkeeper served them coffee, homemade cinnamon rolls, and fresh fruit on the front porch. It was a lovely and relaxing way to start the day. The July heat was beginning to build, but the trees in front of the house shaded them entirely.

After breakfast, Mary went inside to talk to the innkeeper about staying another night. Sylvia stayed on the porch, sipping the last of her coffee and staring blankly at the trees. Their presence gave her some peace, but she was still too roiled up inside to be able to see their auras. What she saw, was something like rain. Sylvia blinked. When she opened her eyes and looked at the sun-drenched landscape again, her vision was almost blurry with the movement. She rubbed her eyes. It reminded her of the time the Green Man gave her extraordinary sight to see auras. She breathed slowly in and out. She thought of the Green Man, wishing for him to come to her, to bring her some comfort.

With a rustle of leaves, there he was. Sylvia flung herself into his arms, locking her arms around him as if she would never let go. He held her tightly while she buried her face in the brocade, leafy fabric on his body and breathed in the spicy, woodsy scent. They didn't talk. Peacefulness from the Green Man emanated from him and into her. She didn't speak. Neither did he.

Approaching footsteps caused Sylvia to step back and the Green Man vanished. Her mother and the innkeeper came out to the porch. Disappointment washed over Sylvia.

"Can I get you more coffee?" the innkeeper asked.

Mutely Sylvia nodded and held out her cup for one more splash of java as she softly murmured her thanks. Mary introduced Madeleine.

Madeleine was tall, very tall. She swayed a little as she stood, reminding Sylvia of a giraffe or even more of a lithe dancer. Her gray hair was short and chic and her kind eyes reminded Sylvia of Marian. Madeleine extended her hand and told Sylvia she was sorry to hear about the trouble she and Owen had on the bay. She told Sylvia and Mary she would have a treat for them when they returned that evening, freshly baked, chocolate chip cookies. Mary groaned in delight, thanking her in advance. Sylvia smiled in response.

Owen was sitting up and looking brighter when they arrived at the hospital. He was hoping he could be released the next day. Mary left the hospital, shortly after dropping off Sylvia, to pick up some more clothes for Sylvia, Owen and herself. Sylvia noticed the hospital floor had a rhythm to it. She could see this from her vantage point in Owen's room, and when she assisted Owen with a walk down the hall, to the nurses' station and back, trailing his IV pole.

The morning was busy with the ins and outs of the nursing staff and various medical personnel checking on Owen. She had Owen call his parents. She knew her mom had called Anne and

Phil last night, but thought Anne would want to hear her son's voice. Phil was teaching a summer class, but Anne insisted on driving to Marian's to stay for a few days. Sylvia could hear a catch in her voice through the phone. Later, Sylvia called Carol and caught her up on what had happened and talked to her about the upcoming Bay Days. It only seemed a short time had passed when Mary came back to pick up Sylvia to take her to lunch.

They drove to nearby downtown Chestertown. Sylvia and Gwen had often haunted a small café where they had signature coffee drinks, homemade pastries, and hearty sandwiches. The restaurant was sparsely filled. It wasn't long before they had their sandwiches and drinks. They sat in what was once a large window in a store and let the sunshine pour in on them. It felt good. Sylvia closed her eyes for a moment.

"Are you all right?" Mary asked her daughter.

Sylvia nodded, not opening her eyes. "I'm weary, I think," she answered her mother. "It's all still so jumbled around. I can't seem to get a straight thought. I keep asking myself, 'why.'" Sylvia opened her eyes. I'll be happy to go home," she admitted honestly.

"I'm hoping that will be tomorrow," Mary told her. "Owen is looking well. Also, I wanted to let you know that I asked Anne to stay in the guest room and not at Marian's. She's so anxious about Owen and we can tag team taking care of him and you can get back to Thurmont.

Thurmont, Bay Days, this was not a good week for Sylvia to be away from the job. But, it couldn't be helped. Sylvia nodded in agreement with her mother's statement.

"I'm going to need to talk to Carol," she told her mother.

Mary nodded, "I know," she said.

But, Sylvia couldn't bring herself to dial Carol's number. Instead, she hid behind a cheery text that they were hoping Owen would be released tomorrow and that Sylvia would return to Thurmont on Thursday. Carol's response was a smiley face, but no other words.

Sylvia was a little puzzled, but brushed it off, knowing that Carol was likely very, very busy, doing work on Bay Days and other work that Sylvia was responsible for. She would need to make it up to her somehow.

They returned to the hospital and received word that Owen would definitely be released the next day. While Mary and Sylvia had been at lunch, the chest tube had been removed. Owen had been given additional pain medication. Now he was sleepy. Sylvia gave Owen a light kiss on the cheek and promised to see him in the morning to take him home.

Mary took Sylvia back to the bed and breakfast for the warm chocolate chip cookies Madeleine had promised them that morning. Still weary, she asked her mom to get sandwiches or pizza for dinner, rather than going out. Her mom complied and went out to get dinner. Sylvia wandered the campus about one hundred yards from the bed and breakfast. Memories of her years at Washington College flooded her as she strolled around the grounds. Her phone buzzed. It was her mom asking where she was. Briefly, Sylvia told her where she was and she would be back in a minute.

Mary had picked up sandwiches and a bottle of Sylvia's favorite wine. She had dinner set in the dining room when Sylvia walked in.

"Looks good," Sylvia commented at the sandwiches on the table. She picked up her glass of wine and held it aloft in a toast. "To this nightmare being over soon," she said to Mary.

Mary clinked her glass and nodded. "Here! Here!" she agreed and drank to the toast.

CHAPTER TWENTY-ONE

"Once you choose hope, anything is possible."

— CHRISTOPHER REEVE

Sylvia was never so glad to head home in her life. Finally discharged from the hospital, late in the morning, Owen fell asleep just minutes after climbing carefully into the car. Sylvia and her mom chatted quietly as they drove north on Route 213 towards Deerton. The July heat and humidity was in full force. Heat seemed to rise from the fields of corn and soybeans along the road.

When they arrived in Bayside, Sylvia saw Anne's little compact car and Marian's ancient Volvo wagon parked across the street in the open space in the neighborhood. Sylvia saw Marian industriously planting something by the back door of the house that faced the road. Mary pulled into the driveway and Marian stood up and brushed off her denim capris and came toward the car.

As soon as she opened the car door, Sylvia could hear Percy barking crazily from inside and Anne's voice telling him to 'calm down.' The side door to the kitchen opened and the large, white, standard poodle flung himself out of the door and catapulted himself towards Sylvia.

"Percy! Percy!" Sylvia crooned and bent down to hug him.

He danced his happy, doggy dance where his entire body quivered in happiness to see them. Mary was helping Owen out of the car while Sylvia kept Percy at bay for a moment, but he raced over to Owen. He seemed to sense that Owen was hurting and wiggled and jiggled and sniffed and whined.

Owen reached a hand toward Percy, who licked it enthusiastically. "Hi, Percy," he said weakly.

Anne went to her son, tears in her eyes and hugged him carefully. She didn't say anything, just sighed and held him.

Owen carefully hugged back, wincing from the pain in his shoulder. "It's okay, Mom. I'll be fine," he assured her.

Anne nodded, her eyes full of unshed tears when she pulled away from her son.

"Let's get you inside," Mary suggested.

Sylvia gave Marian a fierce hug. Tears threatened to spill from Sylvia's eyes. She wiped at her eyes distractedly with the back of her hand. Sylvia looked at the gardening tools in Marian's hand and at the plants by the door.

"What are you planting?" Sylvia asked Marian curiously.

"Rosemary," Marian state succinctly. "You and Owen have been beleaguered by bad luck. Rosemary is said to be protection. In times of trouble, I say, use anything you can." She grinned at Sylvia, "and, as you know, it never hurts to call on the Old Gods."

Sylvia blushed. Yes, she had called the Green Man often.

"So, now you have rosemary at the front and the back doors," she told Sylvia as she pointed towards the front door of the house facing the water and the back door on the road, "for protection."

"Thank you," Sylvia told her and hugged her again. She was feeling in need of some sort of luck after their experience a few days ago.

They walked to the kitchen door and went inside. Owen was already ensconced on the couch with a pillow and a light blanket. Anne and Mary were setting up lunch items on the dining room table. Sylvia took a minute to give Anne a big hug and then looked at the dining room table. The table was laden with a chicken Caesar pasta salad, rolls, Insalata Caprese and fresh melon.

Sylvia sat cross-legged on the floor next to Owen. Percy had climbed up on the end of the couch and placed his head on Owen's leg. Owen was staring out the window at the "True Love."

"Our poor boat," he said sadly. "We'll have to get her repaired. I'll have to call the boat yard."

"Do you think they can get it repaired before the wedding?" Sylvia asked.

"Don't know," Owen said. "I certainly hope so. She'll have to go into dry dock for them to fix it."

Sylvia nodded. She looked up and saw Anne gesturing her to come and fill up a plate. She got up and filled a plate for Owen and took it back to him.

"Food!" he breathed, "*real* food."

"Come on," Sylvia scolded, "the hospital food wasn't *that* bad, was it?" she queried.

He tried to shrug, but stopped, wincing in pain.

"Owen! Are you okay?" Anne asked, coming into the living room and seeing grimace.

"Okay, but not too smart," Owen explained, "Don't shrug your shoulders after a collapsed lung and a gunshot wound."

"It's a good thing I'm ambidextrous," he quipped, launching into his food.

Sylvia agreed. Mary and Anne came in with plates and sat down while Sylvia went to get food for herself. She returned and sat again, cross-legged on the floor next to Owen. Sylvia answered Anne's questions about their trip between bites. Mary told her of the bed and breakfast in Chestertown and Owen updated Anne on Scotty and his career.

When they finished lunch, Owen was worn out. Mary brought him his medications and they tiptoed out of the room as he took a nap. Sylvia took her laptop to the deck to catch up on work emails. Anne and Mary cleaned up lunch and went for a walk. It was definitely a hot, July day, but the humidity was down and so was pleasantly warm. Sylvia spent a lot of her time staring at the water, sky and the auras over the trees on the shore. They danced with a bright, white light that leaped and danced in the air. She was so very glad to be home. Sylvia sighed with pleasure. Everything seemed fairly copacetic at work. She was glad she had worked so hard on Bay Days in the last few weeks. She hoped everything would come off without a hitch. Last year's Bay Days was a complete nightmare with Mr. Carter's heart attack, the lecher Richard Headley and Ed Davenport's graffiti about Thurmont. Unsettled at the memories, she looked at the water, trees and sky again to absorb the sense of peace that permeated Bayside.

She heard Owen cry out in his sleep and she rushed to him. He was still asleep but agitated. She sat next to him on the floor and took his hand gently. She leaned her head against the couch. He stirred a few minutes later and woke up. She looked into his eyes and kissed Owen gently.

"You were having a nightmare," she told Owen.

He nodded slowly. "Not a good time," he said. "Can you help me up?" he asked her as he squirmed painfully on the couch.

"Of course," she said.

She helped Owen stand up. They held each other as best they could.

"I love you," he whispered to her.

"I love you too," she answered. She felt tears welling up again but refused to let them spill over. Shakily, he took a breath and held her face up for a kiss. Their lips were about to touch when the kitchen door opened and their moms walked into the house. Owen gave her a quick kiss and turned to face the mom's.

"Anne and I are heading out to the grocery store to pick up some steaks," Mary told them. "We'll grill and enjoy the sunset."

"Sounds good," Owen said. He yawned and turned to Sylvia, "Can you get my laptop? I should check my email."

Sylvia chuckled. "Just what I've been doing. Side by side on the deck?"

He nodded and went out to the deck. The moms left for to the grocery store and Sylvia went to get Owen's laptop and set it up for him. She logged on and got his email up. He hunted and pecked carefully with his injured arm. Sylvia logged into the cloud network and continued to work.

"Pretty nice working digs," Owen commented, looking up from his laptop, at the water and then at Sylvia.

She was biting her lip in concentration. She nodded. She stopped working and looked up at the water, the sky and at Owen. She smiled at Owen, nodded again and went back to work.

The afternoon waned and wended its way toward evening. Anne and Mary brought some bruschetta and toasts out to the deck along with a beer for Owen and a glass of wine for Sylvia.

"Only one for you," Anne told her son. "You're on pain meds."

Owen made a face and his mother smiled back at him serenely. He knew she was right.

"Time to close the laptops," Mary told them.

"Gladly," Sylvia said.

She logged off and shut her laptop down. Sylvia stood and stretched before reaching for Owen's laptop to take them inside. A few minutes later she rejoined the family on the deck. They had a relaxed evening. Mary and Anne insisted that Sylvia relax and stay with Owen while they prepared dinner. Steaks and corn were grilled. Anne had prepared tomatoes with fresh oregano, feta cheese, and a vinaigrette.

They talked about little things and watched the sun set over the water. Twilight was beginning to envelop the evening as the sun set in a burning line on the opposite shore. Boats chugged their way to their ports. There was a silver streak of water in the center of the bay. Wavelets moving towards the shore were ribbons of silver, blue and black as darkness gathered. Lights on the bows and sterns illuminated boats as they traversed the bay. A mid-week party boat was lit up like Christmas decorations on a house. There was more boat traffic than usual for mid-week. Sylvia knew that Bay Days drew thousands of people into the town of North Bay and the county. In addition to all of the activities planned for Saturday, there was a bass tournament. Bass boats trolled the bay looking for good spots to fish. She couldn't help but wonder if some were looking for places before the tournament. Apparently the prize monies ran into the thousands of dollars. There was a boat, with only a bow light on, relatively close to their property. It slowed and looked like it stopped. She asked Owen about it.

"Looks like the light on their stern is out. Remember our light being out? It probably saved us," Owen told her. "That's what the police said. If they had known we were there, those goons would have killed us sooner than later."

Owen squinted at the boat, "I think it's headed further out into the bay," he said. That's why we can't see the bow light any longer."

"Actually, I think they're backing up," Sylvia said, watching the boat as the bow light came back into view. "Weird."

The boat seemed to reverse in the water and then moved forward again and headed out into the bay. For some reason, it made

Sylvia uneasy. She tried to shake it off and focus on the ribbons of silver, blue and increasing black of the waves hitting the beach. The sound was soothing.

"Work tomorrow, Syl," her mother advised, "you should get to bed."

"And you too, young man," Anne told her son in a faux stern voice. "Off to bed with you."

"Okay, Mom," Sylvia and Owen said in chorus.

"I've never known my mom to send me off to bed with a woman," he whispered in her ear. "It's a shame that I'm injured," he continued, "But, maybe we could think of something."

Sylvia couldn't help but blush as she imagined creative ways to handle Owen's injury in bed.

"But, our moms are here," she hissed. "We can't."

"We'll see. I can be very quiet," Owen told her, "but, can you?" he asked.

Sylvia blushed even more and they closed the door to the bedroom firmly.

CHAPTER TWENTY-ONE

*"Life isn't about waiting for the storm to pass. It's about
learning to dance in the rain."*

— Vivian Greene

W hen Sylvia walked into the office suite at Thurmont, Carol
practically flew around her desk and Sylvia found herself
swallowed in a bear hug.

"Oh, Sylvia!" Carol cried, tears spilling down her cheeks. "How
are you? How is Owen?"

Sylvia returned Carol's hug.

"I'm okay, Carol," she assured her friend. "Really."

Sylvia gently pulled away from her friend. "Let me put my stuff
down and we can talk a few minutes," Sylvia told her.

Sylvia opened her office door. The air inside was stale. She wished she had a window she could open. She put her purse in a drawer in her desk and her briefcase on top before she went out to Carol.

"Sit!" Carol commanded. "Mr. Carter is off today and things are in good shape for Bay Days. We can catch up!"

Sylvia sat and told Carol all that had happened that weekend, about the sailing, Fells Point, Scotty, the scary trip back, the gunshots and Owen's injuries. Carol listened intently.

"Wow. I think you need a lucky rabbit's foot or something, girl-friend," Carol joked unintentionally. "Wow."

Sylvia gave her friend an infinitesimal glare. "C'mon," Sylvia said, "really?"

Carol shrugged.

"And what about you?" Sylvia asked Carol. "What's been going on here at Thurmont? How are things with you and Joe? You two seem to be getting hot and heavy."

At this comment, Sylvia's bright friend, usually full of chutz-pah, crumpled. Her shoulders slumped and she started crying again. Sylvia was stunned.

"Carol! What's wrong? What's happened? Is it Joe? Is he all right?" Sylvia asked in a rush and it was her turn to envelop her friend in a bear hug.

Carol was hiccoughing, trying desperately to stop crying. She wriggled from Sylvia's hug and grabbed a bunch of tissues.

Taking a deep breath, she told Sylvia, "Joe and I had our first fight," she wailed, "and I don't know what to do!"

"What? You had a fight," Sylvia paused before she asked, "with Joe? Whatever happened? You two are crazy about each other! Do you want to tell me what the fight was about?"

Carol took a deep breath, "Joe asked me to move in with him. I...I said no," she wailed and started to cry.

"That's what the fight was about?" Sylvia said.

"Yea," Carol said. "I am not sure I'm ready to do that. He took offense. He's willing to move on to bigger and better things with us and I'm not sure I'm willing to take that step."

"I'm surprised, Carol," Sylvia told her friend. "That's what you've talked and talked about – a great guy, moving in, getting married, the house, the picket fence, the two point five kids…"

"I know," Carol told Sylvia, "but, in truth, I'm a chicken."

"What does your mom say?" Sylvia asked gently. "Is she part of your reason not to move in with Joe?"

"Joe thinks so. He said I'm still trying to protect her. I don't know, maybe I am. Mom says to go. She *loves* Joe and thinks I'm crazy not to move in with him," Carol admitted.

"Do you love him?" Sylvia asked Carol, already knowing the answer.

"Yes!" Carol moaned. "I can't imagine life without him."

"Go to him," Sylvia stated, "Tonight! You two need to talk. Trust me, I know!"

Carol gulped. "I know you're right, but…" she stopped.

"No 'buts,'," Sylvia told her friend and then slyly said, "and trust me, the make-up sex will be terrific!"

"Sylvia!" Carol remonstrated, pretending to be shocked.

The two friends broke into giggles.

"We really should get some work completed," Sylvia said.

"Things are actually pretty well set for Saturday," Carol told Sylvia. "Mr. Carter and I used the KISS principle. Mom and I stuffed the information bags a couple of nights in front of the television, facilities knows how and where to deliver the boxes, the tent, table, and chairs. Mr. Carter took today as his comp day. I'm taking tomorrow. We'll all be at Bay Days on Saturday. It should be hot, but okay."

"Better than last year," Sylvia said drily.

"You bet!" Carol said. "Mr. Carter is bringing a cooler, ice, and sodas. Mom's baking cookies. We can go to one of the food booths for sandwiches. It should be fun!"

They talked the morning away. Carol rehashed all of her concerns with moving in with Joe. Sylvia urged her to text Joe to see if she could see him that evening. He replied that he would be home all evening.

"Put on your sexiest dress and take his favorite beer," Sylvia advised.

"And some of my mom's cooking," Carol joked.

"Probably couldn't hurt," Sylvia replied.

Sylvia talked Carol into leaving a little early to get ready for Joe. Sylvia left promptly at five and headed home.

Owen was much better. He seemed brighter and his pain level was dissipating. He had spoken to the fiberglass repair place at the marina thanks to Skip's insistence. They were going to take the boat for repair tomorrow. He had emailed and later spoke with his boss, Tom Green, who said he indeed missed Owen. Tom wished Owen well and asked him to return to work as soon as he possibly could. His mom had scheduled a follow-up appointment with the doctor. Owen was ebullient with joy, thinking he could return to work if the doctor cleared him.

Mary and Anne were busy in the kitchen making tacos, one of Owen's favorite meals. Sylvia went up to change into shorts and a t-shirt. She padded downstairs in bare feet. They came out to the deck to eat again. Sylvia told everyone about her day and what was going on between Joe and Carol.

"Oh, no!" Mary commented, "That could be awkward at the wedding."

"I think they'll be okay," Sylvia replied.

Owen agreed. "They definitely belong together," he said.

Sylvia was surprised that he said this but pleased. Mary told them she would be leaving the next day. Anne would stay until next week when Owen could return to work. He still wasn't permitted to drive, nor did he want to, with the pain in his shoulder from the gunshot wound. They told him it would be three to six months to heal, but he was determined to get back to work in the next week or two. All three women looked at him skeptically.

"Wh-aa-t?" he asked in a heavily accented, gangster type of voice.

Owen was rewarded with chuckles from all of them.

"Stubborn," Anne said firmly in a stage whisper, "he's always been stubborn."

"You think?" Sylvia asked rhetorically.

The next morning, Mary got up with Sylvia to get an early start towards home.

"Mom," Sylvia told her. "Thank you for everything," she said as she hugged her mother.

"I'm glad I was able to help. I'll be talking to you. You and Owen have the wedding stuff under control. Call and let me know how things are going and what I can do to help. I'll see you in a couple of weeks. I'm heading to the shore with John and Donna for a couple of days. I'm beginning to enjoy being retired!" she told Sylvia.

"Good," Sylvia said, "You deserve every moment. You worked so hard to keep us okay after Dad died. I'm beginning to understand now."

Sylvia hugged her mother. Mary's eyes grew moist.

"Good," she whispered to Sylvia.

Sylvia arrived to find Mr. Carter already at his desk. He gave Sylvia a big, bear hug. He asked how she was and how Owen was doing. She repeated her story to him as she had to Carol the day before. They went over last minute details for Bay Days and met briefly on some upcoming projects. The day flew by and she kept busy with little projects.

Home again, Anne told Sylvia that Marian and Jon were bringing dinner that evening. Owen had been resting most of the day. They had watched the marina helpers take the True Love and motor her towards the marina where she would be pulled out of the water for dry dock and repair. Skip had supervised the entire operation and Anne told Sylvia that Owen was happy with how they treated his baby, the 'True Love.' Anne told her she enjoyed giving Percy long walks in the neighborhood. Sylvia noticed that Percy was particularly subdued. He was tired!

It was wonderful to see Jon and Marian. They enjoyed another one of Marian's excellent meals, but Sylvia was weary. Despite the fantastic support of their families and friends, she wanted things to return to normal. She wanted Owen to be well and be back to their lives at Bayside with Percy.

Marian, of course, picked up on her discomposure. She raised an eyebrow and asked Sylvia to help her in the kitchen, directly after dinner. Anne started to protest stating she would help.

Quickly, Sylvia jumped in saying, "Anne, you've been helping us so much. Please take a moment to relax."

Marian winked at her and they cleared the table and met in the kitchen.

"So, what's going on, Sylvia?" Marian asked.

"I don't know," Sylvia stated and paused, "Well, I think I might. I just want everything to return to normal. But, what is normal?" she returned.

Marian sighed, "That's a good question. You two have certainly been through the mill. It's not a wonder you're jumpy. You deserve some peace. I hope all of the bad things are out of the way and you can enter into your marriage with clear skies, calm waters and full sails. I know your mom and Anne are just trying to help."

"I know, I know!" Sylvia said, "They've been wonderful. And, I feel like a spoiled brat, wanting everyone to just go away and leave Owen and me to have our life again."

"Sylvia," Marian assured her, "You are *not* a spoiled brat. You and Owen have had an amazingly stressful time of it, actually, since the beginning of your relationship. The last couple of months you've been planning a wedding. That's been a stress in itself. Now, you've been shot at. But, it's really great that Mary and Anne can take the time to help you so that you can get back to work."

"I know, I know," Sylvia said again.

Marian gave her a hug. "It will all work out," she advised. "Things usually do."

Sylvia nodded mutely, afraid her voice might catch. What was wrong with her? She was getting emotional again.

"Let's get this dessert out to everyone before they send in a search party," Marian suggested.

Marian pulled out a homemade peach cobbler that she had placed in the oven on low to keep warm. Sylvia pulled vanilla ice cream from the freezer and together they spooned and scooped. They took the dessert out to the deck.

The sun was setting and clouds obscured a beautiful sunset. Owen and Jon were in a deep discussion on sailboats. They were both speculating on the time it would take to repair the bullet holes in the boat. Jon and Owen waxed poetically on how the True Love handled in the water. More boats traversed the bay. It was definitely the beginning of a weekend on the water. Jetskis zoomed near the shoreline and dangerously wove in and around some of the boaters. Sailboats were mostly motoring due to the heaviness of the building humidity and the lack of wind. Power boats zoomed up and down the bay. There were cigarette boats that stopped their conversation as they roared past.

Marian and Jon left shortly after sunset. Owen was happy but apparently fatigued. Sylvia helped him get ready for bed and then returned to Anne, who was sitting on the deck, enjoying a glass of wine. She smiled as Sylvia stepped out onto the deck with her own glass of wine. Sylvia sat in the Adirondack chair next to her future mother-in-law.

"How are you doing, Sylvia?" Anne asked gently.

Sylvia took a sip of wine, considering her answer. "Fair," she finally admitted. "I really appreciate your help, but…" she trailed off afraid of how she would sound with brutal honesty. And, she was fortunate her mom and Anne had the time and energy to come to help take care of Owen. She flushed at her own thoughts.

"You must just want things to be normal again," Anne said, "I can understand that."

Sylvia looked at her future mother-in-law gratefully. "That's exactly it," she said with relief.

"It will happen," Anne said. She patted Sylvia's hand that was resting on the arm of the Adirondack chair.

They sat quietly watching the stars pop out over the water and the lights begin to twinkle on the other side of the bay. The water rippled blue and black under the stars. A few boats were meandering slowly through the water. Sylvia, remembering how dark it was on the water, thought they were brave to traverse the bay with just their running lights.

Anne said good night, patting Sylvia on her shoulder when she went inside. Sylvia sat, absorbing the peacefulness of the evening. The insects sang to her. Sylvia's worries melted away.

CHAPTER TWENTY-TWO

"What lies behind us and what lies before us are tiny matters compared to what lies within us."

— RALPH WALDO EMERSON

Morning came much too soon for Sylvia. Percy was not a barky-barky dog, but something disturbed him and he barked sharply, once, twice, during the night which set Sylvia's nerves on edge. She couldn't sleep for more than an hour before she would wake all of a sudden. She had a difficult time returning to sleep. Now, the sounds of the cigarette boats and motor boats roaring down the bay beginning at five in the morning also disturbed the last vestiges of her slumber. The bass tournament started and boats were racing to their favorite fishing spot. She knew they would be announcing the winner at Bay Days.

Owen was still sound asleep. He usually slept heavily, but his medications really zonked him out. Sylvia got up early and actually had to wake Percy to let him out. He scooted back upstairs to bed once she let him out in the yard to do his business. This surprised her, but Sylvia remembered he had barked during the night. He must have been awake and listening for something too. She wished she could join Owen and Percy in bed.

Instead, Sylvia enjoyed her coffee and breakfast on the deck, relishing the slight breeze that came up from the water. She held her breath as a blue heron glided into shore. It kept its eye on the water as it carefully waded along the shoreline, its head bobbing slightly. A bald eagle soared overhead and gulls wheeled in the sky. The water was a bright, French blue this morning and the surface echoed the clouds in the sky in the reflection. The boats involved in the bass tournament had already raced down the bay leaving calm waters until the pleasure boaters woke up.

Sylvia went back inside to get ready for Bay Days. She thought of crawling back into bed for a few minutes to snuggle up to Owen but found Percy, stretched out, sound asleep next to Owen, leaving little room for her.

When she was ready, Sylvia slipped out of the house quietly, not waking anyone. Pulling out of the driveway, she saw their mailbox had been smashed. There was not a lot of crime in Bayside, but every once in a while, petty crime, like broken mailboxes and minor break-ins occurred. Disgusted, she stopped her car and examined the mailbox. It would definitely need to be replaced. This must have been why Percy had barked in the night. Sylvia did not want to go in and wake Owen to tell him the bad news, instead, she texted Owen and Anne what had happened. She hoped they would take the time to get a new mailbox. Then Sylvia realized that Owen would not be able to replace it with his injury. Knowing Marian was likely awake, she called her to ask if Jon could help out. Marian volunteered his services and said she would send him over to check it out. Sylvia thanked her profusely and asked her to thank Jon too. Now running late, Sylvia quickly texted Owen and Anne an update in the mailbox situation and scooted down the road out of Bayside.

Sylvia had planned to pick up donuts but was running too late. She stopped at the small grocer in town, remembering they had cakes and cookies from an Amish bakery. She adored their carrot cake but thought it would be too messy for the day's events. Sylvia settled on a large, raspberry and cheese Danish. She also picked up coffees for Mr. Carter, Carol and herself.

The local VFW graciously granted parking spaces to vendors at Bay Days. She showed the gentleman her Thurmont badge and told him at which booth she would be working. He pointed to a parking area. Sylvia parked and balanced the food and coffees and went in search of the Thurmont booth.

Carol just grinned at Sylvia when she approached the booth.

"In your words from a year ago, you glow, girl!" Sylvia told Carol. Carol actually blushed.

"I take it you will be moving in with Joe?" she asked coyly.

"You are correct," Carol said, as she grinned at her friend.

"My little girls are growing up," Mr. Carter remarked. He had caught wind of the conversation when he approached the booth.

Sylvia passed out coffees. Carol couldn't stop smiling when she said she would need a couple of days off to move in with Joe. Sylvia told Mr. Carter and Carol what had happened to their mailbox as they sipped coffee, ate the Danish and set up the booth. People began trickling in before ten and wandered among the booths. Delicious smells from the food vendors began wafting towards them just after eleven. Smells of kettle corn, hot dogs, and barbecued ribs filled the air. The July heat and humidity seemed to always peak on this weekend. Sylvia was grateful that Mr. Carter had brought a cooler of ice water. Carol and Sylvia kept an eye on him to make sure he was well hydrated and keeping as cool as possible.

"Stop being mother hens," he complained good-naturedly. "See, I brought one of those bandanas and hats that have the chill thingy in them. I'm all right."

Sylvia checked her phone and saw a text from Owen. He had received her news about the mailbox. He said that Jon was working on it. He wished her well and told her to stay cool.

It was a successful day. Sylvia was pleased with an increasingly positive response from the community about Thurmont. She hoped that some of her programs were a catalyst for this. By the end of the day, they were all hot and exhausted. Mr. Carter offered to take them out for dinner at an air-conditioned restaurant, but all Sylvia could think of was a refreshing swim. She invited them back to the house, but they both declined. The facilities team came at the end of the day and efficiently packed up the tent and Thurmont paraphernalia. They wearily walked back to their cars and said they would debrief on Monday morning.

"Enjoy the rest of your weekend!" Mr. Carter said as he climbed into his car.

"Don't you worry, I will!" Carol assured him with a smile and her usual sense of chutzpah.

"Calm would be enough for me," Sylvia said.

She drove home and noticed the lovely, new mailbox Jon had installed when she pulled in the driveway. She would need to pick up a bottle of his favorite scotch for all of his help. He was particular about his libations and preferred an expensive, single malt scotch.

She parked and told Percy to hush as she walked up to the kitchen door and went inside. Anne was chopping vegetables. She greeted Sylvia with a cheerful hello.

"Owen has a glass of wine waiting for you in the living room," she told Sylvia.

"I think I'll go and say hello and either go for a swim or get a shower," she told Anne. "Are you interested in a swim?" she asked Anne hopefully.

"That sounds beautiful," Anne told her. "Dinner's done. Cold shrimp salad and some crusty bread."

"Yum," Sylvia told her. "You're spoiling us."

Anne smiled, "Just wait until I get grandchildren!"

Sylvia shook her head, smiling and went in to see Owen. He kissed her happily and cupped her breast in his good hand.

"I've missed you," he told Sylvia.

"Same here," she said. "Your mom is already planning grandchildren."

Owen rolled his eyes and his hand dropped from her breast, "Oh Gawd," he stated.

"Hey, I'm hot and I'm sweaty," Sylvia began.

"And not in the right way," Owen interrupted.

Sylvia brushed him away, "I'm going swimming with your mom," she told him.

Sylvia scooted upstairs to change into her swimsuit and water shoes. She met Anne on the deck and they walked to the water with the long, colorful, floating noodles. The water was as warm as bath water in the hot July sun. They strode out until the water was up to their breasts and Sylvia plopped onto the noodle with a small splash. They floated and walked, searching for the cooling, natural springs.

"This is wonderful," Sylvia said as she floated with the noodle.

"Absolutely!" Anne said. "When Owen was little and he threw a tantrum or was unhappy, I could always put him in water – pool, river, bath, whatever, and he was a happy boy. I think that works for most of us."

"I agree," Sylvia replied. "Are you suggesting that's what I need?" she asked Anne, a little coyly.

Anne nodded and then splashed her. They both laughed.

They splashed around a little more and Sylvia broke the news to Anne, "You know, Anne, Owen doesn't want to have kids for a while. A long while, he told me."

"A future grandmother can always hope," Anne said to Sylvia, almost smugly.

The thing about Anne, Sylvia thought, is that she was so sweet. Sylvia just loved her. They continued to paddle and float until Owen called them in.

"I'm starving," he shouted to them. "Come in for dinner!"

Percy howled in agreement. Sylvia and Anne laughed and headed to shore. After brief showers, they fed the starving men of the household.

The next morning, Sylvia felt incredibly lazy. She slept later than usual and Owen got up to let Percy outside while she returned to sleep. It was luxurious. She woke up much later with the sun streaming through the windows. The smell of coffee wafted up the stairs and then there was Owen, spilling some as he carried a very full cup in his good hand.

"Time to wake up, Syl," he said.

He tried to give her the cup carefully, but coffee spilled on the sheets and comforter. Sylvia reached for the cup with two hands and took a sip. It was scalding but tasted fabulous. Owen went around to the other side of the bed and carefully sat down.

"Are you okay?" he asked.

"I will be," Sylvia answered, "Actually, I think I am. Being at home, sleeping next to you and getting a good night's sleep was wonderful."

"Good," Owen said. "Bill called. He's coming over in an hour."

"What?" Sylvia cried. She gulped more coffee. "No rest for the weary, eh?"

"Bill's cool," Owen said. "Mom's got brunch handled. You can come down when you want to."

Sylvia stared at the bottom of her now empty coffee cup. "I'll be down in a few minutes," she promised Owen, "especially, if you can bring me another cup of coffee?" she asked pleadingly.

"Be happy to," he told her and gave her a swift kiss.

Sylvia went down a few minutes later. Owen had been correct, Anne had brunch handled and did not need or want any help from her. Sylvia took her at her word and went to finish her coffee on the couch where Owen was seated.

Bill arrived. "Hey, Bro!" he greeted Owen enthusiastically but avoided giving Owen a manly slap on the back when he saw the lump of bandages.

Bill gave Sylvia a huge hug and a kiss on her cheek. Owen introduced Anne to Bill.

Anne offered him a Bloody Mary, but he declined, asking if he could indulge in a beer instead. Sylvia went to get him one which he opened and quaffed a huge gulp.

Bill often talked with his hands and he waved them now, asking what happened. Owen gave him a brief version of the story. Bill shook his head, muttering, "Unbelievable, man. Unbelievable."

Sylvia, weary of their story turned the conversation to Bill asking him what he had been doing this summer.

"Just got back from Maui!" Bill exclaimed enthusiastically. "Amazing trip. I took a group of students to find tardigrades."

"What's a tardigrade?" Sylvia asked.

Bill laughed, "A tardigrade is a very cool micro-organism. They sort of look like a live gummy bear. In fact, they call them water bears or moss piglets. You can find them in every phylum in the world. They're nearly indestructible and they come up on those extreme animal shows all the time. I won a grant so it was a perfect opportunity. And, Maui rocks, to say the least!" He continued talking about the tardigrades and the experiments and pulled up a photograph of one on his phone, along with photos of the students working in Maui on the project.

Anne left for a few minutes and went to the kitchen. She returned to say brunch was ready. Sylvia went to the kitchen to assist with placing things on the table. Anne brought in a platter of crisp bacon and sizzling sausage. Sylvia carried in a pan of oven baked cinnamon French toast. She was practically drooling by the time she brought it to the table. Anne returned to the kitchen for butter, syrup, and whipped cream.

As they served themselves, Bill asked Sylvia if she had been dowsing since he last saw her. She flushed a little and shook her head. She didn't want to think of the kidnapping today.

"But, you're a natural!" Bill insisted. "I was thinking of having one of the "Science and Spirit" seminars on dowsing. What do you say? Would you be willing to help?"

"Sure," Sylvia answered tentatively. "I guess so." She took a bite of the French toast and found it was stuffed with a sweet, warm, cream cheese filling. It was divine. She almost groaned.

Sylvia asked Bill, "Do you have a list of topics for the Spirit and Science seminars this year?"

Bill became animated again. "When I was in Maui, I met Garret Lisi!"

Anne, Owen, and Sylvia returned blank looks to him. Bill sighed.

"Garret is the guy who talks about the eight-dimensional universe! He's a particle physicist and when they look at the particles smaller than atoms, they are finding they fit into a pattern!" He said excitedly before he turned to Sylvia and said, "You know what it is, Sylvia."

"The Flower of Life?" she asked.

He nodded enthusiastically.

"Yeah!" Bill continued, "Check out his TED talk. He talks about the E8 pattern and how nature keeps a perfect balance. But, what the really neat thing, Sylvia, is that the flower of life pattern is at the smallest, most microscopic level!"

"So everything, everything, everything, fits into this pattern?" Sylvia questioned.

"Yes!" Bill almost shouted in his excitement.

"And the pattern moves, and always changes and keeps a perfect balance, right?" Sylvia asked.

Bill turned to Owen, "Where have you been hiding her?" he asked, jerking his head in Sylvia's direction, "she should be in physics!"

Owen raised his eyebrows at Sylvia and smiled.

"Well, it just makes sense," Sylvia insisted. She was relieved to find and learn that the pattern that the Green Man referred to, or the pattern she *thought* he referred to, was something like what Bill was talking about. But, she couldn't help but think it was even more than this.

"This is fascinating," she told Bill. "You said it was particle physics?"

"Yup!" Bill told her. "I think you need to get a masters degree in physics."

"I don't think so," Sylvia replied. Sylvia changed the subject and asked, "What about a talk on fractals?"

Bill pondered for a moment, "Not a bad idea. I think I could find a guest speaker to talk about them."

"But, aren't fractals more a math concept than science," argued Owen.

"Math and science," Bill corrected.

"And art," Sylvia added.

"Fractals would fit in well with Lisi's theories," Bill said thoughtfully.

"How?" Owen challenged.

"Fractals are part of every living thing," Bill insisted. "They are the poetry of mathematical language. They're part of the new geometry. There's order beneath the chaos of fractals," he said.

"So it all fits," Sylvia established. "It's part of the code in nature?"

"And that's where it bleeds into science," Owen said.

"Exactly," Bill repeated what Sylvia said, flashing her a grin.

"Exactly," Sylvia agreed.

"Whew!" Anne said, "This is a pretty heavy conversation! Boys, eat up."

"Anne, this French toast is amazing! I could eat the entire pan, but I wouldn't be able to fit into my wedding dress."

"As I just said, boys, eat up!" Anne insisted.

"Speaking of the wedding," Owen started with a slight hint of trepidation. "You're okay with not being a groomsman?" he asked Bill.

"Oh, my God, yes!" Bill exclaimed. "I haven't been in a monkey suit in…in…, well, I can't remember. I can't stand the things." He rubbed around his neck as if he was wearing a tight collared shirt and tie. "I will be a happy, audience participant," he told them brightly. He said he had received the invitation and would send back the confirmation.

Anne began talking to Bill about academia and Sylvia started to clear the table. The academic politics bored her to tears. Owen said he grew up with this kind of conversation and he participated on the fringe. Sylvia was so tired. She put the things in the dishwasher and made a pitcher of Bloody Mary's and took it into the table along with a beer for Bill. He gladly accepted.

Even with the food, the other Bloody Mary hit Sylvia hard. She had a hard time keeping her eyes open.

"Would you excuse me?" she told the group? She kissed Owen and gave Bill a one-armed hug. "Thanks for cooking brunch," she told Anne. "It was yummy."

"She's exhausted, poor girl," Sylvia thought she heard Anne, in a stage whisper.

She was exhausted. Sylvia went upstairs and lay on the bed.
What she thought was only a couple of minutes, turned out to be
hours. She woke up briefly when Owen asked if she wanted dinner. She mumbled 'no' and only wanted to go back to sleep, but
he insisted on pulling off her dress and tucking her in bed. Percy
came up a bit later and she felt the comforting weight of the dog
against her legs. Sylvia didn't remember Owen coming to bed.
She slept like a baby.

CHAPTER TWENTY-THREE

*"Life is not a problem to be solved, but a reality
to be experienced."*

— SONJE KIERKEGAARD

Sylvia woke the next day feeling a million times better. Sylvia gave Percy a resounding smooch on the top of his head when he put his nose in her hand in the morning. The alarm was about to go off and she silenced it before it woke Owen. She took Percy out through the French doors in the living room and had him gambol, do his business on the front lawn while she made coffee. Being able to come out on the deck in her nightgown in the early morning was an incredible luxury in the summer. Sylvia appreciated the time, and the moment as she sipped from her steaming cup. It was still warm and humid. Sylvia knew thunderstorms were predicted in the evening. Percy was panting after a few minutes of play, leaping to catch the small insects that flew up from the grass.

The grass. She would need to mow it very soon. She had become used to Owen doing the job. Today was the day Anne was taking him to the doctor to look at his wound. She wished she could go, but she had missed so much time with the emergency last week. She wanted to save her vacation for their honeymoon.

Percy ran himself out and came onto the deck. Sylvia settled in an Adirondack chair and looked out over the water. A bald eagle sat in Kim's tree and stared at the bay while blue heron flew in to stalk the water at the shoreline. She heard the newspaper lady zip through the neighborhood at a speed faster than she was supposed to and heard the occasional slap of a newspaper hitting the ground. Songbirds twittered from the bushes and the grove next to the house. Percy sat quietly beside her. Sylvia was at peace. This time of the morning was almost like a meditation. Its subtle perfection entirely filled her. She sighed in contentment as she sipped her coffee and relished the quietude.

Sylvia went inside and made a second cup of coffee, looking at the time. She was running late. Percy climbed into bed with Owen as she dressed for her workday. She didn't take time for breakfast but instead promised herself a drive-thru sandwich. Rushing out to the car, Sylvia stopped. Her front tire was flat! Really flat! What had happened?

"Shit!" she said involuntarily, using the swear word she seldom used. "Shit!" she said again and she stomped her foot. She went to find the passenger side front tire was flat as well. "Shit!" she said a third time.

She ran back inside and up the stairs. She shook Owen gently and called his name.

"Owen!" she hissed. "Owen! Wake up!"

He rolled over and opened his eyes. "Hi," he said sleepily and reached for her.

Carefully she moved his hand. "No, Owen," she said succinctly. "Listen, my two front tires are flat!" Hysteria now edged her voice. "I need to take your car to work. I need you to call someone today to get it fixed."

Owen was awake now. "Tires?" he asked. "That's weird."

"I'll say. I don't remember running over anything. Sorry to have woken you, but I needed you to know and I need your keys," she told him.

He pointed to the bureau where his keys were in a small, carved wooden holder. What had Owen called it? A valet tray, she remembered.

"Thanks," she whispered and gave him a swift kiss.

Owen turned over and fell asleep again almost immediately. Percy had only cracked one eye open. He nuzzled her briefly and she gave him a pat and a kiss before going back down the stairs.

Owen's car was in the garage. She opened it and backed it out carefully. His was a standard transmission. She knew how to drive one, but, after driving an automatic for a long time, she jerked a little. She didn't want to hurt his car. After a rough start, she got the hang of pushing in the clutch and changing gears by the time she left the neighborhood.

She was only a couple of minutes late to work. Sylvia explained to Mr. Carter and Carol what had happened. Carol looked worried.

"You don't usually have this much vandalism in Bayside, do you?" Carol asked Sylvia.

"It's usually seasonal," Sylvia told her. "Likely, teenagers getting their kicks. But, I'm pretty upset about this little trick, I can tell you."

"I told Joe about the mailbox. He agreed with you that it was kids," Carol said. "I'm just going to text him about the tire thing," she told Sylvia.

"Okay," Sylvia said. "Thanks. Owen and Anne are there now. They have a late morning doctor's appointment. Gosh, I hope

Anne's car is okay. I never checked. Owen's car was in the garage and that's the one I took."

Her day didn't go from bad to worse, but it was challenging. The Board of Directors liked her idea of the teacher grant but were balking at the idea of two dinners for the educators. Sylvia thought this was silly, but she was able to get prices from caterers and sample menus for the board to make a decision. It took her the entire day and she was frustrated and tired when she left.

It was one of those days that if Carol had breathed the word 'happy hour,' Sylvia would have jumped at the chance. But, Carol was in her happy place of moving in with Joe. She hummed to herself, most of the day, oblivious to the carnage from the Board of Directors. Mr. Carter had been busy with other meetings, so Sylvia had to handle this on her own, and she did. She was happy to climb into Owen's car at the end of the day and head home.

She had promised Owen and Anne she would pick up Chinese food on the way home. She had called in the order from the office and it only took moments, once she arrived at the restaurant. Owen's car was filled with savory smells and her stomach rumbled.

Shiny, new tires graced her car, she noticed, when she pulled into the driveway. Percy, hearing Owen's car, started barking his happy bark. Anne let him out the door to greet her. She claimed Percy as her first grandchild and she smiled fondly at his antics. She was definitely spoiling him while she was here, giving him a beef bone on a nightly basis. He happily chewed away and now bones littered the house.

Once again they ate on the deck. When they were nearly finished with dinner, Joe and Carol surprised them. Percy had barked and wagged his tail happily when Carol's car pulled in.

"Hi!" Sylvia greeted them. She stood up to give them both a hug. "Come and sit. I'll get you a couple of beers."

Joe and Carol sat at the table. They all sat and sipped at their drinks, making small talk for a while.

"It's lovely to see you, but what brings you here?" Sylvia asked.

Carol looked guilty. "I told Joe about your tires," she said, "and he's a little worried."

Joe had his 'cop face' on. He had shaken his head before he said, "Sylvia, you have a way of begging trouble. The mailbox was one thing, but I'm a little concerned that you've had this second incident. No one in the neighborhood has reported any other vandalism. Do you know if other neighbors were hit with this?"

Sylvia shook her head. "Not that I know of."

Anne spoke up, "The tire repair people caused a stir in the neighborhood. No one else had their tires slashed."

Carol looked at Joe. Joe put his hand on her knee.

"So, what's going on?" Joe asked them.

"Nothing that we know of," Owen told Joe. "We haven't heard from the police or Coast Guard about the shooting in Worton Creek. Jon said it would likely be awhile. They didn't stick around, nor did we, after I was shot. I don't think they know who we are."

Joe nodded. "I think I'll put a couple of feelers out," he told them, "for everyone's peace of mind."

"Now you're getting me a little worried," Sylvia said.

"Me too," Anne added.

"I think Tony has some clout, even from prison. He would be my main cause of worry. And, I think he's crazy enough to try something. Remember the elaborate schemes and the dirtbags he hired last year when he murdered Joyce *and* has similar plans for you, Sylvia," Joe added.

"What's that old saying," Carol intoned, "better safe, than sorry?"

Sylvia shivered at the thought that Tony might try something. She wouldn't be overly surprised. His obsession was indeed irrational. If he got wind of the engagement and wedding…well, it could be something that would put him over the edge. She voiced those fears out loud. Joe nodded.

"We really don't have the resources to have a protection detail to be with you without more concrete information. I'll make sure a car comes through on a regular basis. That might deter whoever is doing this. And, I'll check out what's going on with Mr. Capaselli," Joe assured her.

"Thanks, Joe," Sylvia said. "You're wonderful."

They left a few minutes later. Percy needed to be walked.

"Are you up for a little walk?" Sylvia asked Owen. "I think I'm a little spooked."

He nodded and said, "Let's go."

"How did your doctor's appointment go today?" she asked.

"Mmm," Owen grumbled, "they called to reschedule it for Thursday."

"Sorry," Sylvia said. "I know you want to get back to work."

They walked on in the gathering twilight. The air was getting heavier and brief, yet intense bouts of little breezes turned the leaves so that you could see their backs. Whitecaps were beginning to form on the bay.

"Hurry, Percy," Sylvia told the dog. "I think that storm is coming up."

They continued their walk toward the marina and passed by Tony's house. It was a large, dark, shadowy lump on the shoreline. Sylvia shivered.

"Do you think it's Tony sending someone to harass us?" Sylvia asked Owen, her voice barely above a whisper.

Owen ran his good hand through his hair before he answered, "I really don't know," he said, "but, if Joe thinks it's a possibility, I believe him. Tony is really, really delusional."

"You don't need to tell me twice," Sylvia replied drily.

Lightning flashed in the distance and a few seconds later, they heard thunder.

"C'mon, Percy," Owen ordered, "let's turn around and go home."

They hurried back to the house with the storm on their heels. The clouds were getting darker and darker over the water and the wind had picked up more. Sylvia gave a sigh of relief when they were all inside safe and sound.

Anne rushed into the kitchen, "I'm so glad you're back," she cried. "I was worried when I saw the lightning and heard the thunder. The television is sending out that horrible alert sound about a severe thunderstorm."

"Then we need to batten down the hatches," Owen told his mother.

"I'll work on the windows upstairs," Sylvia told them. "Anne, if you can get the ones down here, it would be appreciated." She glared at Owen, "No and no!" she ordered him. "You can't do anything to help with that shoulder injury. We can handle it."

"Hen-pecked and not even married yet," he teased her.

She swatted him on the bottom before heading upstairs.

"Promises, promises," she heard him mutter so that only she could hear as she passed him. She shot him a smile and winked at him.

"Maybe," she teased. "Maybe when you're all better."

Sylvia scooted up the stairs before he could reply.

The storm hit with full force. Wind and rain lashed the neighborhood. Lightning lit the sky like it was daytime. When the lightning blazed and the thunder struck immediately, Sylvia knew the storm was right above them. Percy crawled low to be close to them. They heard another loud crack, and the lights went out. The storm raged directly above them.

"Never fear," Owen said, "the trusty cell phone light is here."

Sylvia used his cell phone to help her dig for candles and matches in the drawers under the bookshelves. Some candles were already on the dining room table and she lit those as well. They sat in the living room and looked out at the riotous, uninhibited waves crashing against the shoreline when the lightning lit up the sky. Small bits of branches and leaves struck the window. They heard the loud crack of a larger branch that hit the roof.

They sat, while the storm raged, conversing about whether or not the mailbox incident or slashed tires could have been due to Tony Capaselli hiring more goons to do his dirty work. Owen was insistent it was. Sylvia was confused. Anne had no idea as she had only heard portions of the entire tale with Tony. Sylvia was already weary of the talk. Tony was someone she definitely did not want to think about.

The storm abated. It moved on. Sylvia found herself counting the seconds between the lightning and the thunder. The electricity returned. Each, in turn, breathed a sigh of relief. Even Percy.

"After that excitement, I think I'm ready for bed and an excellent book," Anne commented.

"Sounds like a plan," Sylvia said.

"I'm restless," Owen told them. "I'll be up in a few minutes."

"Will you be all right?" Sylvia asked him.

"I'll be okay," he told her. "I'm going to check my email and play a game or something."

"Okay," Sylvia said. "Good night."

"Cabin fever," Anne whispered to Sylvia as they went upstairs. "I'll need to find something for him to do to distract him until this doctor's appointment."

"I'll think about it too. Good night, Anne," Sylvia told her future mother-in-law.

Percy followed Sylvia into the bedroom and promptly jumped up on the bed and turned three circles before settling down.

"Leave some room for us, boy," Sylvia told him.

His head was between his paws. He just looked at her with his big eyes. He blinked in a doggy wink.

CHAPTER TWENTY-FOUR

*"In the end, it's not the years in your life that count. It's
the life in your years."*

— ABRAHAM LINCOLN

The doctor grudgingly gave Owen clearance to return to work the next week. Owen had to promise to follow directions, like not lifting anything over five pounds, and taking it easy. Owen was thrilled. He had Anne pick up a bottle of Champagne to greet Sylvia with when she returned home from work on Thursday. After the doctor's appointment, he had spent the afternoon emailing and talking with the people in his lab.

Carol had talked Sylvia into a girls' afternoon on Sunday. Sylvia mentioned her mom was coming down but knew from Anne that they were going on a shopping spree for 'mother–of-the-bride' dresses. Carol kept telling her 'not to worry' that she would 'handle' everything, so Sylvia wondered what they would be doing. Carol had talked recently, about finding local wines for the wedding and suggested they go on a wine tour in southern Pennsylvania. Carol rattled off the names of several wineries in the local vicinity. Sylvia was intrigued, and it would be a fun afternoon.

Mary and Anne left for their shopping expedition late on Sunday morning. They giggled like two schoolgirls and talked, what seemed to Sylvia, very loudly about the colors they were considering. Carol came to pick up Sylvia a short time later, promising her good food and good wine on their winery tour. Owen gave her a kiss goodbye and said he was going to nap and catch up on rest before he went back to work on Monday. And so they went.

It was a beautiful summer's day. Carol kept up a lively conversation about Joe's house and their plans for renovations, including the picket fence he told Sylvia about a year ago. Carol had plans for a large cottage garden in front of the house.

"Now, who's acting like an old, married couple," teased Sylvia.

Carol blushed a little, but grinned at Sylvia, "I know, I know. Ain't life grand?" She shot Sylvia a dazzling smile.

They drove through the rolling hills of southern Pennsylvania, slowed down a few times by Amish buggies. Sylvia loved the old fieldstone and brick farmhouses along the way.

"If I didn't adore Bayside," she told Carol, "I wouldn't mind restoring one of these."

"They are beautiful," Carol agreed before telling her, "By the way, we're starting at one of the wineries furthest away. We're heading to their tasting room in West Chester. They have an event going at the Vineyard today. A wedding, I think. Wouldn't that be cool to be married in the vines?" Carol asked rhetorically.

"Yes," agreed Sylvia, "but, I think you and Joe would rather be married at a brewery. I wonder if Yuengling, Iron Hill or Dogfish Head are starting events like that."

Carol laughed. "That would be a lot of fun!"

"I haven't been to West Chester in years," Sylvia remarked. "I just remember a charming, little town, with brick sidewalks and cute boutiques."

"I haven't a clue," Carol admitted. "That's why I'm glad I now have a GPS app that will tell me how to get there."

They continued to chat about work gossip, the upcoming wedding, Joe's house, men and assorted, sundry things. When they finally got to West Chester, Carol told Sylvia to check around for parking. They found a space, about a block away from the winery's tasting room.

"Ooh, hold on," Carol told Sylvia, "I promised Joe I would text him when we got here."

"Really?" Sylvia asked, surprised.

Carol typed on her phone, somewhat frantically, Sylvia thought.

"Oh, and I forgot to tell you, this place is dog-friendly. They have a 'yappy hour' where you can bring your dog and drink wine. You and Owen can come and bring Percy!" Carol told her.

"Cool," Sylvia said. "That might be a fun evening."

They walked down the street, peering at some of the boutiques along the way. Sylvia's stomach grumbled and she saw a Mexican restaurant and an Irish bar close by.

"You said they had some food, right?" Sylvia asked.

"Oh, yeah," Carol told her distractedly. "And, if you're still hungry we can get a late lunch before we head to the next one."

"A very late lunch," Sylvia said drily.

"Don't worry," Carol told her. "Here we are."

Carol opened the door on the storefront advertised as a tasting room.

"After you," Carol told Sylvia.

Sylvia walked in, her eyes tried to adjust from the bright sunlight outside to the darkened room. She was blinded at first and only heard some movement and then a chorus of "Surprise!"

As her eyes are adjusted, she saw her mom, Anne, Marian, Gwen, Claire, Maureen, Kim and some friends from Thurmont and from college. She was stunned.

"We did it!" Carol crowed. "She had *no* idea!"

Everyone gathered around Sylvia to say hello and chat a few minutes before Carol introduced her to the vintner. The Vintner, Margaret, was kind but had a no-nonsense attitude. She asked everyone to sit quietly, told everyone a brief history of the vineyard, and the types of wine they would be tasting. They enjoyed tasting different whites and reds and ended with dessert wines. Afterward, a caterer brought cheeses, fruit, crackers and assorted small sandwiches to each table. A lovely tower of scrumptious cupcakes decorated the gift table. Cell phone cameras snapped candid photos. The tasting room personnel kept the wine flowing. Sylvia still could not believe that Gwen and Carol had pulled off the surprise so well.

Gwen called Sylvia over to a chair near a table stacked with gifts. She had a tablet and pen to log the gifts and givers as Sylvia opened gifts. Carol took the bows to create the bow bouquet Sylvia would use at the wedding rehearsal.

Everyone seemed to enjoy themselves and Amber, Carol's mom, had made wine cork keychains and wine charms to add to a gift bag with a heart shaped wine stopper for each of the guests. Amber blushed when Carol announced her mom had made the favors. Everyone applauded politely. The winery generously offered discount coupons and a calendar of events.

Claire sidled up to Sylvia and whispered, "We thought the wine tasting would be more fun than those bridal shower games."

Sylvia laughed at this and nodded in agreement. Her mother and Anne were giddy with delight over the surprise. They had definitely bonded during the stress and aftermath of the shooting.

Anne approached her, "Congratulations, Syl," she told her future daughter-in-law, "I'm going to head home – back to Millersville."

"Oh! Anne!" Sylvia exclaimed and turned to give her a hug, "Thank you for everything! You have been amazing! And, thank you for your wonderful gift."

Anne and Phil had given Sylvia and Owen a stay at The Old Brick Inn, in St. Michael's, Maryland. She had explained that they might like a 'real' bed while they were boating on their honeymoon. Anne gave her a hug and told Sylvia she would see her soon. Her mother left shortly after that, being fairly close to her home in suburban Philadelphia. The other guests were leaving in small groups, congratulating Sylvia again and saying goodbye. Marian stayed as Gwen and Claire had stayed with her as part of the surprise. Maureen stayed a bit longer too. Sylvia thought she looked happier than she had in weeks. She squeezed Sylvia's hand.

"Good things," Maureen stated. "Happy things. This is good."

"We need to catch up," Sylvia told her.

Maureen nodded. "Soon," she said. "Soon."

"Please thank Skip for taking such good care of the True Love," Sylvia told her. "Owen was a basket case about his baby."

Maureen smiled at this. "Typical," she said, laughing. "I will pass on the message."

"Are things returning to normal at the marina?" Sylvia asked.

Maureen shrugged. "I don't know," she said. "I can't explain my trepidation. It's still bothering me that they can't find George's killer. From what I understand, it's pretty normal to take several months."

"How's business?" Sylvia asked her.

"Okay," Maureen said gravely, "It dropped drastically after the murder and has returned to a low normal." She shrugged. "People are spooked. I don't blame them. I feel the same way."

Carol interrupted them, "Hey, Bride-to-be, we need to begin packing up. Sorry," she said as she turned to Maureen.

"Did you drive up on your own?" Sylvia asked Maureen.

"No, I came with Kim. Here she comes," Maureen nodded in Kim's direction.

Kim came over and gave Sylvia a hug, congratulating her.

"I just love the pottery you gave us," Sylvia told her. "Thank you. It fits the theme of the wedding."

Kim had given Sylvia lovely serving pieces with leaf patterns on them.

Kim smiled, "I'm so glad. They seemed to fit you in some way," she pondered as she answered Sylvia.

Maureen and Kim left for Bayside. Kim said she would be around for a couple of days to take advantage of the beautiful weather. She promised to come over for a glass of wine at sunset tomorrow. Claire, Gwen, and Marian helped Carol gather the gifts and take care of things with the tasting room. Sylvia thanked the tasting room's hostess, Margaret, and told her she and Owen would be back sometime for the 'yappy hour' with Percy.

Claire ran over to Sylvia and whispered excitedly in her ear, "Marian is the coolest, ever!" she told her. "Wow! Her house! Jon! Wow!"

Sylvia laughed delightedly at Claire's enthusiasm. "I know," Sylvia said. "She and Jon are pretty amazing."

"You're not kidding!" Claire expostulated as she gave Sylvia a quick kiss on the cheek, "Got to run, my bus is leaving."

Gwen, Marian, and Claire headed towards their car, laden with bottles of wine. Sylvia had a brief conversation with Gwen and was glad she was feeling better from her earlier morning sickness. Gwen wore the pregnancy glow well. Sylvia noticed Gwen's aura had a second layer. Was that the baby? Carol motioned to her from the door that it was time to go.

"You guys are pretty amazing," Sylvia told Carol. "I never dreamed you were throwing me a shower today."

"I know," Carol said smugly.

They discussed some of the gifts that Sylvia had received. Sylvia had registered, under duress from Mary, Anne, Marian, Gwen, and Carol, for several items. She and Owen had registered for new towels, bed linens, and new cookware. They had received many of the wished for items.

"I'll need to get busy this week and write thank you cards," Sylvia mentioned.

"Do four or five thank you cards a night and you'll get them done in a flash," Carol suggested. "And by the way, Gwen and I picked up thank you cards that match the invitations. Owen has them for you."

"You two are definitely my BFF's!" Sylvia said. "You two are amazing!"

CHAPTER TWENTY-FIVE

"The truth is you don't know what is going to happen tomorrow. Life is a crazy ride, and nothing is guaranteed."

— EMINEM

Sylvia accused Owen of giving her the bum's rush to get out of bed quickly on Monday morning. He was very anxious to return to work. He, in turn, promised her an extra-large coffee and a breakfast sandwich if she hurried.

Owen had taken Percy on a very short walk. He looked hopefully at Sylvia when she came downstairs.

"Sorry, Percy," Sylvia apologized to the dog. "Daddy wants an early start. And, you'll be all alone again for the first time in weeks. Poor baby!"

She reached into the cupboard for an extra dog treat. Percy took the treat gently from her hand and went to put it near the

French doors. When he came back to the kitchen, Owen was urging Sylvia out the door, but she took a second to give Percy a smooch on his pouf.

As promised, they went through a drive-thru on the way to work. Owen kissed her swiftly outside her office and promised to email her about meeting for lunch.

Sylvia was hard at work on the late summer newsletter for Thurmont. She was trying to coerce and cajole the people from research and development into giving her a hint on upcoming products. She wanted to carefully suggest in the newsletter about new products for the consumer. They were deliberating with her when Carol came to the office door. She had a funny look on her face.

"Sylvia, you need to take the call on line one," she said gravely.

"I'll be finished in a minute, can I call them back?" she asked Carol.

"No," Carol was insistent. "You need to take the call *now!*"

"Okay, okay," Sylvia said. She huffed and got back on the phone with the research and development team.

"Do you think you could think about it, and let me know by tomorrow?" Sylvia asked them. "I'll call you back then," she said sweetly after saying 'thank you.'

"What's wrong, Carol?" Sylvia asked, puzzled.

Carol didn't answer but shook her head while Sylvia pressed line one on the phone console.

"Sylvia Ash here," she answered, "How can I help you?"

Sylvia recognized Kim's voice with its edge of hysteria, "Sylvia! Sylvia! You need to come home now!"

"What's going on, Kim? What's wrong? Is Percy all right?" Sylvia asked, getting worried and a little scared between Kim's hysteria and Carol's frozen, inscrutable countenance at the doorframe.

"Your house! No! It's your garage! It's on fire! Oh my God! Oh my God!" Kim was hysterical.

"Kim! Kim!" Sylvia now shouted into the phone, "Did you call the fire department?"

"Yes!" Kim told her, "They're coming down the road right now. Come home, please!" Kim pleaded.

"I'll get Owen and be right there," Sylvia told her neighbor.

Sylvia hung up and she looked up at Carol. "I can't believe it! Our garage is on fire!" and talking more to herself than to Carol, Sylvia gathered her purse and a few belongings. "Owen! I need to get him."

"I'll call him, tell him what happened and to meet you at the car right away," Carol told her, "and I'll call Joe."

Carol must have called Owen immediately because Sylvia saw him walking swiftly down the hallway when she entered the bright, sunlit Thurmont lobby. She waited for him anxiously.

"I can't believe this," Owen muttered. He took her by the elbow, and they walked swiftly to the car.

"Me either," Sylvia said.

Sylvia never drove so fast in her life, trying to get home as quickly as possible. As she drove through the trees towards Bayside, she could see a large plume of smoke rising down by the water. Two firetrucks, with lights ablaze, were at their house.

"Oh, not the house, please! Percy, please let Percy be all right!" she begged the Universe.

She pulled swiftly into the open space in the community and jumped out of the car. She put her hands over her face for a moment and then heard Percy's wild barking.

"Oh, God!" she cried. "Percy!" she called to him. "Percy, I'm coming!"

A fireman detained her. "I need to get to my dog!" she cried. "He's in the house!"

"He's safe," the fireman told her. "You need to wait. We need to make sure this fire is under control."

Owen stood with her and put his good arm around her. Kim saw her and hurried over. The police and the fire marshal pulled up. Joe was in one of the black and white's.

"Oh, Joe!" Sylvia cried, and she threw herself into him. "Why?"

He gave her a comforting hug and patted her back. "When they get this under control, we can investigate. That's this gentleman's job," he told Sylvia and Owen, nodding to a man who had come near their little group. He pulled Sylvia gently from his arms to turn her towards the gentleman.

"Sylvia and Owen, meet Ned Polk, our fire marshal," Joe introduced them.

Mr. Polk reached out to shake their hands. "I have some questions," he said.

"Why don't you come over to my place next door," Kim offered. "I have tea and coffee, hot or iced," she suggested.

Mr. Polk nodded. Kim led them to her kitchen. She had clearly been at work in her studio. She was wearing old black shorts and a t-shirt that were spattered with clay and had dots of glaze colors on them.

They sat at Kim's table. Her home was tiny. There was a relatively small great room that wasn't much larger than an efficiency apartment. It was whitewashed pine paneling with a wall of windows that looked out over the bay. It was an eclectic mix of art and antiques. Craig and Kim had a small, loft bedroom above the kitchen. Sturdy wooden stairs led up to the loft. The previous owners had a guest house in the garage, but Craig had turned that into a studio for Kim. Kim brought out pitchers of iced coffee, iced tea, cream, sugar and lemon.

"Who called in the fire?" Mr. Polk asked the group.

"That would be me," Kim said. "I was in my studio and I heard Percy barking. I had smelled some smoke earlier, but it isn't unusual for the residents to burn some of the driftwood that washes up on the beach, so I wasn't worried, until I heard Percy, and I knew something was wrong."

"What did you see when you went to look?" he asked Kim.

"Smoke and some flames, coming from the garage. I called 911 immediately, and then I called Sylvia at the office," Kim said.

They heard a small explosion. Sylvia put her hands over her face. She wanted to get up to see, but Owen and Joe put a hand on her.

"I don't think you want to look," Owen said.

"What is in the garage?" Mr. Polk asked Owen and Sylvia.

"Garage stuff," Sylvia said.

"Tools, lawn mower, gasoline and," Owen said acerbically, "my car."

Mr. Polk wrote it all down. "We'll need a list," he told them, "as comprehensive as possible. Also, did you have greasy rags lying around?"

They both shook their heads.

Mr. Polk also asked, "Do you know if someone had sour grapes with you two? Is there a chance this is arson?

Sylvia and Owen looked at each other and then they looked at Joe.

Joe cleared his throat and answered for them, "Sylvia and Owen have been having some petty crimes committed against them. Their mailbox was smashed and tires slashed. Things are escalating. We're going to be opening an investigation. I have a few ideas," he told Ned.

"I also owe you two an apology," Joe told Sylvia and Owen. "Things got crazy in the office, and I wasn't able to check out the Tony connection."

"It's okay, Joe. This isn't your fault," Owen said.

"When can I check on Percy, our dog?" Sylvia asked Mr. Polk anxiously.

"I'll check," Mr. Polk said and he stood and went outside.

He came back to Kim's house moments later.

"You can go to your house," he told Sylvia and Owen. "Go around the front."

Sylvia rushed out of Kim's house. A group of neighbors had gathered in the open area, close to where Sylvia, Joe, and Mr. Polk had parked their cars. Sylvia ignored them and rushed to the house. Owen followed with Kim.

"Uh, oh," Kim intoned, "the poison-ivy vine is beginning. The rumor mill will be running rampant. I'll go see if I can spray a little Round-Up on it."

Owen nodded and continued to follow Sylvia to the house. She was inside the front door, kneeling on the floor and crying into the big, standard poodle's fur.

Percy had panicked with the fire and had scratched the door to pieces. Sylvia didn't care. They could get it repaired.

"We should go look at the damage," Owen told Sylvia quietly. He brushed some hair stuck to her cheek from her tears. He kissed her gently above her ear.

Sylvia nodded and got up slowly. She felt as though she was a hundred years old. She went out to the kitchen to get Percy's leash. She caught a glimpse of the garage, or what was left of it, through the windows in the kitchen door. What had been the garage was only a heap of smoking rubble. She felt sick. When she didn't come back right away, Owen came out to the kitchen.

"Come on," he said gently.

They went outside to look at the garage. It was a heap of burned wood over what was left of Owen's car and the small things inside. Sylvia just stood, shaking her head.

"I know you wanted a new car," she said faintly to Owen so that only he could hear.

Owen chuckled and shook his head. "You know, you're right," he said. "It's always funny how things work out. I'm not sure I like this way, though."

Joe joined them. "I'm so sorry," he said to Owen and Sylvia and a serious note entered his voice as he continued, "I promise you, I will check out if Mr. Capaselli has *anything* to do with this. I need to go, but when this cools down, a team will be out to investigate." He turned to Sylvia, "I'll call Carol. You probably have a bunch of calls to make. The firemen will clear up here. We'll be sending a black and white to keep an eye on the area and shoo off any curiosity seekers," he told them and nodded to the knot of neighbors still hanging out in the green, open space.

Joe left them and walked over to the neighbors. Sylvia and Owen stood and looked at the smoldering rubble of what used to be the garage. They went inside. Owen called his parents and Sylvia's mom, Mary. Sylvia called the house insurance company and gave them as much information as she could. She also called the local carpenter and explained about the door. Then she called Marian.

"Hi Marian," Sylvia began.

"What's wrong, dear?" Marian asked, "I can hear it in your voice."

"The rosemary didn't work," Sylvia told her. "We should have planted some around the garage."

"What?" Marian asked, "What are you talking about?"

Sylvia reminded Marian that she had planted rosemary for protection a little more than a week ago. She explained to Marian what had happened to the garage.

"Oh, my!" Marian exclaimed, "What do you need, Sylvia? Do you and Owen need to stay here?"

"No, no thank you, Marian," Sylvia told her, a sad note in her voice. "The house is okay. Just more stuff to juggle." Sylvia sighed deeply.

Numb, Sylvia walked to the hammock, swinging gently in a breeze from the water. She sat in it wearily, too tired and numb to cry. The wind from the water kept some of the acrid smell of the burnt building away. The question 'why' kept playing over and over in her head. Was Tony behind all of this? She asked herself again and again.

The rustle of leaves jerked her to attention when the Green Man stood before her.

She put her question to him, "why?" she asked quietly.

The Green Man put his hands of living wood on her shoulders. He looked at her with concern.

"I know it's selfish," she said, "but, what have I done in this life or in past lives, if there are any, to deserve all of this?" she asked.

"You haven't *done* anything," the Green Man told her gently in his deep, baritone voice. His voice almost sounded like a scolding.

Sylvia interrupted him, "Well, *why*, do bad things keep happening? I wish and try so hard to be a good person, consciously *attempt* to be a good person. From my perspective, these things have been pretty bad!"

The Green Man's voice had a soothing quality, "There will always be good and bad. Things are always in a balance. There's a universal law of cause and effect. But, as I have said to you before, the better, the more hope, the more joy you can bring into the world, the more of the evil stuff, as you say, will be squelched. You," he explained, "and all of humanity, co-creates together."

"I don't know anymore," Sylvia said in weary frustration. "I'm so very tired of all of this."

The Green Man kissed her gently on both eyelids. It was like when she was in Chestertown, and she saw the brilliant connectedness between everything. She gasped in awe, but she was still frustrated.

"I can't see the future," he told Sylvia, "that's not part of my gift. I am here to help keep the balance of this beautiful, living earth and its environs. We are all manifestations of the same thing. Our core spirit essence is represented by the different manifestations and their states at any given moment."

"Does that reach beyond the earth and into space?" Sylvia asked.

He smiled at this and said, "through space, through time, but more on that another time," before he disappeared with another rustle of the leaves on his leafy brocade.

CHAPTER TWENTY-SIX

"Life is a song - sing it. Life is a game - play it. Life is a challenge - meet it. Life is a dream - realize it. Life is a sacrifice - offer it. Life is love - enjoy it."

— SAI BABA

Sylvia walked back to the house, slowly. Owen was in the study, watching something on television. Percy was at his feet. Both looked up when she came into the room.

"Are you okay?" Owen asked her.

"I will be, I think," Sylvia told him.

"I would have come down to the hammock, but you looked like you wanted to be alone," Owen said. "And, I didn't think this," he hitched his head to his injured side, "could take the hammock."

"How are you doing?" Sylvia asked, "Have you talked to the insurance company about your car?"

"I'll be okay. I'm angry, I think," he said and then with a growl, continued, "I'm *furious* at Tony Capaselli!"

"I know, I know," Sylvia said. She went to Owen and gave him a light kiss on the lips. "What kind of car do you think you'll be getting?"

"No idea," he told her, "yet."

Sylvia sat, thinking about nothing and not really paying attention to the television. The doorbell rang at the back door. Percy began to bark frantically. Puzzled, Sylvia and Owen looked at each other. Sylvia stood up. At the back door was a pizza delivery guy. Sylvia looked at him.

"But, we didn't order anything!" she told the pizza guy.

"It's got your address, lady. And, it's been paid for," he told her. "Here, happy dinner." He winked at her.

Owen had come to the door, carefully shutting it before Percy had a chance to escape. He was whining.

"What's up?" he asked Sylvia.

"Apparently, someone sent us dinner," Sylvia said, taking a couple of pizzas and a huge paper bag from the delivery man.

"Good night," the delivery guy said, and he got into his car with its lighted sign.

"I wonder who..." Sylvia began.

"Wonder no more," Kim said, coming across the yard with a six-pack of beer and a large bottle of wine in her hand.

"Thanks!" Owen said.

"Yes, thanks," Sylvia told her. "I hadn't even thought of dinner."

"I wondered," Kim said. "If this had happened to me, I think I would have returned to bed to wake up later to see if it was all a dream. By the way, there's enough for the guys in the black and white, too." She nodded in their direction.

"Owen, hand me one of those pizzas," Kim said.

He did so and she took it to the two policemen in the car. They grinned in appreciation. Sylvia ran inside for extra napkins, bottles of water and some paper plates that she ran out to the car.

"Let us know if you need anything," Sylvia told them.

"Yes, ma'am," they returned.

Sylvia, Owen, and Kim settled onto the deck. Sylvia realized she had skipped lunch and was famished. Owen was too. They talked about everything, except the fire, even though a wisp of wind would bring acrid smoke around the corner.

"Are you going to work tomorrow?" Kim asked.

"Have to," they both replied at once.

"We've missed so much time," Sylvia said, "we need to work every second so we have a few hours as a honeymoon!"

"I'll be around," Kim said, "if you need anything."

"And, I think the Black and White will be here as well," Sylvia added.

"I might need to stay home an afternoon or two when the carpenter comes to repair the door," Sylvia said.

"Or Marian and Jon could come over then," Owen offered, "or maybe one of the moms can come down."

"Marian and Jon are supposed to be going on another trip," Sylvia reminded him, "but, I can't remember where or when, right now."

"Oh, yeah," Owen said.

Kim cleared her throat, "and, my friends, you can call me too. I'll be happy to help out if you need me."

"Thank you so much, Kim," Sylvia told her again.

"It's not a problem," Kim told them. She picked up her paper plate and napkins. "I'm going to bid you good night," she said.

CHAPTER TWENTY-SEVEN

*"Do not dwell in the past, do not dream of the future,
concentrate the mind on the present moment."*

— BUDDHA

Sylvia didn't have much time to think in the next couple weeks. She was focusing on work, and juggling the last few plans for the wedding, as well as handling the repair of the garage and the door. She wanted the garage to be a re-creation of what had been there, but with some of the modern conveniences and added storage. Fortunately, pictures of the property gave the builder an idea of what she wanted. His schedule was full, but he said he would get it completed by mid–October.

It was August. Sylvia was beginning to feel the pinch of even more last minute details for the wedding. One evening, Joe dropped by with Carol in tow. He had his 'cop face' on. They settled on the couch in the living room.

"This isn't about the wedding, is it?" Sylvia asked carefully.

"No," Joe and Carol said together.

"And, are you two going to elope?" Owen asked.

"No!" Carol cried, not realizing at first, that Owen was teasing. She blushed.

"I have some good news and some bad news, with regards to the investigations," Joe told Sylvia and Owen. "The good news is that we caught George's murderers."

"What? Who? Who is it? Who are they?" Sylvia asked.

"Fish poachers," Joe told them, "It was a ring of fish poachers. Their last haul was over three tons of striped bass. They've been running the ring through various marinas, using extortion with some fishermen and showing a violent side. George apparently caught wind of the ring. They killed him because he threatened to turn them in. They knew he would. They feel they didn't have a choice, but to end his life. As with most criminals, they don't think they'll get caught. They thought it was a perfect crime. They moved on to another marina."

"Poor George," Sylvia said sadly, her eyes tearing.

Owen came and sat beside her and took her hand in his. He gave it a squeeze.

"Do Maureen and Skip know?" Owen asked.

Joe nodded, "Yes, I told them this afternoon, just before we came here. They are relieved the nightmare is nearly over."

"And, what's the bad news?" Owen queried.

"It's apparently *not* Tony Capaselli who has been stretching out his arm from prison to harass you," Joe said.

"Are you sure?" Sylvia insisted.

"As sure as I can be for the moment," Joe told them. "I'm still having him monitored pretty carefully in prison, but we cannot find any connection whatsoever."

"Then who?" Sylvia asked. "I don't think…"

"I was *sure* it was Tony," Owen interrupted vehemently.

"You and me both, bro," Joe said. "Now, we're back to square one."

"Shit!" Owen returned.

"My sentiments exactly," Joe told him.

"What about Mr. Headley?" Sylvia suggested. "He was pretty crazy too."

"I can check it out," Joe told her, "but, I don't think so. That's not what my gut is telling me."

"And, usually that's right," Carol smiled at Joe.

"It's right often enough," Joe admitted, "but, I still need to follow leads and get the job done right."

"Well, sorry to disturb you two, but I wanted you to know as soon as possible," Joe said and then he mentioned, "Bluegrass this weekend at a farm outside of town if you two are up for it."

"Sounds good," Owen said.

Joe and Carol left. Sylvia and Owen were alone.

Sylvia stood up and Owen held her. Percy, worried, circled around them.

"Now, what?" Sylvia murmured.

"I don't know," Owen told her honestly.

CHAPTER TWENTY-EIGHT

"Life isn't a matter of milestones, but of moments."

— ROSE KENNEDY

August. Sylvia was so busy, she thought her head might fly into a million pieces. Meeting her deadlines for work before the wedding and the wedding itself, were the prize, which Sylvia had her eye on. Owen was busy at work and looking forward to getting the True Love home. The vandalism stopped. The black and white left the neighborhood. Life seemed to be returning to normal.

The carpenter called and was finally able to fix the door. He was going to come and take off the door, take it to his workshop to sand it down and refinish the vintage door that graced the house. Sylvia offered to take off and make some calls to confirm things for the wedding. She drove Owen to work and returned home to wait for the carpenter.

He arrived just after ten in the morning. He brought a substitute door to take the place of the one needing repair. It wasn't pretty, but it fit and they could close and lock it. Sylvia told herself it would only be for a couple of weeks. The carpenter left and she and Percy went back inside.

The heat was building, but it wasn't humid. Sylvia turned on the whole, house fan, got a large glass of ice water and put on her lightest shorts and tank top. She sat in the study, trying to wrestle the paper tiger of wedding plans and the current bills. The shredder was making a grinding noise. She had jammed it with too many papers. It was hot and she pulled her hand away when she touched it. Annoyed, she pulled the plug. Percy was barking and barking and barking. She listened. It was an odd bark. She wondered why and started to get up out of her chair. She thought she heard a strange noise. It was like a pop. She thought she heard him yelp.

"Percy?" Sylvia called, "Percy? Where are you? What's going on?"

Sylvia stepped out of the study and saw Percy, lying in a puddle of his own blood in the hallway.

"Percy?" Sylvia cried, "Oh, Percy!"

Sylvia ran and knelt beside him. A thwack on her head made everything go black.

When Sylvia came to, there was duct tape over her mouth. Her hands and ankles were tied. She was seated with her knees in her face. She must have been sitting there awhile as her feet and legs were numb and sore. Sylvia was against the wall in the living room. She could see into the hallway where Percy lay. Tears blurred her eyes.

A man came into the room. "So, you're awake," he growled. "When's your old man coming home?"

Sylvia obviously couldn't answer him. The tape was on her mouth. He ripped it off quickly and she cried out in pain.

"Shut up!" he yelled at her and he slapped her across the cheek. Instantly, Sylvia was quiet.

"Well?" the man asked, "when's he coming home."

"He's, he's working late tonight," Sylvia lied. "I really don't know when he'll be home."

If she didn't pick him up, Owen would call. If she didn't answer, he would get worried. If he got worried, he might call Carol or Joe. Sylvia could only wish.

"Shit!" the man snarled.

Sylvia had thought Joe's eyes were cold when he was working on a case. They were nothing in comparison to this man's eyes. His were like chips of ice with dead shark pupils. His mere glance chilled Sylvia to her bones. Her stomach clenched tightly in response to his terrible gaze. Even worse, she could tell that he knew how she was feeling. He felt he was the hunter and she was his helpless prey. His mouth curled in an unattractive sneering smile. She had to look away. Fear filled every cell in her body. There was something more frightening about this man than Mr. Headly, Ed and Maureen Davenport, or even Tony Capaselli.

"I have to figure this out," he muttered, more to himself than to Sylvia, "Boss man wants both." He turned to Sylvia with an evil smile. "Well, we're just going to have to wait for him," he said in a low, menacing voice that sent more fear racing through Sylvia.

Sylvia was confused. Who was he? Why was he here? He was scary, but he was also odd. He smelled funny, almost like ammonia. He was sweating, profusely. Much, much more than needed, even on this hot, humid, summer's day. She wrinkled her nose.

"What are you starin' at?" he asked her.

Sylvia hesitated.

"Answer me!" he screamed at her and just stopped shy of hitting her again.

He was rail thin, almost emaciated. He seemed really, really nervous. She had heard of home invasions, but nothing like that had happened in this area, as far as she knew. She knew of some drug stings, through Joe, but North Bay and Bayside were still pretty nice places to live, without a lot of crimes. Or so she thought.

He leaned over her again. Sylvia saw bruises on his arms and it looked as though his skin was turning black on his fingers and his hands. It didn't look like dirt.

"Answer me," he growled, in a low and savage growl.

Frightened, Sylvia squeaked, "Why are you here? If you're robbing me, take anything you want!"

He sneered at her. "I'm not a thief," he told her, "But, thanks for the offer, anyway." He was jumpy and looked out the windows and at the door. "I'm here because you saw us. You could identify us. My boss doesn't like that."

"What are you talking about?" Sylvia said.

"You saw us!" he screamed, grabbing a fist full of her shirt and dragging her to her knees. His scream in her ear blocked her hearing for a minute. Her ears rang. He got her off balance and she slumped to her knees, nearly falling over.

"Where?" Sylvia said, completely puzzled.

"On that damn boat," he said.

Sylvia's eyes widened at this.

"Near Worton Creek?" she whispered.

"Now, you're getting it," he sneered at her.

"You're a drug smuggler? From Mexico?" she asked incredulously.

"Baby, I'm *not* from Mexico or Central America. Our stuff is purely homegrown," he told her, almost proudly.

She was naïve about drug use. The thought of heroin and the needles totally freaked her out. She really didn't know a lot about recreational drugs, other than the pot smoke that occasionally seeped out of one of the rooms in the dorm on campus.

He was sweating more now, and his pupils had dilated. He clutched at his chest as if he could slow down his heartbeat. She saw his pulse had increased and was throbbing in his neck. She wondered if he was going to have a heart attack.

"Flakka," he told her. "Better than PCP. Better than angel dust. You can eat it, vape it, smoke it, snort it, inject it. It's cool, baby. And, it turns me into Superman! I am invincible!"

He was serious. He was terrifying.

"I don't understand," she quavered.

"You saw our operation! We're bringing the thrill of Flakka to the North East!" he told her, "and you and your boyfriend saw us. My boss doesn't want anyone getting in the way on our way to being millionaires."

"But, we didn't see you!" Sylvia insisted in a panicked voice, "It was dark! All we saw were red flashlights! There's no need to hurt us. I'll never tell! We *really* don't know anything!"

"I have my orders," he told her darkly. "I am to make you disappear."

Sylvia closed her eyes for a moment. She wondered what time it was.

"But, my dog," she started to say, "why," but, grief captured her voice.

"Yapped too much," the man told her quietly. He turned his eyes on her that had dilated even more. They were evil eyes, with no light whatsoever.

Sylvia thought of the Green Man and what he said recently, about manifesting good things. How could she do this? She was so very frightened. She saw Percy's still body on the floor and couldn't think. Her head pounded from where he had hit her.

He was sweating more profusely now and looking crazier. Sylvia wondered if he had a fever. He was making a weird sound in his throat and tearing at his clothes. He started to tear off his clothes. She stared.

Then she remembered. Her reality. She thought about her Green Man.

And he was there, the vast, great, green, angel of a figure. He was there, and he stood in front of her protecting her from the crazy man who had ripped off his clothes and had run from the house screaming at the sight of the Green Man.

The man ran into the water, shouting and yelling. Sylvia could hear the word 'monster' screamed from his mouth. The Green Man turned to her, but before he could say anything, Sylvia heard someone at the door. The Green Man disappeared in a rustle of leaves.

"Help!" Sylvia sobbed. "Help!"

Joe burst in. His weapon was drawn. He checked to see if Sylvia was all right but glanced out the French doors at the man writhing in the water. Another cop was coming in the back door. Another was coming around the side of the house. The man in the water was having a seizure. Joe and the other cop ran down to the beach. They pulled the man out and his body flopped wildly on the ground. Joe reached on the ground to put something between his teeth, but the man was frothing blood at that point. His body seized again and then lay still. Joe checked for a pulse. He shook his head. He went back to Sylvia.

Joe cut the ropes and helped her to sit on the couch. He rubbed her feet and ankles and hands. She couldn't talk. More police and an ambulance arrived. Carol came in with Owen. Sylvia looked at Percy again and reality hit her. Percy was dead. He was gone. Forever. Sylvia passed out as Owen cried out her name.

She wasn't out long. The paramedics held smelling salts under her nose and Sylvia came to, coughing and choking at the smell. The questions began. Owen brought her a shot of scotch. Sylvia sipped and choked. Joe was patient.

While she gathered herself, Joe told her Owen and Carol knew something was wrong when she didn't answer the phone calls or texts. Carol had called Joe and he had responded and had back up. He didn't know what he would be walking into. Sylvia glanced at his pale face. Realization hit her that he didn't think he would find her alive.

Sylvia told her story of the day, what she knew of the man, and why he had come to the house. She shuddered. Joe probed gently. Carol brought her ice to put on her head. The paramedics checked her out and thought she should go to get an x-ray to see if she had a concussion. Sylvia shakily said she would be okay. Joe probed with more questions. In a few hours, everyone had gone.

In bed, Owen held her as closely as he could. Sylvia couldn't stop shuddering.

"What next?" she said to him. "What's going to happen when they realize that guy failed? Do you think we're still in danger?" she asked Owen.

"I think Joe's going to do his best to protect us," Owen said. "Probably no privacy," he sighed, "but, we'll be protected."

"Percy," she whispered. "Poor Percy. He was trying to protect *me!*"

"I know," Owen said. "I know."

The tears started to come, slowly at first. Owen held her as sobs wracked her body. She cried until she was asleep.

CHAPTER TWENTY-NINE

"You have enemies? Good. That means you've stood up for something, sometime in your life."

— WINSTON CHURCHILL

Sylvia woke up feeling as though she had been on a drinking bender. Her head throbbed and her face was sticky with the tears she had shed. No cold nose woke her this morning. She was going to begin to cry again but stopped herself.

"Owen," she said gently, "Owen! Are we going to work today?"

He groaned, "I don't want to," he said, "but, I think we should."

"I agree," she told him. She didn't want to, she couldn't spend the day in the house today.

Sylvia went to the shower and stood under the spray for a long time. Owen knocked gently on the door and still, she jumped.

"Coffee," he said, "just coffee."

Sylvia went to get dressed while he had his turn in the shower. They went downstairs together. Someone had picked up Percy's body and had cleaned the spot where he had lain in his own blood. She couldn't look at it. Outside an unmarked police car was parked, stolid in their watch. Sylvia picked up her purse and they went out the door.

Carol was shocked when Sylvia walked into the office.

"Sylvia! What are you doing here?" she asked her aghast. "You should be at home!"

"And do what?" Sylvia asked bitterly. "Cry? Wait for another crazy person to try to come to kill me? Anyways, it's probably safer to be here at work."

Carol was quiet, but eventually she nodded in agreement, and then said, "Yes, you're right."

Sylvia went through her tasks woodenly. She was grateful Mr. Carter was at another division for meetings. She didn't want to see people or answer questions. Owen brought lunch to her in the office. They ate quietly. Carol left them alone.

At the end of lunch, she knocked quietly on Sylvia's office door. "Syl? Owen?" They looked up at her.

"Joe's going to come by," she said, gently. "He has a little information."

"Okay," Sylvia said, "Thanks."

Owen gave her a kiss. "Call me when he comes, all right?"

Sylvia and Carol nodded at his request. Sylvia couldn't concentrate. She put her head down on her desk, wondering how Owen was staying awake. He had been awake most of the night, listening and waiting for something to happen. There was a knock on her door. She lifted her head and there was Joe.

"Hi Sylvia," he murmured. "How are you doing?"

She shrugged, in response, not able to trust her voice.

"I see," he said. "Owen's on his way. Are you okay, if I come in and sit down?"

Sylvia nodded. Joe sat. He put his hand over hers and squeezed. They didn't talk while they waited for Owen. He arrived. He sat. Owen and Sylvia looked at Joe. There was a hint of pleading in their eyes.

"The man that attacked Sylvia yesterday was under the influence of Flakka," Joe told them.

"Flakka?" Owen asked.

"What's that?" Sylvia asked.

"It's a new sort of designer drug. It's very, very dangerous. It's cheap and easy to manufacture. It can be smoked, snorted, vaped, chewed and ingested in almost any way you can think of," Joe began.

"That's what that man said," Sylvia said faintly, "He said he felt like Superman."

"Yes," Joe agreed. "It gives one the feeling of superhuman powers, paranoia, and an elevated body temperature. And," he hesitated, "sometimes extreme violence without remorse. Flakka is making its way North from Florida, Kentucky, and Tennessee. It's easy and cheap to manufacture. A hit is only five dollars on the street. You can even get a free sample online!"

"Shipped in a plain, brown wrapper, no doubt," Owen interjected acerbically.

"Exactly! Whoever this guy worked for is trying to bring it to the I-95 corridor." Joe took a breath and continued, "They moved their operation out of the Fairlee and Worton Creek area after you stumbled on them. We're looking and the Coast Guard is looking. The problem is that the Chesapeake has thousands of small coves, tributaries, and possible points to marinas and nearby roads." Joe sounded frustrated.

"How did they find us?" Sylvia asked, finding her voice.

"Someone saw the name of your boat. All boats are registered. It was a pretty easy way to find you," Joe told her.

"Now, what?" Owen asked. "How are you going to find them?"

Joe tugged at his very short, blonde hair. "I don't know yet," he said. "We're working on it. That's the only news I have."

Sylvia closed her eyes. "But, we didn't even see anything! Just some red flashlights in the dark!" Sylvia argued.

"Sylvia," Joe said gently. "They don't care. They know you were there. They are paranoid. They are violent. You *are* in danger. *They do not care if you die,*" he finished unswervingly.

They were quiet for a few minutes.

"Owen," Sylvia whispered, "if they haven't caught these people by the wedding, I don't think I want to go sailing for our honeymoon. I think these bad guys might blow us out of the water and never look back."

Joe looked at Owen, "Smart lady. She's right, you know."

Owen groaned, "Catch them, Joe. Catch them.

"I'm trying, bro," Joe told Owen, "the Narcotics team and the Coast Guard are working together. It's probably inevitable, but they do not want Flakka in this area. We've heard stories from other precincts..." his voice trailed off. "They're not pretty," he said in a very quiet, very firm voice.

"Smuggling, and in particular, drug smuggling in the last century, on the bay, happens all the time," Joe told them.

"But, I don't hear about it in the news," Sylvia protested.

"Nor will you," Owen answered her drily, "we only listen to what they want us to hear. That's why I listen to NPR and look at news from other news agencies in the world."

"There's been a little bit out about Flakka," Joe told them. "You hear more about it in Florida. I've seen small news pieces on the national news, but really blips in comparison to other news. There was a short piece in the USA Today newspaper a couple of months ago. It's coming out more and more as the drug gets more popular. These amphetamine things hit peaks and valleys in popularity. The effects of this one, though, are really scary. The violence..." his voice trailed off again. He stopped as if he had said too much and stood, shaking his head and putting his cop face on.

"What's next?" Owen asked.

Joe looked at both of them. "Try to continue on as normally as possible. We'll be watching over you two as well as we can," he told them.

"I feel like shark bait," Sylvia said.

"I won't sugar coat it," Joe said, "In some ways, you are. You two are the information link about these guys coming up the Chesapeake."

Joe left. Owen and Sylvia sat in silence.

"You okay?" Owen asked, rubbing her back.

"As okay as I can be," Sylvia answered, "and you?" she asked him.

Owen shrugged. Both Sylvia's and Owen's eyes widened at this gesture. It didn't cause him pain. A smile broke out on his face at being able to shrug pain-free.

"It's those little things," Owen said. "We'll be okay," he told Sylvia.

Owen went back to his office to get his things. The afternoon had flown by. Carol came in to check on Sylvia.

"How are you doing?" she asked carefully.

"As well as I can be, I think," she told her friend. "It's just so frustrating to—to be so helpless in all of this. It's just a wait and see, sort of thing on this end. But, I'm a little paranoid."

Sylvia became quiet, but she had to ask. "What happened to Percy?" she asked Carol.

Carol took a shaky breath, "We took the body to be cremated," she told Sylvia. "Joe and I did."

Sylvia stood to hug her friend. "Thank you," Sylvia said, trying not to cry.

Carol began to tear up and pulled from Sylvia's hug to get a tissue.

"Let's lock up and get out of here," Carol said.

CHAPTER THIRTY

"Maybe all one can do is hope to end up with
the right regrets."

— ARTHUR MILLER

Their lives continued on as normal as they could with the police watching their every movement. The wedding was creeping closer and now their honeymoon was up in the air. The True Love had been repaired and anchored where they could see her from their home. Looking at her was bittersweet for both Owen and Sylvia.

Sylvia felt a hole in her life without Percy. She was sure Owen did too, but he didn't talk about it. They had agreed to wait to get another pet until after the wedding and honeymoon. But, it didn't help Sylvia fill her need to be close to something furry in her life.

It surprised her, in many aspects, the depth of her need to have an animal in her life.

At the end of August, Joe and Carol came over with a small, wooden box with an engraved brass plaque. It contained Percy's ashes. The plaque had the poem "The Rainbow Bridge" engraved on it as well as an engraved photograph of Percy. His name was inscribed under his picture and the phrase "Beloved Friend" beneath his name. Joe and Carol also brought champagne, to celebrate Percy's life. Everyone toasted Percy solemnly while Sylvia held the box in her lap.

After the champagne, Sylvia had to ask Joe, "Any more news?"

Joe shook his head, "What we're hoping," he said, "is that these guys will forget about you once they realize you didn't see anything. They won't want to draw more attention to themselves. This guy has already made his money," Joe said with frustration. "He made the drop in Worton Creek. They got it out of there lickety-split when they realized you guys were there. I'm sure it's been distributed and is on the streets in one of the major cities."

"Good for us, I guess," Owen said. "And, we'll be able to go sailing on our honeymoon," he added hopefully.

Sylvia still looked skeptical, but Joe nodded in agreement to Owen's suggestion.

"Yeah," he said, "I'm feeling pretty confident these guys are long gone. And, so do the other authorities. Not sure if you noticed, but the vigil of people watching you has been dwindling. This Flakka stuff is imported as a chemical. It's not even illegal in China, where it's manufactured. We don't have a lot of control over it. It has the Feds, all the law enforcement agencies, and the Coast Guard in a tizzy. We're all expecting a storm of this as the storm of crack-cocaine several years ago. With the online samples, and sales, and drugs being manufactured from inexpensive and legal substances, we're fighting a whole, new, drug war."

This news caused them all to be silent again.

"We need to explain the last couple of weeks to our family," Owen said gravely.

The authorities had asked them to keep quiet about the incident, as to not hinder their investigation or draw more people into danger. Owen and Sylvia had become ingenious at skirting questions.

"Why don't you ask them to come to a picnic this weekend?" Carol suggested. "Joe and I can come and then we can fill them in on what happened."

"Good idea, sweetie," Joe told Carol. "What do you two think?" he asked Owen and Sylvia.

They both nodded in agreement.

"Jon and Marian will be back too," Sylvia said. "We've been keeping an eye on their home and picked up the mail while Jon and Marian were in Watch Hill, Rhode Island, visiting former colleagues of Jon. We'll need to tell them as well."

"And, Maureen and Skip," Owen added.

"And, Mom," Sylvia said, "We'll need to tell Mom a little early. She'll wonder why Percy isn't here when she comes on Friday."

"Do you want me to be here?" Joe asked, "to answer any questions?"

"Yes, please," Sylvia answered and Owen nodded as well.

"Okay," Joe said. "Plan in place."

The weekend came quickly. Sylvia, Owen, Carol and Joe took off a couple of hours early to beat Mary to the house. Joe and Carol pulled up to the house as Mary pulled into the driveway.

"This is convenient," she said, after giving each a hug. "Can you help me carry stuff in?"

"And you," she ordered Owen, who had come to the kitchen door. "You stay where you are. I talked to your mother and I know you're not to lift anything heavier than five pounds."

"Yes, Ma'am," Owen answered, giving her a small salute, "Okay if I hold the door open?" he asked her.

"Of course," Mary said and gave Owen a kiss on the cheek as she walked into the kitchen.

"Oh, Mom!" Sylvia cried as she gave her mother a hug, "It's so good to see you!"

Her mother put down the packages and hugged her daughter back. She was surprised, and happy, at this unexpected, animated show of affection from her daughter.

Joe and Carol followed Mary inside.

"Where's the big guy?" Mary asked, looking around for Percy.

"Oh, Mom," Sylvia began.

"Why don't you come and sit down Mary," Carol said, leading Mary into the living room.

Sylvia sat next to Mary and took her hand in her own. Tears pricked her eyelids.

"What's happened?" Mary asked concerned.

"We have quite the story to tell you, Mary," Joe began.

The sound of authority in Joe's voice brought Mary to attention. She looked at Joe, Sylvia, and Owen.

Carol, had slipped into the kitchen to pour two glasses of wine for Mary and Sylvia. She took three beers out of the refrigerator for Owen, Joe and herself. Quietly, she handed the drinks around.

Joe began the story, telling Mary the incident that had happened with Sylvia and the crazed Flakka addict. Mary gripped Sylvia's hand harder and harder. During the story, Mary occasionally put her hand over her mouth. Once she took a gulp of wine. She looked at Joe, Carol, Owen and Sylvia aghast as she heard of the events. When Joe had finished, Mary put her arms around Sylvia. And then she reached around Sylvia and put her hand on Owen.

"Oh, my poor baby!" Mary said to Sylvia. "My brave, sweet girl. Poor Percy!"

"We couldn't tell you what had happened in the last few weeks," Sylvia reiterated what Joe had told Mary. "I'm sorry, Mom."

"I'm just so grateful you are all right!" Mary said. "That's what counts."

"That's why we're having the picnic tomorrow. We need to let our family and close friends know what happened," Owen explained.

Mary asked many questions that evening. Sylvia was grateful that Joe and Carol were there. They had sent out for pizza and they sat and ate, drank and talked until long after sunset. Sylvia and Carol had lit candles, to drive away any mosquitoes. The end of summer insects played their percussion-like song. If their conversation had not been so sad, it would have been a lovely, summer's evening. Joe and Carol said their good-byes and said they would see them tomorrow for the picnic.

Mary stood in the kitchen, hands supporting her against the counter after they left.

She kept shaking her head, "Sylvia," she whispered, "Sylvia."

"It's okay, Mom. It's all going to be all right," Sylvia told her. "We're okay."

"And, Percy," her Mom said faintly.

"Percy died trying to protect Sylvia," Owen said to Mary. "He's a hero in my eyes."

Mary nodded.

"Let's get a good night's sleep," Sylvia suggested.

And they all went up to bed.

CHAPTER THIRTY-ONE

"Life is ten percent what happens to you and ninety percent how you respond to it."

— Lou Holtz

A solemnity pervaded what should have been a festive, pre-wedding gathering of friends and family as Joe told the story of what had happened, again. He answered questions, sometimes more than once, but he answered each one with patience. Sylvia, Carol, and Mary prepared the food while Joe spoke. Mary had gone out that morning to pick up champagne. Carol and Sylvia passed out paper cups filled with the bubbly liquid.

"To Percy," Sylvia said, raising her glass.

"To Percy," they all chorused and took a drink.

"To our wonderful law enforcement," Mary said, raising her glass.

And they toasted again and again. A little more relaxed with the alcohol, and a lessening of tension, the subdued atmosphere exited and excited talk of the wedding began.

Carol and Sylvia took some of the things into the kitchen to clean up.

"I'm sorry Gwen and Frank couldn't make it this weekend," Carol said, "but, I filled her in on a FaceTime call," she told Sylvia.

"Thanks," Sylvia said. "Sometimes, it all seems so surreal. It's like I'm watching this from the outside looking in. Almost like déjà vu."

"I always knew there was something different about you," Carol teased. "Maybe you actually live in another dimension."

Carol chuckled, but Sylvia paused, thinking of a few comments that the Green Man had made about many other times and dimensions. Maureen and Amber came inside, interrupting her thoughts.

"We thought we would work on the bird seed packets, to throw after the ceremony," Maureen said.

"They're actually packets that look like roses," Amber explained. "Carol, be a love and get the stuff out of my car." She tossed her car keys to her daughter. Carol caught them neatly and went to the car to bring in a large, plastic tub of things. Marian, Anne, and Mary came in as well. They all sat around the dining room table. Amber showed them how to create the flowers. She had already sewn the sage and white satin fabric into small tubes. She demonstrated putting a small part of a cardboard tube inside, gluing the one end of the stem, filling it with birdseed and pushing in the top, so that it looked like a rose.

Maureen had a beautiful basket to put the completed roses in.

"Why do they throw stuff at weddings, anyways?" Carol wondered out loud.

"To wish the couple prosperity and fertility," Marian answered her.

"Didn't it used to be rice that they throw at brides and grooms?" Sylvia asked.

Anne answered her this time, "and rice isn't good for birds and it's a waste of food."

They worked together, putting the favors together in a short time.

"Just two more weeks as a single woman," Carol teased Sylvia as they finished the roses.

"Do you need help with anything else?" Anne asked.

"I can't think of anything," Sylvia assured her future mother-in-law. "The boys are taking care of everything for the boat. I've been able to get everything organized thanks to all of you here." Sylvia waved her hand in a sweeping motion, taking in everyone at the table.

CHAPTER THIRTY-TWO

*"Nothing in life is to be feared, it is only to be understood.
Now is the time to understand more, so that we may
fear less."*

— Marie Curie

The next two weeks went by frighteningly fast for Sylvia. Work and wedding planning, wedding and work. Sylvia spent hours and hours, double checking every minutia for both. Owen and Sylvia had blood drawn and picked up their wedding license. Sylvia asked Marian repeatedly if she had heard from the mysterious minister that she had arranged. Sylvia trusted Marian, but she thought it odd that this man was always unavailable. Marian assured her that it would be all right.

Gwen and Frank came the Wednesday before the wedding. Gwen, Carol, and Sylvia went to get the last minute tailoring check on their dresses on Thursday morning. Gwen's tummy had popped a little, but not enough to cause hysterics with the tailor. She glowed with her pregnancy and with happiness.

Scotty came on Thursday night. He was more than surprised to hear all that had happened since he saw them in Baltimore. He told Owen he should write a novel because you couldn't make up this stuff.

"You write it," Owen insisted, "You're more the creative guy."

Skip and Maureen took them out on one of the 'Buick' Regal boats for a combined bachelor and bachelorette party. Skip definitely would not let Sylvia live down her faux pas regarding the name of the boat and still chuckled, sometimes, when he saw her.

Sylvia was in awe of the regal. Skip had a Regal 53 Sports Coupe. It wasn't a Buick, it was more like an Aston Martin of boats. She thought of George's fifty-eight foot, Chris Craft Roamer. His boat was not as elegant, but it was large and spacious as this one.

Skip zoomed down the bay, past the clay cliffs at Turkey Point, past the lighthouse and out into open water. Maureen had the event catered by the marina's restaurant, and they were served delicious hors d'oeuvres. Champagne flowed freely and Skip had micro-brew growlers for the beer lovers. Gwen and Sylvia were sitting with Carol and Maureen on the boat's patio.

"Marian would love this," Gwen thought aloud and asked Sylvia where she and Jon were.

"No, she wouldn't," Sylvia insisted, "Believe it or not, she doesn't like boats! Besides, she's getting ready for the rehearsal dinner tomorrow. Mom, Anne and Phil have joined her."

"I thought she was catering it," Carol said.

"You know Marian," Sylvia said, "It's not a party, but an event."

They motored around the bay and headed back towards North Bay at sunset. It had been a lovely, relaxed evening.

On Friday, Sylvia wished she had gone to work to keep her mind busy. Owen moved back to Marian's for the night so he could follow the tradition of not seeing the bride before the wedding. Owen and Sylvia had mixed feeling about the tradition. Mary, Anne, Maureen, Gwen, and Carol whisked Sylvia away in the early afternoon to get manicures and pedicures and a hot stone massage.

When it was time for the rehearsal dinner, Sylvia donned a lovely, long, white lace and gauze dress and strappy sandals. She was pushing the old rule of wearing white after Labor Day, but she figured she was a bride and it was appropriate. It was also Indian summer and the evening was quite warm. They were all meeting at the Pergola before heading to Marian and Jon's for an elegant picnic. Sylvia kept her fingers crossed that the mysterious minister would be there. Her mother drove them down the street so they would have the car to take to Marian and Jon's house. Gwen and Frank were staying with Sylvia and Mary at home. They took their SUV on the short drive to the marina.

Maureen was already in the pergola. She had hired one of the dock girls, Jeanne, who pumped gas for them, to handle the music during the ceremony. Maureen stationed Jeanne in back of the pergola, with a table and stereo. Skip had had the pergola wired for sound. The white, translucent curtains embossed with leaves, fluttered in the evening breeze. It was lovely. The chair rental people had arrived and were beginning to set up the chairs. Maureen hurried away from Jeanne and went to give directions to the men on how to set up the chairs. Scotty had walked over to the marina from the bed and breakfast. He approached Sylvia.

"Are you nervous?" he asked her.

"Terribly," Sylvia admitted, "and I don't even know why."

"It will be okay. Here comes the groom," he said, pointing at the approaching car.

Indeed, Owen and his parents were coming down the road followed by Jon's SUV.

Owen hurried over to Sylvia and Scotty. He gave her a long kiss and whispered to her that she looked beautiful.

Sylvia looked up. Owen's kiss had distracted her. There were Marian, Jon, and the mysterious Dr. Luis coming towards them. Sylvia gasped when she saw the tall, nut brown skinned man with a flourish of a mustache as he walked toward her. She thought she saw double. She blinked. With one moment, she saw this elegant gentleman and in the next moment, it was the Green Man. Sylvia felt as though her eyes would pop out of her head. She looked at Marian, who grinned, joyfully at her and winked.

Marian made introductions and the Dr. Luis/Green Man came to her, he said, "I think Sylvia remembers me from the party now," in his rich, baritone voice.

His firm handshake held her up.

Owen looked at Sylvia, "Are you okay?" he whispered.

"Fine," she said, almost giddy, "I'm all right," and she flashed him a dazzling smile.

Sylvia shot Marian a glance with wonderment at how Marian had pulled off such a thing, but Marian and the Green Man had gone on to other introductions. Joe and Carol arrived with Mr. Carter. Sylvia had not been able to decide on one person to walk her down the aisle since her Dad was gone. So, she had decided to ask Mr. Carter and Jon to do the honors.

When everyone had arrived, Maureen asked everyone to get quiet. They all took their places to practice the ceremony. The rehearsal went off without a hitch – or mostly so. Owen couldn't seem to say her name – particularly her middle name of Beithe, and they all erupted in giggles. The Green Man / Dr. Luis patiently taught Owen the correct way to say the Ogham name of the birch tree.

Marian had pulled out all the stops for the rehearsal dinner, with definite touches by Anne. Like the first party Sylvia had attended, white, fairy lights adorned the fence and the trees.

Beautiful, glass, candle filled lanterns added more of a magic touch. It was a relaxed and happy time. Sylvia spent as much time as she could with the Green Man. It wasn't a time he could drive her crazy with didactic or spiritual lessons, but a time that she could just enjoy being near him. He laughed and talked with the guests. His eyes never stopped twinkling with the surprise he and Marian had given her.

"I think I could be jealous," Owen whispered to her as he gathered her into his arms for an impromptu embrace and a kiss.

Sylvia nearly blushed, but returned a kiss in a way that he knew he had absolutely nothing to worry about.

"Just think," he said, "Twenty-four hours from now, we'll be married and on our honeymoon."

"I know," Sylvia said, "I can hardly believe it." She shivered inside with pleasure at the thought. "But, I think I need to be heading home for some beauty sleep before tomorrow."

He nodded and kissed her one last time. Sylvia said good night and after a round of good nights, climbed into Gwen and Frank's SUV with Scotty and her mom.

CHAPTER THIRTY-THREE

"A happy marriage is a long conversation which always seems too short."

— ANDRE MAUROIS

Sylvia woke early. It was her wedding day! She couldn't help it, she still looked for Percy when she got out of bed. A sudden wave of sadness came over her as she headed downstairs for coffee. She was shocked to see her mother up. Mary and Frank were having coffee at the kitchen table.

"Good morning," she greeted them.

"Good morning to you!" they returned.

"Are you nervous?" Frank asked her.

"A bit," Sylvia admitted.

"Trust me," Frank said, "It's all good." He smiled at Sylvia as she made her café au lait.

She sat with her mother and Frank for a few minutes, sipping her coffee. Then Sylvia excused herself and went out to the deck to look at the sky and the water. She could not have asked for a more perfect day. The sun was shining, the humidity was low. There was a slight breeze. The water was a silvery blue. It was a bright, beautiful, early, autumn day. Perfect. Part of her wanted the Green Man to appear, but she knew she would see him later that day, and that was all right. She went upstairs to shower.

Carol arrived a short time later with pastries. She knew Sylvia wouldn't feel like eating that morning, so she foisted a carrot cake muffin on her friend.

"You play dirty pool," Sylvia teased.

"You have to eat *something*," Carol insisted.

"Yes, you do," her mother intoned.

"Or this starving, pregnant lady might steal it from your hands," Gwen announced as she came into the kitchen. "I think this baby is growing again. I think I could eat anything that isn't nailed down."

They laughed.

"Listen, girls," Mary said, "The hairdresser is coming shortly. Gwen, why don't you get a bite or bites to eat and run up and shower."

Sylvia had hired her local, favorite hairdresser to come to the house that day to do their hair and make-up. Sylvia admired her talent and artistry with haircuts, even though her own was relatively simple. She always felt pretty when she left the salon. And, Zoe, the salon owner, had been frank with Sylvia on possible up do's for the wedding day. Sylvia appreciated Zoe's honesty and creativity.

Anne arrived. Zoe came. Frank cleared out. He went over to the Bed and Breakfast to talk to Scotty. They were planning to pick up Owen and head out to breakfast.

The moms were first. Mary looked chic and Anne looked like a darker haired Judy Collins with her charcoal gray and black hair. Carol was next. Sylvia thought Carol's hair was too short to put into a fancy hairstyle, but Zoe managed to pull off a lovely style with some creative curls, twists, and rolls. Sylvia knew Gwen's hair would look stunning with it pulled up. Gwen was stunning to begin with and now, with her pregnancy glow, she was drop dead gorgeous.

At last, it was Sylvia's turn. She had brought out the leafy headpiece that Marian had given her. Zoe designed her hair with elaborate braids and twists. She left a curl or two draping down, romantically. As a gift to Sylvia, she pinned up part of her hair with tiny, rhinestone leaf bobby pins. They sparkled in Sylvia's hair like diamonds.

"You look beautiful," Zoe assured her when she had completed her handiwork and looked at it critically.

She gave Sylvia a mirror to look in. Sylvia was stunned to see her reflection.

"I feel like a princess," she told Zoe.

"You are!" Zoe insisted. "Especially today."

The next stop was Maureen and Skip's house where they had their dresses. Maureen had been busy supervising the florist and setting things up. The photographer was going to meet them there to begin taking before wedding photos. The men were dressing at the bed and breakfast down the street where Scotty was staying. Mr. Carter, Joe, and Jon were meeting them there for photos as well.

Sylvia gave Gwen and Carol beautiful necklaces by Michael Michaud of Silver Seasons. Sylvia had fallen in love with his jewelry at Longwood. She treasured the holly necklace and earrings she had received from Owen and Marian. She gave the girls a beautiful, contoured necklace and earrings of basil leaves in bronze and green that picked up the color of their dresses.

Maureen brought the photographer in. He had just come from the bed and breakfast and having just finished taking pictures of Owen and the groomsmen. The photographer set up several photographs, some serious, and many fun with Sylvia, her mom, Gwen, and Carol.   Mary had called Anne and insisted she join them as well as Marian. The photographer had them laughing at silly things while he snapped away with many candid photographs.

Finally, it was time. Maureen excused herself to check on things and get the music started. Marian, Mary, and Anne left to get seated.   Sylvia's stomach fluttered terribly. Maureen returned. She nodded. She was followed by Mr. Carter and Jon, who both teared up when they saw Sylvia in her wedding gown.

"Don't start," she warned them, tearing up herself.

The processional began.   Carol strolled out Maureen and Skip's back door, through the yard and down the aisle Maureen had created with the chairs and runner. Gwen followed. Sylvia, flanked by Mr. Carter and Jon, stopped at the end of the aisle and waited for the "Ode to Joy" to begin. It was one of her favorite pieces of music. Sylvia had requested that one of her favorite music artist's – David Garrett's version, be the music accompanying her as she walked down the aisle. Walking down the aisle, Sylvia looked up and saw the Green Man, standing and smiling at her. She looked at Owen and was lost immediately in his eyes, which held so much love for her. His eyes drew her towards him. She smiled tremulously at him when she reached him and she took his hand.

The wedding ceremony was a blur. In her mind, Sylvia remembered the vibrational quality of the Green Man's voice, his touch as he held Owen and her hands together. She remembered his blessing her, and feeling that all was right with the world as he sealed their love for one another. She remembered when the Green Man said, "You may kiss the bride," to Owen. Owen's kiss swept her away. Everyone cheered. And they went down the aisle, hand in hand. Not being in a church, the wedding party lined up along the bay front to greet the guests. With the small gathering of family and friends, it did not take long.

It was time to go to the reception and Owen led Sylvia amid a shower of birdseed, to a hunter green, Mazda Miata that Scotty had rented for his trip. Scotty, Joe, and Frank had outfitted it with crepe paper, signs and a streamer with old shoes and tin cans. Owen and Sylvia waved to everyone and they drove through the neighborhood, honking the horn. Owen had·been given orders to drive through town and give people at least fifteen minutes to make the five minute trip to the yacht club. He obliged and pulled the car over to give Sylvia another kiss.

"Hello, Mrs. Anderson," he said.

"Hello, Mr. Anderson," she said.

He kissed her again. He sighed and turned to pull out into traffic. When they reached the Yacht Club, almost everyone had arrived. Scotty gave him the thumbs up when they pulled in. The guests sampled hors d'oeuvres and drinks while the wedding party had more pictures taken at the yacht club with the vista of the Chesapeake Bay behind them.

The evening was magical. Joe's group entertained them well and when it was time to dance, he played and sang Sylvia's favorite Elvis song, "Can't help falling in love with you." As he sang, he never took his eyes off Carol.

They broke into lighter bluegrass music after that. Sylvia was spun around the floor by Owen, Jon, Mr. Carter, Frank and finally, the Green Man.

"So, Dr. Luis," she asked. "How did that name come about? Should I call you that from now on?"

The Green Man threw back his head and laughed and dipping her low. When he pulled her back to continue dancing, he told her, that Luis is the Ogham word for Rowan tree. The Rowan, she knew, had been classed as a magical tree for millennia. At the end of the dance, Sylvia threw her arms around his neck and gave him a kiss on the cheek. Having him there, to officiate her wedding with Owen was more than a dream come true. He always brought her peace and joy.

Sylvia made sure Carol caught the bouquet and Owen made sure Joe caught the garter. They both were surprised and pleased. Carol had a hard time looking at Joe after that, but she wore a grin for the rest of the evening.

Finally, it was time for the night to end. Maureen orchestrated the lighting of the wish lanterns that Sylvia had requested. Like magical stars, the wish lanterns filled the night sky as they floated up and out across the Chesapeake Bay. Among the lights and the well-wishers that lined the sidewalk to the pier, Owen and Sylvia walked to the True Love.

The boat had been decorated with lights and a Japanese lantern hung mid-mast. Everyone cheered as they got on board. Owen and Sylvia waved as they motored away from the yacht club, the wish lanterns floating in the air above them.

They motored away from the yacht club and down into the bay. Sylvia stood beside Owen at the helm.

"We're not going to motor too far tonight," he told her. "I thought we could anchor off Bayside, and have some champagne and spend the night?"

"That's perfect," she told him. "Let me go below and release myself from this dress, while you guide us to our port."

Sylvia went below. It took her several minutes to free herself from the dress. She left on her wedding lingerie, garter belt, and stockings. Sylvia took some champagne from the cooler and two glasses and went up on deck, much to Owen's surprise. He was very pleased to see her outfit. He hastily secured their mooring and told Sylvia huskily it was time to go below. There, he conveniently helped her from her remaining clothing, slowly, sensuously, one piece at a time and they began a long and languorous wedding night.

They sailed from port to port this trip, instead of finding hidden coves as they had dreamed of earlier. The Flakka dealers had seen to that. They kept in contact, via text, with Joe to let them know where they were and where they were headed. It was on the third day of their honeymoon that Joe texted them to say the Flakka dealer and her henchmen had been caught. The danger was over. They would be safe. An enormous weight was lifted from their shoulders. They both felt they could relax and really enjoy themselves, instead of looking over their shoulders for someone to harm them.

They meandered to St. Michaels, where they used Anne and Phil's gift certificate to celebrate their honeymoon in a 'real' bed, as Anne had suggested. What was considered the honeymoon suite was, fortunately, open mid-week, and Owen and Sylvia took advantage of it. They sailed to Oxford, Maryland and to Solomons Island, Maryland before sailing home again. The Indian summer weather held true. The days were warm and the nights were cool. It was a magical time for Sylvia. She thought Owen felt it too. A large part of her didn't want this honeymoon to end. It was one of the few times in their relationship, over the past year, that strife had not insinuated itself into their lives. They returned home happy and relaxed, planning their next trip down the bay.

EPILOGUE

Sylvia sat in an Adirondack chair on the deck and watched Owen on the bridge of the boat. In her heart, she knew she had new life inside of her, even though they had taken precautions on their honeymoon. Sylvia could just feel it. She could see the small, extra layer added to her aura. It pulsed with life. She would need to find a way to break the news to Owen.

There was a rustle of leaves. The Green Man was beside her. They stood side by side, not speaking, just watching the water and the sky in companionable quiet. She could feel his positive energy pulsing into her body and she inadvertently leaned in closer to him.

His deep tenor voice interrupted her thoughts, "You asked once, 'why me?'" he stated to Sylvia.

She turned to look into his eyes and nodded.

"There are many names for those who are like you," he told her. "You will find them and they will find you. As long as there is one or more who believe," the Green Man told Sylvia, "then there is hope for the human race. All will be well."

With a rustle of leaves, he was gone again. A twinge of sadness filled her as the air next to her was suddenly empty. But, she knew he would return sometime soon. There was a comfort in that knowledge.

Sylvia suddenly thought of the quote she had read on a Green Man site on Facebook, *"Our ancestors said to their mother Earth: 'We are yours.' Modern humanity has said to Nature, 'You are mine.' The Green Man has returned as the living face of the whole earth so that through his mouth we may say to the universe: 'We are one."*

Sylvia looked out at the trees, the sky and the water. She put her hand on her abdomen, protectively. All at once, Sylvia knew, without a shred of doubt, of the interconnectedness of everything. From the small life the size of an apple seed pulsing within her to all of humanity that crowded this living, breathing being of a planet and all other realms as well. All was well and life was good.

The End.

29853474R00166

Made in the USA
Middletown, DE
04 March 2016